The Aviary

The Aviary

KATHLEEN O'DELL

Alfred A. Knopf   New York

Visit us on the Web! www.randomhouse.com/kids

Educators and librarians, for a variety of teaching tools, visit us at www.randomhouse.com/teachers

Library of Congress Cataloging-in-Publication Data is available upon request.
ISBN 978-0-375-85605-1 (trade)
ISBN 978-0-375-95605-8 (lib. bdg.)
ISBN 978-0-375-98935-3 (ebook)

The text of this book is set in 12.5-point Goudy.

Printed in the United States of America
September 2011
10 9 8 7 6 5 4 3 2 1
First Edition

Random House Children's Books supports the First Amendment and celebrates the right to read.

For Alexia Sophia Ramirez Franco,
with love

Chapter 1

As a young child, Clara Dooley had felt that the Glendoveer mansion contained the whole world. George Glendoveer had been a famous magician and illusionist, and he and his wife, Cenelia, filled their home with curiosities from around the globe. Even the construction of the house owed its beauty to the arts and crafts of far-flung places: intricately carved woodwork with birds and flowers from Germany, Italian murals that made the ceilings into night skies scattered with stars, glowing Persian carpets in the shades of peacock feathers.

Clara, however, had never seen the house in its prime. Mr. Glendoveer had long since passed away. Mrs. Glendoveer was aged and frail. Many parts of the house were shuttered and closed. But Clara had lived there so long that she looked past the gloom and decay. Her mother, who cared for Mrs. Glendoveer, and Ruby, who cooked for them all, filled the rooms with their bustling energy. It was a circumscribed world, but for Clara it had seemed just enough.

Now, at nearly twelve, Clara felt she was outgrowing more than just the small desk that had been set up in Mrs. Glendoveer's bedroom for her studies. The room, with its elegant Chinese paper and French green enamel stove and shelves of foreign bric-a-brac, seemed to tease Clara. Because of her weak heart, she was not allowed to attend school—or run or play or exert herself in any way. And though there was a large rose garden in back where she might take the air, she hated attracting the attention of the birds in the mansion's outdoor aviary.

The enormous black iron cage, almost as big as Clara's own room, was backed up against the corner garden wall and sheltered under a pergola with a tattered roof. At the sight or sound of a human being, the birds inside would flutter and scream as if they were on fire, grasping at the bars with their sharp claws.

Judging from the noise, anyone nearby would have thought there were at least a dozen birds, but Clara knew there were only five—a mynah with a saffron mask surrounding blood-red eyes, a white, sulfur-crested cockatoo, a noisy black grackle, a fearless yellow kiskadee, and a terrified foam-green honeycreeper who pulled at his own feathers. Many times Clara wished for the birds to disappear so that she could roam the garden in peace. But strangely, old Mrs. Glendoveer loved the birds as much as Clara feared them.

This late afternoon when Ruby brought out the birds' feed, their piercing cries snapped Mrs. Glendoveer awake. She wore such a look of anxiety that Clara leapt up and took her hand until the squawking subsided. "Everything's all right," she said, looking into the woman's pale blue eyes. "I'm sorry they gave you a start."

Mrs. Glendoveer's voice quavered. "It's gotten worse since I can't get down to feed them myself. They're lonely, poor things. And they're getting so old too. It's a pity they don't have a Clara of their own to keep them company."

Mrs. Glendoveer talked about the birds to Clara the way a mother might tell stories about her precocious children. The cockatoo, for instance, could pick a lock. The mynah would nest only in the pages of old books and newspapers. Even the common grackle was gifted. "Better than a watchdog," she would say as he screeched to bring down the heavens.

When all was calm, Clara perched again on the edge of the bed and leafed through an old volume with color pictures of sea animals separated by the thinnest sheaves of tissue paper. She pointed to a scarlet-shelled creature covered with horns. "When I get well," she said, "I'm going down to the sea and gather a bucket of shells just like these. And I'll line them up here so you can see them when you wake up from your nap."

"Dear," said Mrs. Glendoveer, "you'll have to go to

Indonesia for those, I'm afraid. It's a prickly sort of urchin that grows only in warm water. Can you imagine what it's like to step on one?"

Clara didn't know what kind of water was in the sea that glittered in Lockhaven Bay. She could catch a glimpse of something that looked like a pool of mercury on the horizon, but she'd never been to the shore. "What lives in our sea, then?" she asked.

"Nothing too colorful," Mrs. Glendoveer said. "The ocean here in Maine is gray and ill tempered. I'm glad that my window faces south, so I don't have to gaze on it every day. . . ." She shuddered. "I prefer the garden. Thank goodness for all those sturdy old roses George planted. I believe that we have everything here a contented person could possibly need."

Yet Clara was not content. She fervently hoped that there was a doctor right now creating a cure for weak-hearted children so she could go out into the world. In the meantime, she must try to follow the precepts offered in *Advice for Young Ladies*, a pretty little book buried on the reading room's shelf:

> *Life has many ills, but the mind that views every object in its most cheering aspect bears within itself a powerful and perpetual antidote.*

Whenever she felt twinges of envy watching her mother go out the door with a market basket slung over her arm, she reminded herself that her yearning could only cause her own suffering, and redoubled her efforts to become the "antidote" to her own ills. And when she talked about her future, Clara was sure to include the phrase *When I get well,* intent on banishing clouded forecasts from her heart and mind.

The only doubtful habit she still clung to was a twice-daily ritual at the window seat, spying on the neighborhood children on their way to and from school. "I'll quit tomorrow," she'd say. But invariably the urge proved irresistible, and Clara permitted herself to fantasize that she was among those children, burdened with their books and overcoats, rushing along with *somewhere* to go.

"Clara!"

She hurried down the hall, looked over the banister, and saw Ruby, red in the face as always, blotting her upper lip with her apron.

"Your ma says come to tea," Ruby called.

"Four o'clock already?" Clara skipped down the stairs and put her arm through Ruby's. "You're so warm, Ruby dear. Too warm."

"Need to have a sit-down. Your mother! Thank goodness our Harriet has the tea habit, or we'd be on our feet from dawn till dusk." She shrugged cheerfully. "Could be worse, I guess. Could have a husband. At least I've got a free hour or two before bedtime to prop my feet up. Never a night off with a husband."

Clara had known Ruby since she was a baby, and she loved her. Ruby's every physical detail—from her graying hair afrizz at the temples to her small red nose and prim cherub's mouth—was endearing as well as soothingly familiar. Clara's mother, Harriet, was originally hired by Mrs. Glendoveer as a nurse and companion, but she was a worker and a perfectionist and soon gave all her time to the maintenance of the vast, crumbling house, marshaling Ruby into joining her in a disciplined and ceaseless round of chores.

The kitchen smelled of nutmeg and was hot and steamy almost beyond comfort, which told Clara they were to have rice pudding. Her mother had already set the table with sugar and cream, bowls, cups, and a china pot. "You two pour while I fetch more cordwood," she said.

"Look at the size of these spoons!" said Ruby, shaking her head. "Your ma's been off to the broker again. She had to choose between the teaspoons and the soup spoons, and it nearly broke my heart."

"The broker?" said Clara.

"The pawnbroker," Ruby said. "Twice in the same month too." She went quiet as Clara's mother came back in through the kitchen door. Clara made up her mind to look up *pawnbroker* in the dictionary as soon as she finished her tea.

"Great goodness," Clara's mother said as she nudged the door closed behind her with her foot. "You could hear a pin drop out there. It's quite unsettling."

Ruby rose and looked out the kitchen window. "Sky's a bit green as well," she said.

Clara's mother loaded firewood on the pile by the stove and pushed her hair back from her brow. "Lord, if there's a storm coming, let it pass us by. This old house won't stand it."

"Come sit by me, Mama," Clara said. "Your tea is getting cold."

Her mother smiled, took her seat, and gave Clara a pat on the head. "I don't think I've said hello to you since breakfast. So, hello."

"Hello," Clara said. She watched her mother relax into her chair and bring the cup to her lips. They never chatted much at tea; but Clara liked the closeness of the women, the lull in the kitchen as they all stared down into their cups, lost in their own thoughts.

Ding-ding-ding-ding!

Clara, her mother, and Ruby snapped to attention.

"It's Mrs. Glendoveer," Harriet said, springing to her feet. Clara rose to follow her.

"No, you stay with Ruby," she warned.

"What do you suppose has happened, Ruby?" asked Clara. "It sounds as if she's about to pull the bell cord off its hinge."

"I don't know, sweet, but look out there." Ruby pointed to the window. "It's black as death, I do declare. And so sudden too."

Clara ran to the window. The clouds appeared to be coming to a boil.

"Ruby!" cried her mother from down the hall. "Fetch the canvas!"

"I'm on my way," Ruby answered. "Shall I fill the bathtub with water? The storm could foul the well."

"We don't have time!"

"I'll do it!" Clara said. She got as far as the foyer when a sheet of white light flared through the transom window and a bone-cracking BOOM shook the house. Grabbing the banister, Clara made it only to the landing before the house shook again. The gas lamps flickered and went dark.

She hugged the wall until she reached the bathroom. After getting the drain plug in place, she sat on the edge of the tub and waited impatiently for it to fill.

"Mrs. Glendoveer?" she called. But there was no answer from down the hall. "Hurry!" she said to the tap. When lightning hit again, the tiled room blazed bright as day, and Clara swore the thunder was strong enough to knock Mrs. Glendoveer from her bed. The rain hit the roof with a few strong splatters before pelting it with hail.

Clara closed the tap and flew down the hall. "Mrs. Glendoveer!"

There, framed in the open window, stood the old woman, her white hair unpinned and coiling weakly down her back. Rocks of ice were bouncing against the floor. She turned to Clara, her eyes wild. "My babies!" she said. "Did you see? The hail is the size of quail eggs."

Clara rushed to her side and pulled the window shut.

"We must get you back to bed," she said. "Why, you aren't even wearing a wrapper."

"I shan't go until I know my birds are safe."

The hail stopped as suddenly as it had started. Clara peered out into the yard, where both her mother and a capless Ruby struggled against the wind with a sail of canvas slapping the birds' cage.

"Don't worry," Clara said. "Look, Mother has already tied down one side. And Ruby is stronger than she looks. There. They've got the ceiling covered completely. It's going to be fine."

The lightning flashed again, and Clara saw the black shapes of the birds moving in a flurry behind the bars. Their cries were electric and out of rhythm: "Awwwk-AWWWWWK! Skeee skeee!"

Ruby slipped on the hail-strewn grass, muddying her knees. The birds took up their cries again as the canvas panel flapped against the cage. Harriet finally caught hold of a corner and tied the canvas down with rope.

Ba-BOOM! With another strike of lightning, the clouds loosed a slanting rain.

"Now aren't you glad I shut that window?" asked Clara. "Imagine your getting wet."

Mrs. Glendoveer allowed herself to be led back to bed, where she shivered violently under the blankets. Clara lit a candle and warmed her feet with her hands.

"You're a dear," Mrs. Glendoveer said. "I suppose you must think I'm a hysterical old woman."

"Of course not."

"I meant to have the old awning replaced on the pergola by now." She clapped her hands to her cheeks. "If anything had happened to them, I never could have lived with myself. Never."

"You do love them very much," said Clara.

"It was George who loved them," said Mrs. Glendoveer. "And he had so many birds. We went through flocks of stage-trained doves during his years in the theater. But these meant the world to him, and I can only imagine what he'd say if he found so much as a single feather endangered on any one of them."

Clara knew the birds were old. George Glendoveer had died at least thirty years ago. She'd heard her mother and Ruby wonder just how long these animals were supposed to live, but no one dared bring up the subject with Mrs. Glendoveer.

Clara's mother came in, soaked to the skin and carrying a lantern. "Ah, Mrs. Glendoveer," she said. "The rain is still coming down in buckets, but the birds are dry. We've got the stove downstairs fired and soup on the boil. Lights are out all over town, though, so I brought you a lamp."

"Thank you, Harriet, but I must insist that you get out of your wet clothes before you do another thing." And then to Clara, "Your mother is a treasure, always putting others before herself."

For the rest of the night, doors slammed randomly with the gusts that blew through the drafty house. Candles extinguished themselves. Branches from the big oak and countless bits of debris scratched outside the walls as the storm heaved.

Although she had slept in her own little room for years, Clara did not refuse her mother's invitation to share a bed this night. They said their prayers together.

"And may the shingles stay on the roof," concluded her mother.

And may the roof stay on the house, added Clara silently. She clung to her mother in the dark, her eyes wide open.

Chapter 2

Sometime during the night, the storm quieted enough for Clara and her mother to fall asleep. But as soon as the gray dawn shone through the lace curtains, Clara's mother was wide awake. "I'm almost afraid to look," she said. Her breath came out in clouds. "You put on your coat and slippers and make sure Mrs. Glendoveer has a coal fire."

Clara did as she was told, and saw that shafts of light were penetrating the dark stairwell. The big window at the top of the landing had its shutters open, and the sunrise was just starting to make the sky glow pink. She leaned against the glass, looked down, and gasped.

The old oak had split in half and now lay against the front door of the house. Bricks were scattered in a corner of the hedge. Two shutters had fallen and smashed, and the one that had protected the landing window was hanging at a precarious angle.

Clara's mother stood outside pinching the bridge of her nose, as she always did when a headache was coming on. Ruby, carrying a hatchet, came around the side of the house to join her. As Clara stared, she heard something like a loud bark coming from Mrs. Glendoveer's room.

She found the old woman in bed with her hands at her neck. "I can't speak," she wheezed. Her breath rattled in her throat. "I've caught cold. How has the house held up?"

"I'm not sure," Clara said, stoking the fire. "Mama is outside now."

"And my birds?"

"I'll find out for you," Clara said, "and bring you something for your throat."

"I'm worried," whispered Mrs. Glendoveer. "It is so awfully quiet."

Clara tried to smile reassuringly. She hoped Ruby had already checked the aviary. When she reached the kitchen, however, she saw that the cage out back was still shrouded in canvas, mud-splotched and hung with dead branches but otherwise untouched.

The sound of chopping came from the front yard, and Clara knew that Ruby and her mother were taking apart the old oak. Clara made a mixture of honey and lemon, stoked the stove, and put a kettle on, stalling really, in the hope that one of the women would come and check on the birds for her, but the chopping outside continued.

Clara squared her shoulders. "They're only birds in a cage," she said to herself sternly. But as she approached the aviary, her heart filled with dread. No sounds came from inside. The sun had risen fully—a time when the birds were usually the noisiest. She stared at the dirty, wet rope for a full minute before she dared touch it.

"Hello?" she whispered through the canvas. "Are you all right?"

No answer. For a moment, all sorts of pictures flashed through Clara's mind: damp feathers like fallen leaves, the black mynah on his back, claws up, red eyes open. She swallowed hard and picked at the knot.

"Please, please, let them be safe," she said. The knot came undone, and Clara unthreaded the rope from the grommets. She counted to three and threw back the flap.

"AWWWWK! AWWWWWK!"

Clara covered her ears and jumped back as every bird in the cage came to life. The cockatoo angled his way across the bars, screaming and scolding. A blur of feathers criss-crossed inside the aviary. Amid the shrieking, someone called. The voice was garbled, as if a human being were trying to talk with a mouth full of water.

"Who's speaking?" Clara said. "What do you want?"

"Elliot! Elliot!" called the mynah, canting his masked head to show Clara one red eye and then the other.

As the mynah chanted, the birds took up the rhythm. Each one settled on a perch until all were still and staring directly at Clara.

"Elliot!"

"Skee-skee!"

"Elliot!"

"Awwwwk!"

A chill ran through Clara as she gazed back at the birds. What kind of omen was this?

She turned toward the house, refusing to look back as the birds loudly reproached her. By the time she reached the kitchen, the kettle on the stove was whistling at a high pitch, and it seemed to Clara that the entire house was in a state of alarm.

Trembling, she poured water into the teapot, set a tray, and took it upstairs. The anxious look on Mrs. Glendoveer's face was transformed when Clara told her the birds had all survived the storm.

"They're a bit upset, of course," she added bravely. "But very lively."

Mrs. Glendoveer smiled and took her cup. "Thank you, my dear," she rasped.

Clara sat on the edge of the bed in silence before she got the courage to ask. "Mrs. Glendoveer," she said, "who is Elliot?"

Mrs. Glendoveer nearly dropped her cup and set it down sloshing onto the saucer. "Did you say 'Elliot'?"

"I did. Or rather, one of the birds did. The mynah. He was quite insistent."

"Extraordinary," said Mrs. Glendoveer. She touched her fingers to her lips, and her wide blue eyes grew watery. "He said they might speak, but I had lost all expectation."

"Who?" Clara asked.

15

"George. My husband."

"Has the mynah never spoken before?"

"Never," said Mrs. Glendoveer. "It almost makes me wonder . . ." She trailed off. "Are you sure?"

"Absolutely," Clara said. "That bird's eyes look as if they could burn through me. I was frightened, to tell the truth."

"Oh, love, don't be afraid." She lowered her voice. "Shall I share my story with you?"

Clara nodded as Mrs. Glendoveer reached into the collar of her nightgown and pulled out her gold locket with a lovely green citrine stone in the center. "The latch is so small and my eyes are so dim," she said. "Could you open this for me, please?"

Clara did, and found inside a tiny key, which she handed to Mrs. Glendoveer. Then the old woman pointed to an alligator chest in the corner of the room. "In that box you'll find a stamped leather book with a lock. Bring it here and I'll show you."

The book was heavy, so Clara was careful to rest it gently on Mrs. Glendoveer's lap.

"It has been a long time since I've opened this," she said. "If you don't mind, would you please turn around while I look inside?"

"All right," Clara said. She could hear the key clicking in the lock and the sound of turning pages.

"Ah, so there he is. My goodness, I'm quite overcome," Mrs. Glendoveer said. "Please come see, Clara."

The big leather book was shut, but Mrs. Glendoveer had pulled out a photograph in a paper frame showing a beautiful woman in an old-fashioned gown, seated in a cane chair and holding an infant with bright black eyes.

"Is that you, Mrs. Glendoveer?"

"Yes," she said. "And the darling baby is my little Elliot."

"He's precious. Where is he now?"

Mrs. Glendoveer shook her head. "We didn't have him very long," she answered. "I remember him clearly, though. He was a passionate thing with a lusty cry. Curious little boy. Or he would have been had he stayed with us."

Clara remembered asking her mother once why Mrs. Glendoveer never had any children, before she learned that the question was a rude one.

"Don't be nosy, Clara," her mother had warned. "If Mrs. Glendoveer wishes to speak of such things, she will be the one to broach the subject."

Now that Mrs. Glendoveer was telling her about the baby, Clara felt free—almost relieved. "I always knew you must have had a child," she said. "I felt it."

"Did you?"

"Yes. I can't tell you why. Maybe because you have always been so understanding of me." Clara took the picture and studied the baby's face. "I am glad you told me. I only wish he were still here to be a consolation to you. It's always seemed a shame that this house wasn't filled with children."

Mrs. Glendoveer looked over her spectacles. "And that, I suspect, would be a consolation to *you* as well."

Clara blushed. "Oh, I don't mean to complain."

"It's all right. We all get lonely." Mrs. Glendoveer slipped the photograph back in the book and locked it again. "When you first came here with your mama, you quite reminded me of Elliot. Snappy black eyes, taking everything in. It's fitting that you know about him."

"Thank you for telling me," Clara said, taking the book to put away.

"Clara," Mrs. Glendoveer said, "I can't tell you how much it would mean to me if you'd report any other things you might hear from the birds. In fact, if you could go and speak to them, it might bring them out some more."

Clara told Mrs. Glendoveer that she would pass on anything she heard, but doubted she could bring herself to talk to the birds. "You mustn't strain your voice any more," she said. "Today, I can read the rest of my Sir Walter Scott while you rest."

Books were the one way Clara could wander, so she was more than happy to spend her morning with the Black Knight and legendary outlaws of the forest. But on her way downstairs, she couldn't help but kneel again at the window seat. All the house's front windows had been shuttered long ago to discourage stone-throwing children. Thanks to the storm, the view was now wide open, and Lockhaven lay before her in the crystal-clear morning light like a page from a picture book. The tiny Pincushion Islands dotting the bay were green and refreshed by the rain. All the roof-tops and carriages appeared doll-size and fit for her to re-arrange in any way she'd like.

As her mother and Ruby hacked at the fallen oak below, Clara pressed her nose against the glass and dreamed.

"If I went to school, I would never simply walk down the sidewalk. I would run and skip and never get out of breath. I'd be happy and healthy and in a hurry to take my seat in the classroom's first row. Because I am smart. But certainly not conceited. Everyone would like me, I'd make sure of it."

Clara became so immersed in her "made-up" life that she almost began to believe she was the smart, strong, kind girl beloved by classmates who ran here and there boldly and with complete freedom. Then the clock tower struck eight o'clock and broke the spell.

Schoolchildren began to flock down the street. They came waving branches from fallen trees, stomping on the clumps of wet newspaper that had been scattered on the sidewalk by the wind. One little girl picked up an umbrella that had blown inside out and twirled it over her shoulder. Clara marveled at them, celebrating the ruin as they might a carnival.

She put her hand up against the glass and watched a ring of steam form around it, then studied her handprint. "I'm like a ghost in a tower," Clara murmured. "I might as well be invisible."

Just then a girl walking alone, with a red cap and

ringlets, stopped on the street and turned to look at the house. Clara thought she must be close to her own age but didn't remember ever seeing her before. "Look at me!" Clara whispered.

The girl held back, distracted by something—the sound of the oak being chopped?—before lifting her eyes to the turret window where Clara knelt.

The girl froze. For some reason, Clara half expected her to scream. But instead, an amazed smile broke out on her face. She raised her arm and waved.

Clara put her hand to the glass again, this time with a yearning in her heart that was almost like pain.

"Hullo!" shouted the girl, waving madly this time.

Before Clara could smile back, she saw her mother striding to the center of the yard. Clara ducked and slid from her perch to the wooden floor, where she wrapped her arms around her knees.

There was a noise in the foyer, a slamming of the door. Her mother was marching up through the house. Clara grabbed her book, ran to Mrs. Glendoveer's room, and slipped into a chair, but she couldn't take in the words. All she could see before her eyes was the girl in the red cap, bouncing on her toes, waving, shouting "Hullo!"

Chapter 3

By late in the day, Mrs. Glendoveer's cough had turned into a persistent rattle. Clara was put to work brewing a drink from the boneset plant her mother grew on the windowsill. Making the remedy took time, because the herb had to be steeped in boiling water and then cooled or it would cause an upset stomach.

She fanned the pot and tested the broth with her finger, anxious to get a cup of the stuff quickly to Mrs. Glendoveer before the children came home from school at three o'clock. If only she could catch a second glimpse of the astonishing girl in the red cap before her mother fixed the shutters again. Would she look up? Would she wave?

Finally, it occurred to Clara to speed the cooling with a hunk of ice. She took the brass hammer from its peg on the wall and chipped at the great block in the icebox. Her mother was not fond of anyone chipping at the ice, because the smaller it was, the faster it melted, and food would spoil. When a shoe-size hunk fell off the side, Clara winced, knowing she would certainly catch it from her mother later. Nonetheless, she used the entire piece, setting it in the sink with the pan on top of it until all had thoroughly chilled.

As swiftly as she could, Clara carried a mug of the remedy wrapped in a napkin down the hall and up the stairs. "Mrs. Glendoveer," she said, giving the lady a gentle shake.

She barely stirred, and Clara tried again.

Slowly Mrs. Glendoveer opened her eyes. "Ah. Hello, dear," she said. "What time is it?"

"Somewhere near, oh, three o'clock," Clara said, trying to sound nonchalant.

Mrs. Glendoveer coughed and reached for her hankie. She pulled the sleeves of her nightgown up to her elbows, then felt her hair. "I must look a mess," she said.

Clara wished that Mrs. Glendoveer would please hurry and take her medicine. And then she felt guilty for wanting to rush her. "Let's get this down your sore throat where it can do some good, shall we?" she said.

"All right. But I would like to have my glasses first. Can you find them?"

Clara grabbed at the spectacles on the nightstand and unfolded them.

"If you could polish them a bit, I'd be so grateful," said the old woman.

"Of course," said Clara with all the patience she could muster. As she rubbed the lenses vigorously, she began to wonder if the good Lord was trying to test her.

That's when the town's bell chimed the three o'clock hour. Clara felt she could almost cry. She knew that by the time she had Mrs. Glendoveer's spectacles clean and wrapped over her ears, the coverlet pulled up and the pillows propped behind her, and the medicine cup emptied, the children would have passed. She let herself feel the full weight of her disappointment.

When Mrs. Glendoveer finished her cup, she took a tin of peppermints from her bed stand, popped one in her mouth, and offered one to Clara.

"It clears the bitterness," she said.

If only it could, Clara thought. She took the cup and glanced through the turret window on the way back down to the kitchen. Nobody was out there. She trod heavily down the stairs until an unexpected sight stopped her in the foyer. There, in the stained-glass sidelights by the front door, was someone's shadow. Her heart caught in her throat as she watched the mail slot flip open and an envelope fall to the floor.

Clara rushed forward and grabbed it. There on the front, written in violet ink, were the words:

For the Weary Sufferer

She slumped, assuming now that this letter was meant for Mrs. Glendoveer. But then again, there was no specific addressee. She turned the letter over in her hand and noted that it was not sealed. Couldn't she just peek at it and return it to the envelope at the first sign it was intended for someone else?

Trembling, she slid out the letter and unfolded it. The paper smelled of violets too. Tucking herself behind the parlor door, she read:

A Poem for Thee
How thy soul must seeketh,
   Shut away from view,
Comforts, small, from friendship!
     May I visit you?
I hope to ease thy burden.
     Though lonely and enclosed,
You may teach me patience,
     For you know how the rose
Is thorned as well as fragrant. . . .
     In this world of care,
Those who suffer deeply,
     The angels stoop to hear.

Oh dear. That is an AWFUL last line. I did want to say something about "prayers," which would rhyme so much better with "care," but I had to finish this poem between eating my bread and cheese sandwich and pulling bits of paper from my hair flung at me by a horrible boy (Gilroy something or other? Awful, rude, miserable . . .). So you must take the verse in the spirit in which it was intended, which was to lift your spirits and introduce myself, your new neighbor (two doors down, actually), because although haste and verse are not good friends, I was hoping that we two might be. I've asked around about you (pretty, mysterious girl with braids standing in tower window), but no one seems to know anything except that there is someone ill living at your house. And it made me wonder, frankly, about this town, Lockhaven. Are there no CHRISTIANS living here? My goodness, in my old town, someone from the church would have sent you a covered basket by now, at the very least!

I tend to blurt. If I haven't frightened you off, wave at me tomorrow. I shall be looking for you.

Daphne Aspinal

Clara clutched the note to her chest. *Pretty, mysterious girl with braids . . .* The depiction thrilled her. To be seen, to be described—it was as if the plain girl she always saw in the mirror might be magically transformed by the simple act of being observed by others. Pretty? Mysterious? What else might Clara be?

"It's tea, Clara!" called Ruby.

Clara hastily stuck the envelope under her pinafore and hurried to the kitchen. Her mother stopped in her tracks and put down the shortbread she had just pulled from the oven.

"Are you feverish?" she asked, feeling Clara's forehead.

"No," Clara answered, holding very still.

"You're a bit clammy," her mother said. "But you're red as a beet. Have you been running in the house? You know you mustn't."

Clara shook her head no. Her mother looked at her skeptically, so she turned away and joined Ruby at the table.

As soon as Clara was seated, she felt a jab below her ribs. When no one was looking, she reached to her waistband and adjusted the offending envelope. Even if she never heard from Daphne again, she would keep this note forever. It would be her only secret.

"I'm concerned about Mrs. Glendoveer's cough," said her mother. "If it doesn't clear by morning, I'm thinking of calling in Dr. Post."

Ruby's eyes rounded. "Dear," she said.

"I know, but we can't skimp on her care because we're short on funds. Maybe he'll barter. He doesn't have a wife. Perhaps he has mending?"

Clara roused. "But I gave Mrs. Glendoveer the boneset. It's always worked before."

Harriet looked to Ruby and then to her daughter. "It is never a small thing when an elderly person develops a rattle in the lungs. The downhill can be swift. Even among the young, pneumonia can be . . ." She lowered her head and fussed with her napkin, but Clara caught the expression her mother was trying to hide.

"You've seen it happen before, then," Clara ventured.

"Yes," her mother said.

"Before we came to live with Mrs. Glendoveer?"

Clara's mother began to answer and halted. "No use going over that while we're all here and well," she said. "Drink your tea."

Clara was used to being diverted from any talk of her mother's past. Between her mother and Mrs. Glendoveer, Clara's experience of family was so limited that it wasn't until she began to read that it occurred to her that she too must have a father like the children in storybooks. But when she asked about him, her mother only said, "Everyone has a father, and you are no different. But since he isn't here, we mustn't dwell on what we don't have."

"But I'd like to know just the small things. What was his name? What were the things he liked? Anything little. You know, did he have a mustache?"

She softened for a moment. "I have my reasons, Clara. Please don't think me cruel. I can't say more."

"All right," Clara said. But it was hard to swallow these questions once she started.

Her mother turned to leave her but stopped at the doorway. Her eyes shone, and her smile was sad. "No. He had no mustache," she said.

Clara stood stunned, because she had learned the answer to the question that she most wanted to know but hadn't dared to ask. Her mother had loved her father and missed him still. At that moment, his warm presence flickered between them. How sad it was for Clara to see her mother turn her back and let the moment fade.

Part of what made Daphne Aspinal so fascinating to Clara was her curiosity and her complete freedom to satisfy it. Imagine being like that, walking into a new town and shoving poetry through strangers' mail slots! Would she be hurt if Clara wasn't there at the window? She must have a wide-open heart to care enough to want to ease Clara's burden. Maybe she was extremely sensitive. Clara went on conjecturing until the thought of not replying seemed unthinkably rude.

Later that evening, after putting an iron kettle on Mrs. Glendoveer's stove to moisten the room's air, Clara retreated to the kitchen and cut herself a length of string. Next she took an old butter knife from the sideboard. Then she slipped out the back door to the herb bed that her mother had edged with stones. She was on her own secret assignment and squinted in the dark, hoping to find a rock just the right size.

"Elliot!" screeched the mynah from the corner of the yard.

"Shhhh," Clara said. "Hush now." She was surprised that the birds could see her at this distance at this time of night. Never before had she attracted their attention from as far as the kitchen garden.

"*Appropinquo!*" said the bird.

"What did you say?" asked Clara under her breath.

"*Statim!*"

The hair stood up on Clara's arms. "Are you speaking Latin?"

"*Appropinquo!*" repeated the bird. "Elliot!" As the mynah screeched, he tore at his nest of newspaper and flung the bits like confetti.

Clara tucked a stone in her pocket and walked backward slowly as the mynah continued to shout commands. She had only the slightest idea of what the bird was saying. Whatever it was he wanted Clara to do, he was demanding that she act quickly.

"I don't understand," she said. And when she reached the back porch, she ran in, slammed the door, whirled around, and found Ruby standing there with a mason jar and a garden fork. "What are you doing outside at this hour?" she asked.

"They're speaking to me," Clara said. "The birds. In Latin."

Ruby cocked an eyebrow. "Sounds like you've been doing a bit of moon bathing, to me."

"I'm telling the truth. Oh, Ruby, have they ever spoken to you?"

"No, Clara. And if they should want to chat with a human being, you can be sure I'd be the first in line. After all the bugs and crawly things I've bent my back fetching for them." She held up her jar. "I'm just about to

29

go out for earthworms. Let's see if they have anything to say."

Clara waited by the back door as Ruby went forth into the garden. The birds were silent as statues, and as still.

"How are you enjoying this spring evening?" Ruby asked them all. "I'm getting dinner for you, Mr. Kiskadee. Any preferences?" The birds stayed quiet. Ruby turned toward Clara. "I think that means he'll have the usual," she said in all seriousness.

"Don't tease me," Clara said. "I swear, the mynah said the word *statim*, plain as day. That means 'hurry,' Ruby."

Ruby shooed her inside, chuckling. "Now, now. You're not the only little girl to get the phantasms when out alone in the dark."

There was no use trying to convince Ruby, but Clara would tell Mrs. Glendoveer about the Latin tomorrow. In the meantime, she made her way to her bedroom, where she took out her writing paper and pencil.

Dear Daphne:

Your letter made me happy, and yet so sad. Because I am not allowed to have friends at my house, I cannot have you visit. My mother wishes me always to keep still, and this is a difficulty for me. However, I did not want to let your kind letter go without acknowledgment. And so I send you this note in return, though I know I cannot continue a correspondence.

Please don't speak of me to the children at school.

I don't want to attract the curious, especially since we have had trouble on our property with some of them before. And the nice old woman who owns the house needs her peace and quiet.

In the meantime, I will cherish your letter. No one has ever written a poem for me before. You must be the kindest girl. I will think of you always and look for you whenever I find a window open to the street.

With deep affection,
Clara Dooley

Clara paused and put the pencil to her lips. Was it proper to express deep affection to someone she had only waved to on the street? In the end, she decided that it was more important to tell the truth—and she wanted Daphne to know she regarded her with a special fondness.

After folding the page into a narrow strip, she wrote "FOR DAPHNE" in her best script, wrapped the note around the stone from the garden, tied it with the string, and placed it under her pillow with the butter knife for safekeeping until the morning.

Chapter 4

Before anyone in the house had stirred, Clara woke, put on her robe, and climbed to the turret window. She took the butter knife and worked it hard between the casements, putting all her weight against the handle. She was sure she felt a promising creak in the hinges until all of a sudden, the knife bowed in her hand as if it were soft as lead.

"Stubborn old thing," she said, and gave the glass an angry shove.

It opened. Not far—just about eight inches—but that might be enough. Clara was reaching for the stone with the note in her pocket when she heard footsteps on the stairs. She quickly gathered up the crumbs of dirt and chipped paint that littered the sill and threw them down into the yard, then lightly closed the window without securing the latch.

Her mother was at Clara's door by the time she got downstairs. She was carrying a pitcher of warmed water. "Up with the sun, I see," she said.

"Yes, I am," Clara said, hiding her dirty hands in her pockets.

"Good," she said, pouring the water into Clara's bedside basin. "I could use some extra help this morning. I'd like you to wash up quickly and make tea and toast for Mrs. Glendoveer while I go check on her, please."

"Of course!" Clara said brightly. She washed, dressed, rebraided her hair, and headed for the kitchen. As she set the kettle on the stove and put the bread in tongs to toast it, Clara's heart pounded with the thought of the stone in her apron pocket, the note wrapped around it.

"I'm not doing a bad thing, exactly," she told herself. "I'm only letting Daphne know that I can't see her. If you look at it a certain way, I'm really doing what Mama wants." But inside, she heard another voice making plans. Wouldn't it be wonderful to wave to Daphne each morning? What if, after a while, her mother saw that the friendship was harmless and allowed the girls to exchange letters, like pen friends?

Filled with anticipation, Clara readied the tray and went along, humming, to Mrs. Glendoveer's room.

"Please, Clara, help!" her mother said. She was leaning Mrs. Glendoveer forward over doubled pillows as she slapped her pink, bare back.

"What's happened?"

"Her lungs are congested. We need to help her cough it up. Please get her handkerchief and her bed jacket."

Clara set down the tea tray and got her mother a hankie.

"Cough, Mrs. Glendoveer," she said. "Don't be shy."

She did, and the ragged wheeze that followed disquieted Clara.

"Again, dear," said Harriet, wiping Mrs. Glendoveer's mouth.

"It's painful," rasped Mrs. Glendoveer. "Here in my back."

"And it doesn't help, me beating on you," Clara's mother said sympathetically. "I promise you, we're nearly done."

Clara almost couldn't bear to watch. The sharp bones of the old woman's spine seemed ready to break through the skin. And her lovely white hair was damp and stringy, showing her naked scalp.

After Mrs. Glendoveer coughed into the hankie one last time, Harriet motioned for Clara to bring the bed jacket. She clothed Mrs. Glendoveer and laid her back gently, propping her upright with pillows.

"I'm going to call Dr. Post," she said.

Shivering, Mrs. Glendoveer waved her hand as if she wanted no part of it.

"Please, Mrs. Glendoveer," Clara said.

"There's nothing he can do for me that you girls can't," she said.

Harriet put her hands on her hips. "I will give you this

morning," she said. "If your temperature rises or your pain worsens, I *will* call him."

The patient fell back into the pillows without another word.

"I am going to brush your hair, Mrs. Glendoveer," Clara said, "and put a cool cloth on you."

"Would you?" asked her mother.

"Whatever Mrs. Glendoveer wants," Clara said.

"Then I'll leave her in your hands for now. But I'll be back."

Clara took the pearl-backed brush and some hairpins from the vanity, but when she approached the bed, Mrs. Glendoveer laid her hand on Clara's arm.

"Clara Dooley," she said, "I would like to speak to you."

There was nothing playful about Mrs. Glendoveer's demeanor, and Clara listened carefully.

"Shall I tell you something about what it's like turning twelve years old?"

"That's not until July."

"Doesn't matter. You may think I don't remember. But I do. I don't know what your mother has said to you, but—" Mrs. Glendoveer held up a hand. She coughed lightly, then hoarsely. When she began to speak again, the coughing came back worse than ever.

"Mrs. Glendoveer, you mustn't try to talk now," Clara said.

Catching her breath, the sick woman shook her head. "It's now or never," she said.

"I don't know what you mean."

Mrs. Glendoveer's blue eyes focused on her with riveting directness. "You don't know what's ahead. But I can warn you now: at your age, it is not uncommon to be seized with a frightful restlessness. If you haven't felt it yet, you will soon, I promise."

Clara was speechless. How could she know?

"So many things become a source of dissatisfaction. Your heart can pull you in different directions, and you must decide the right way to go."

"What did you do," Clara asked, "when you were my age?"

Mrs. Glendoveer took a deep breath. "I started planning my escape. Oh, I didn't run off until I was seventeen, but I believe it all started around age twelve. I went to every carnival, every traveling show. And when the caravans left, I cried as if I'd been abandoned. Twice, I saw the young magician George Glendoveer, and on the third time, I convinced him to let me assist him onstage. I was very pretty," she said. "Like you."

Clara blushed. This was the second time in two days she had been called pretty. "If you are warning me against joining the carnival, you needn't worry," Clara said. "I don't have the strength to keep up, even if I wanted to."

"No, I'm telling you something else: a mother needs to have her loved ones close. I broke my mother's heart, and in turn mine was broken. Don't do it to Harriet."

Clara shook her head. "I would never, ever."

"This is advice for your mother as well as you. No happiness built on another's pain can come to a good end. I wish someone had told me this when I was young."

"I understand," Clara said.

Mrs. Glendoveer clapped her hands together softly. "Good. That's done."

Clara then took the hairbrush and ran it back from Mrs. Glendoveer's brow. The old woman closed her eyes. "Aah," she said, "I'm so very tired."

When Clara finished smoothing Mrs. Glendoveer's hair into a topknot, she found that the tea had turned cold. "I'll get you a fresh cup," she said.

Clara stood outside the bedroom door for a moment with her hand over the apron pocket holding the letter to Daphne. She had to wonder how Mrs. Glendoveer had chosen that moment to warn her about inner restlessness and bad behavior.

She walked down the hall deep in thought, until a sight in the turret window startled her. There on the other side of the glass was her mother, standing on a ladder, wielding the claw end of a hammer. Clara could make out the squeak of a rusty nail being pulled from the clapboard. She approached the window seat and knocked gently on the glass.

"What are you doing, Mama?"

"I'm rehanging the shutters," she called. "But I'm going to need some larger nails." She held up a bent penny nail. "These are worthless!"

As Clara watched her mother descend the ladder, the

37

clock tower struck seven. Soon the shutters would be hammered back into place. She closed her eyes and imagined Daphne Aspinal staring up at those closed shutters. In time, Clara supposed, the girl would become absorbed in her new life in Lockhaven, find real friends, and stop looking up at the old Glendoveer house altogether.

And then what?

Clara threw the window open. With all her might, she heaved the letter-wrapped rock, hoping to arc it over the yard and box hedge, down onto the sidewalk where Daphne would soon be walking. But she could feel the weakness in her arm as the stone left her grasp and watched it fly high in the air and drop smack into the bushes.

The air left her lungs. Who would ever find that note now? She closed the window and walked slowly down to the kitchen, dabbing her eyes as the terrible hammering began.

Clara fixed tea and brought it up to Mrs. Glendoveer, who had managed to fall asleep despite the banging. She clasped the old woman's hand. It was dry and hot, and she kissed it. By the time the clock tower chimed eight, the shutters were up and fastened with a new latch.

"My dear Mrs. Glendoveer," Clara whispered. "You are my only friend."

Mrs. Glendoveer slowly opened her eyes, which Clara noted were now dark and exceptionally shiny. She smiled like a china doll, a shiny red patch marking each cheek. "George and I are going away," she said.

Clara stood up and pressed the back of her hand to Mrs. Glendoveer's forehead. "You're scorching," she said.

Mrs. Glendoveer smiled again, as if Clara had delivered a wonderful piece of news. "We won't be long, child. Not long."

"I'm getting Mama," Clara said. As she ran down the hall, past its newly darkened window, she had the peculiar feeling that she had run down the stairs before in just this manner. And she knew that no matter how fast she moved, she could not reach her mother quickly enough, and the doctor would be too slow, and tomorrow would be terrible in a way that would make her long for the security of all her old dissatisfactions.

Chapter 5

Sequestered by her mother in Ruby's room, Clara was kept up half the night by the sound of weeping. And though Clara knew her mother meant for Ruby to watch over her, it was actually Clara who rubbed Ruby's back and whispered words of comfort.

"I told them to take her in the cabbage rose quilt," Ruby said. "It was her mother's, you know. Poor old girl."

Clara knew all about it. The men from the mortuary had brought Mrs. Glendoveer out through the back way, hoping to leave as discreetly as possible. That's when the screams started.

"Keee keeee! Awwwk AWWWKK!"

The birds set up a frightening clamor, beating against the bars of their cage until they rang. Most unsettling were the voices. Clara made out a child's wail among the racket.

At times she heard what she swore was a jagged sob. "MAAAAAH! MAAAAAH!" cried the cockatoo, until Clara was sure he was calling out for Mrs. Glendoveer.

They went on this way for over an hour. And when at last they quieted, they stood on their perches, wings hanging limp, heads bowed.

Clara did not cry. In the space where her heart used to lie was a frozen lump. She was vaguely ashamed, wondering what Ruby must think of her blankness.

"What happens now?" Clara asked.

Ruby blew her nose into her hankie. "I couldn't tell you," she said. "Usually, the bereaved are busy planning the wake. And friends of the deceased come with hot dishes, and we all try to make each other feel better."

"But Mrs. Glendoveer had no friends," Clara said.

"I wouldn't say that," Ruby said, taken aback.

"Besides us, I mean."

"I suppose," Ruby replied. "But we did love her, didn't we? She wasn't alone, at least."

"Of course." She didn't want to tell Ruby that the last thing she told Mrs. Glendoveer was that she considered her the dearest friend, because she just might start to cry. And she wasn't ready for that.

The next morning Clara's mother was up early as usual. Clara found her stirring a big iron pot on the stove with the end of a broomstick. Once in a while, she'd lift the stick and extract something like a rag dripping with tar.

"What an awful smell," Clara said.

"It won't be so bad after we've boiled and rinsed it."

"Are we to eat it?" Clara asked, disgusted.

"No, dear. You are to wear it. I'm blacking your pinafore." She removed the pot from the hot part of the stove, turned, and folded her hands. "I've decided you should come to see Mrs. Glendoveer buried."

Clara faltered. "I don't . . . that is, I'm not sure I want to, Mama."

"I can't let the reverend pray over her by himself. We must see it's done properly and with love. We'll go tomorrow afternoon and come back quickly. I've rented a carriage."

At this, Clara was overwhelmed. The thought of taking a carriage ride all the way across Lockhaven was something she had only dreamed of. And now it was coming true, but under the most unfortunate circumstances.

Harriet called Ruby in. "We won't be printing mourning cards or opening the house. But do you think we should put a notice in the paper?"

"I think that would be nice," Ruby said.

"All right, then," Harriet said. "If you write it and take it down to the *Tribune* this morning, perhaps we'll see it published tomorrow."

"Oh, not me," said Ruby, turning pink. "I don't write things."

"I do," volunteered Clara. "If you let me, I'll write the notice and Ruby can deliver it."

"Fine," said her mother. "But, Clara, make it brief and

with few details. And please do not mention our presence in the home. Officially, Mrs. Glendoveer has no survivors. We mustn't presume."

Clara went to her room and took out her pen and paper.

Mrs. George Glendoveer (Cenelia) passed away Thursday evening of pneumonia. She was quite old—old enough to remember Lockhaven when the big sailing ships still stopped here. Her marriage to the magician George Glendoveer took her to many places. Their love was strong, although their lives were shadowed with disappointment. Mrs. Glendoveer was fond of her birds, which appear to be inconsolable after her death. They did not sing when the sun came up on Friday morning. They have not yet sung today. This dear lady will be much missed.

Clara put down her pen. She hadn't felt capable of sympathy for the creatures before; but as she thought of the ragged old birds, sitting silent, wings hanging as if they were broken, a tear rolled down one cheek.

By the time she had folded the notice into its envelope, she could not stop her tears. Ruby took the note from her and rested her hand on Clara's shoulder.

"I am glad it is you who remembered her for everyone," said Ruby. "She would have liked that."

Clara knew that to be true, which made her suffering keener still.

•   •   •

When it was time to leave for the graveyard, the air was filled with a fine drizzle. Clara wore a thick black crêpe veil over her hat, which made the world appear even drearier. The man who drove the carriage lifted her up onto the tufted leather seat and then assisted her mother and Ruby aboard.

"Will they be selling the old place now?" he asked, jerking a thumb at the house.

"Why?" Harriet replied sharply. "Are you interested in buying?"

"Me?" he laughed. "No. Though I have wondered why the house wasn't pulled down before, what with the history that comes with it. Then the company sends me out here today. Could have knocked me over. I thought the last Glendoveer had expired long ago."

"Obviously not," she answered. "May we go, please?"

But the man leaned against the carriage and stroked his cheek. "I bet you could get something for the land if you hold out. People are building now. Brass works is expanding. Who knows?"

"I'd say you could use less brass and more manners," snapped Ruby.

The man pulled in his chin and gaped.

"Please commence to the cemetery, and in silence," said Harriet.

Clara looked at each of the women, but they stared straight ahead. "What was he talking about?"

"A load of nonsense," replied her mother.

Clara stared out the window as the coach rolled downhill. She saw that the houses and yards grew smaller as they approached the flats of Lockhaven. It was impossible to memorize every single one, yet she tried. One house had wash hung out in the yard, another had a tiny silver-haired woman peeling potatoes on her stoop. A little boy and girl laughed and chased a spotted dog dressed in an old lady's bonnet. The cemetery was a sharp contrast to its surroundings. The grounds were encircled in a grand wrought-iron fence and had an open double-door gate with gilt letters set into an arch above it:

~ MOUNT REPOSE ~

On each side of the sign were angels sobbing into the crook of an arm, drizzle dripping from their elbows. Inside, an intensely green lawn stretched for acres. Clara passed statues of men on horseback brandishing swords, obelisks, baby lambs of stone dozing on the graves of infants. But around the bend was the most awesome sight of all: a hulking black marble fortress supported by fat Ionic columns, slick and shiny from the rain.

At the tip of the roof was a sculpture. Clara thought it resembled a peacock. Its head was raised toward the heavens, and its wings were spread wide. Below, in the doorway, a stout minister in a white collar spotted the carriage and bowed.

"What kind of church is this?" Clara asked after the coach had rolled to a stop.

"It's a crypt," said her mother.

Clara got goose bumps. She had read about crypts. They were burial houses in ancient Egypt. "Are there mummies inside?"

"No. It's a place that George Glendoveer built for his family."

The carriage man held his tongue when he helped the ladies down to the walk, but Clara could tell he was taking in all the details of the crypt's strange edifice, perhaps to gossip about to his next set of passengers.

The minister rubbed his palms together to warm them before shaking hands. "It's chilly inside," he said. "I don't think the place has been opened for thirty years."

"It's an interesting building, to say the least, Reverend Tandy," Clara's mother said.

"Yes," he answered. "That bird on the roof is a phoenix, I believe." He looked up and shook his head. "I'm told it has some significance to the family, but I'm afraid I don't know much more."

As they entered the crypt, dimly lit by a gas lantern, Clara was surprised to note a luscious perfume thickening the air. As her eyes adjusted to the darkness, she could make out a black and silver casket heaped with white lilies. Candles in glass cups flickered around it.

"Reverend," Clara's mother said, "who sent the lilies?"

"I have no idea," he said. "We could ask the director after the services, if you'd like. Should we begin now?"

46

Clara reached for Ruby's hand and they followed the reverend closer to where Mrs. Glendoveer lay. Behind the casket a square door opened into the darkness. A plaque bearing the names GEORGE AND CENELIA GLENDOVEER was mounted above the opening. The reverend lifted his Bible and began to read in a round-voweled voice more dignified than his own:

Behold, I shew you a mystery; we shall not all sleep, but we shall all be changed, in a moment, in the twinkling of an eye. . . .

The words echoed in the marble chamber and seemed to Clara to gather power. She pictured Mrs. Glendoveer inside the heavy casket turning golden with light, readying herself for heaven. Tearing her eyes away from the casket, Clara noticed that there were many doors built into the wall. Each door had a plaque mounted above it.

ELLIOT, read the first. *Baby Elliot,* thought Clara. And then she read the next one: HELEN. *Would that be Mr. Glendoveer's mother?* she wondered. And there were more: ARTHUR, PETER, FRANCES, GEORGE WILLIAM.

None of those names were familiar to Clara. She supposed that Mr. Glendoveer must have come from a large family.

Just then, Clara heard footsteps from behind. She turned her head but was quickly prodded by her mother to face forward. Two men had joined them in the crypt. One wore a pince-nez and a long black coat, and carried his hat in his hand. The other was short and ruddy, and wore a baggy striped suit.

"My friends," said Reverend Tandy, "it has pleased Almighty God to take from this world the soul of Cenelia Glendoveer here departed. We now commit her body with the sure and certain faith in the resurrection to eternal life."

The reverend summoned one of the men. "Oscar?" he said.

The man in the baggy suit stepped forward and put his shoulder to the butt of the casket. Clara said a silent goodbye, expecting the box to glide gracefully behind the door. Not so. Oscar pushed until he was red in the face, but succeeded in moving the box only a few inches. The stone slab the casket rested on scraped and squeaked dreadfully, and so little progress was made that the reverend joined him and pushed too.

The scene repelled Clara. It was almost as if Mrs. Glendoveer did not want to go! By the time the box was finally shoved inside the crypt and the door closed, Clara was shaking with emotion.

Her mother knelt down and examined her. "You look pale," she said.

"I'm all right," said Clara, but her knees were wobbling. Before she knew it, she was lying among the muddy boot prints on the floor.

"Allow me," said the man with the pince-nez. He helped Clara to her feet and she retreated into her mother's arms. "These ceremonies are difficult for children. It's not uncommon for them to swoon. Should we get some air?"

"Thank you," said Harriet, pulling Clara close. "You must be the director. Would you know who sent the lilies?"

"Oh, I'm not the director," said the man. "But I can tell you who sent the lilies. It was George Glendoveer."

Now Clara's head was swimming. She had no idea how many Glendoveers there were, either alive or dead.

The man extended his hand. "I'm Clayton Merritt-Blenney, of the firm Fitzmorris Blenney. I'm the attorney for the Glendoveer estate."

Mrs. Glendoveer received so little mail that Clara remembered seeing letters from Fitzmorris Blenney Partners and wondering who they might be. She heard a little gasp and saw that her mother might be the one now in danger of fainting.

"Ruby," Harriet said, "please take Clara to the carriage."

Ruby's strong hand was at Clara's back, and Clara felt herself pushed down the walkway at a quick clip.

Ruby stayed quiet until the nosy driver had closed the carriage door. "Do you know that man?" Clara asked.

"I know of him," she said, peering through the window. She took out her hankie, wiped her face, and began to fan herself.

"Is Mama in trouble?"

"We'll see," Ruby said.

"But why?"

Ruby threw up her hands. "Because," she said, going red in the face, "we could be out on the street, bag and baggage!" She began to sob. "So sorry. Deary me, I don't know how your ma does it. Excuse me if your old Ruby wasn't born with a cast-iron constitution. . . ."

Clara pressed against the window. Her mother was listening to Mr. Merritt-Blenney, bobbing her head, but her veil obscured her expressions. Finally, the lawyer reached into his breast pocket and produced a card. Harriet studied it and curtseyed quickly as the man tipped his hat to her.

"Here she comes," said Ruby. "Marching like a soldier."

No sooner had the coachman helped Clara's mother aboard and closed the door than she threw back her veil and showed her gleaming face.

"Great merciful God," she said. "We are given a reprieve!"

Ruby fell upon her, crushing her in an embrace. Clara was happy too, but still felt unsettled. She had been on the verge of peril and never had an inkling.

"Tell us," Clara said. "Who saved us?"

"George and Cenelia Glendoveer, that's who," her mother said, letting out a laugh. "The story is strange. In short, Mr. Glendoveer provided for the house to be kept open and in readiness for fifty years after the disappearance of his youngest child."

"You mean Elliot?" said Clara.

"Yes. You knew about him? I must say I'm surprised."

"Mrs. Glendoveer showed me the baby's picture. But I thought he had died."

"No," said Ruby. "The baby was taken. No one knows who did it or what happened to him after that."

"Which is why George Glendoveer wanted the house maintained in case of his return," her mother said. "And Mrs. Glendoveer did him one better. She added a codicil to her will, leaving the house to us along with a modest trust to run it."

"Isn't the fifty years up yet?" asked Ruby.

"Almost," said Harriet. "I believe there are only four or so more months before the fiftieth year ends."

"And then what?" Ruby asked. "The house is falling down around our heads. A small allowance won't go far with the old place."

"I believe we would be permitted to sell the property and split the proceeds. As long as we provide for the birds, of course. They must be kept together and cared for as long as they live."

"Would you really sell, Mama?"

"I don't know. There are other provisions in the document. I'm to meet with Mr. Merritt-Blenney in his office on Sunday to get the full picture."

Clara was thinking how terrible it must have been for Mrs. Glendoveer to never know what happened to her lost baby, Elliot, when she saw her mother draw a blue leather box from her reticule.

"This is for you, Clara," said her mother. "Mrs. Glendoveer told me long ago that she wished you to have it when she passed on."

Clara took the box and opened it. "The locket," she said when she saw the oval citrine stone on its face. The necklace was cold to the touch, which made Clara feel the dear woman's absence concretely. She opened it and glanced at the little key held inside. Then she took off her hat, lifted her hair, and had her mother fasten the chain around her neck.

"I'll wear it always," she said, and spent the rest of the ride home with her hand over her heart.

Chapter 6

The bit of relief that Ruby, Clara, and her mother had felt evaporated when they entered the door of the house. Inside, the rooms were dark and chilly, and Clara noted that today was the first day in as long as she could remember that the house had been left empty.

As Ruby and her mother went to the kitchen to make supper, Clara climbed the stairs to Mrs. Glendoveer's bedroom. The door was ajar, and Clara peeked in and saw that the bed was neatly made. The desk where she had sat and read looked very small.

For many years, Mrs. Glendoveer, a natural teacher, had praised Clara for being a quick study and an ideal pupil. Now Clara realized that her schooling might well be over.

Time seemed stretched out before Clara in a way that actually frightened her. Would she spend her days in isolation until someone carried *her* out in an old cabbage rose quilt?

Gong!

Clara pricked up her ears. She could have sworn she heard the doorbell ring.

Gong!

"There it is again," she said, rushing down the stairs. The bell seldom rang and was so muffled it couldn't be heard in the kitchen.

"One moment!" she called before flinging open the door.

A woman in a full skirt, shawl, and pearl-gray brimmed hat stood before her holding a large covered basket. "Hello," she said, smiling shyly. "I do hope we aren't inconveniencing you."

"We?" Clara said.

A girl with blond curls stepped out from behind the woman. "Yes, we!" the girl said. "The notice of Mrs. Glendoveer's passing was in the papers, and I told Mother we had to come by."

Clara couldn't find words. Here, in front of her, was Daphne Aspinal, and yet she, Clara, stood mute as a fish.

"Mother," Daphne said, "this is Clara Dooley."

"How did you . . . ?" Clara gasped.

"And this is my mother, Delia Aspinal," Daphne went on. "And I'm Daphne."

"Oh! I know!" said Clara. "I received your letter."

"May we come in?" Daphne asked.

"Daphne!" said her mother. "We can't impose like that." Then, to Clara, she said, "Please accept this basket, and tell your mother the Aspinals send their condolences."

Clara took the basket and looked pleadingly at Daphne. "I don't know what to say," she told her.

"No need to say a thing," said Mrs. Aspinal. "Good afternoon, dear." She picked up her skirt and turned to the street, but to Clara's delight, Daphne stayed behind.

"I got your rock," she whispered.

"Oh, I'm so glad," said Clara.

"I almost missed it. I do wonder why you hid it in the shrubbery."

"Daphne!" called her mother.

"Coming!" she called.

"I wish you wouldn't go," Clara said.

"I'll come back for the casserole dish." Daphne tapped her forehead. "See? There's always a way."

"Yes," Clara said, her heart beating wildly. "Yes. And thank you! Thank you both."

"Who you hollering at?" Ruby hollered from down the hall.

Clara shut the door and carried the basket to the kitchen. "The lady from two houses over brought us a hot dish."

Her mother frowned. "Which lady?"

"Her name is Delia Aspinal. Look, she sent a note."

Harriet unfolded the letter and scratched her head. "Says they're new to the neighborhood," she said.

"Well, that explains it," Ruby said.

Clara's mother raised an eyebrow.

"You know darn well that none of the old-timers will call," Ruby said.

"It's awfully nice of them, don't you think?" Clara said.

"Wait until the rumor mill catches up with 'em," Ruby said. "Then we'll see."

"That's enough, Ruby," Harriet said under her breath.

Clara's fists tightened. "What rumors? Please. I want to know what you're talking about. Does this have anything to do with what the carriage driver said?"

Ruby's head shrank into her shoulders, and her mother didn't answer.

"In one day, I hear a baby's been taken and that the house should have been pulled down. What was he talking about?"

"Who knows?" said her mother. "The house is quite a shambles from the outside. Maybe people make up stories about it. I wouldn't be surprised."

"That's how people are," Ruby said. "Why, when I was a girl in Nova Scotia, there was an old lady said to drink the blood of cats."

"Honestly!" said Harriet.

"And don't you know all us children believed it. Whenever a cat went missing, we said it had gone the way of Mrs. Lynch's goblet."

"How horrible," Clara said.

"It wasn't entirely bad," Ruby added thoughtfully. "They do say she kept the population down."

"I suggest we change the subject," said Harriet, "or we won't be able to enjoy this supper so kindly provided to us." She peeked in the basket. "Oh, look, there are hard rolls in here still warm."

"Let's eat early, shall we?" said Ruby, lifting the lid on the casserole. "And I'll say no more about cats."

Clara set the table while Ruby went out back to check on the aviary. "They still haven't made a peep," said Clara to her mother. "Don't you think that's odd?"

"Animals are sensitive," she said. "And these birds have been in the family for I don't know how long. I wouldn't be surprised if some passed away, frankly, from the shock."

When Ruby came back inside, she clucked her tongue. "They spilled their grain on the floor and left the earthworms to dry."

"Just as I was saying to Clara," Harriet told her, "those birds may not be long for this world."

"One would think so," Ruby said, "and not because our Mrs. Glendoveer is gone. All of them except for the cockatoo have lived far beyond their natural limits."

"Due, no doubt, to your exceptional care, Ruby. Now will you get the butter? I believe we're ready to eat."

Ruby and Harriet ate heartily, but Clara couldn't help but think of the starving birds. She had to admit that she sometimes saw in them a reflection of herself, cooped up with nothing but the same faces to look at day after day.

But today, she'd gone on a carriage ride and opened the door to Daphne. Perhaps her own cage door might be rattling open. Just a little bit?

On Sunday, Harriet Dooley put on her veil and took the streetcar down to Fitzmorris Blenney Partners. "Mr. Merritt-Blenney is meeting her there after church," Ruby told Clara. "I'm guessing your ma told him how empty our pockets are. Why else wouldn't they wait until proper business hours?"

"Maybe she doesn't want to sell any more of the Glendoveer silver," Clara said.

"Oh, that," Ruby said. "I just hope Mrs. Glendoveer never knew how desperate we had been to keep the household going."

"I'm sorry you had to worry so much. I'd have found a way to help."

"You did help Mrs. Glendoveer. She adored you, you know." Ruby sniffed and dabbed one eye with her apron. "Now I've got to get myself out back to turn over the soil for spring planting. And, no, you can't join me. Your ma would have my head."

Clara watched Ruby pull on her cap and rough coat, wishing she could keep her company. Instead, she wandered through the house to the parlor listening to the various clocks tick their way through the late morning. At last she rested her head on the old horsehair sofa and dozed until she heard a voice in the foyer.

"Hellooooooo! Anyone home?"

Clara went to look and had to laugh. The mail slot in the big front door flapped open and shut as if it were speaking. She fell to her knees and peered out, and was greeted with another pair of eyes.

"Oh!" said Daphne. "It's you. I tried to ring the bell, but no one came."

"I was asleep," Clara said. "I can't believe it's really you!"

"Did I get you from your bed? Now I feel terrible."

Clara flung open the door. "I've been up for hours. It's just that there's nothing to do around here."

Daphne looked past her into the hall. "It looks like a castle inside. May I see?"

Clara recalled with a start that her mother was not at home. "Please come in," she said.

Daphne stared up at the starred ceiling. Clara followed as she ran her hand down the heavily carved banister leading upstairs.

"You should see my house," Daphne said. "It's *sober*, which is supposed to be tasteful, I guess. Nothing but a box covered with shingles. But this . . ."

"You like it?"

"Of course," Daphne said. "Don't you feel you're living in a fairy tale sometimes? With the romantic turrets and crooked shutters? I would."

Clara shrugged. She was embarrassed by an urge to smile constantly.

"What?" Daphne asked. "Am I prying? I am. I ask too

many personal questions and am always poking into the out-of-the-way places. My mother says to learn to say things in my head before I state them, but that slows everything down to a snore, don't you think?"

"I . . . ," Clara said. She hid her face with her hands. "I've never had anyone in my house before. Not another child, I mean."

"Then I'm the first? Extraordinary! How old are you?"

Clara peeked through her fingers. "Almost twelve."

"How amazing," Daphne said. "I've always been surrounded by *masses* of girls. At boarding school, we ate together and roomed together and went to chapel together and all the rest. There is no mystery in that kind of life. Absolutely squashing."

"But why are you in Lockhaven now?"

Daphne looked over her shoulder, then whispered, "Booted."

Clara stood uncomprehending.

"Kicked out. Sent down." She clasped her hands beneath her chin. "Don't think I'm bad. I did a foolish thing. Our headmistress had it in for a girl who was a bit distracted. And the meaner this headmistress got, the more distracted the girl got, until she was unable to answer in class and kept forgetting to refill the cistern and sat up all night with insomnia and spent all morning falling asleep in chapel."

"So why did they send *you* down?"

"Well, we knew the headmistress had written the girl's parents about discipline, and the girl was sure her parents were going to write back saying, 'Do whatever it takes! Give her a birching if you like!'"

"A birching?"

"A whipping," Daphne said.

"No!"

"Yes. So I . . . stole her parents' letter. And got caught. And I was sent home just in time to move with my parents to rainy old Lockhaven, Maine. My father moved his importing business to this town. Says it's cheaper to keep ships here at the bay than in the larger ports. But, my goodness, weren't there other places that would have suited just as well? He doesn't care, of course, because he's always in Cádiz or Tangier or somewhere that isn't here." Daphne sighed. "My mother got me a cat to cheer me up. A little blue one, if you can imagine that! But Mother had its claws taken off so it won't climb the curtains, and I'm afraid it's as miserable as I am. Poor thing sits at the window, yearning to break free!"

"You don't like Lockhaven at all, do you?"

"I didn't," Daphne said. "Until now."

Clara reddened. "Why is that?"

"Because of you, of course," she said simply. "Why, you're a complete living mystery."

Clara felt flustered. "I'm not mysterious at all. Not really."

"Yes, you are! And I want to know all about you. In

fact, I could kick myself for wasting so much time talking about myself. Have I bored you?"

"Not at all!" Clara said. "You are utterly surprising in every way." And unlike anyone she'd read about in *Advice for Young Ladies*, she almost added. But a door slammed back in the kitchen. Daphne craned her neck and looked past Clara down the hall. "Is that your mother?" she asked.

"No," said Clara. "It's Ruby." She shook her hands loosely at the wrists and wondered what to do. "Follow me," she said firmly.

Clara led Daphne into a coat closet that smelled of mothballs and closed the door behind them.

"What are we doing?" Daphne asked, giggling.

Clara felt the floor for a latch, and lifted the trapdoor that led to the boiler room below the house. A faint light glowed from the tiny windows in the basement. "Step down here," she said. "And be careful. There aren't handrails."

The girls crept down into the cement room crowded by the old metal hulk of the boiler, which was now cold and silent.

Clara swept cobwebs aside and led Daphne to a rickety door behind the boiler leading to the outside. A skeleton key had rusted in the lock.

"Let me try," said Daphne. She jiggled the key and pulled until she felt it grind free. "Here!" she said triumphantly, pushing open the door. The odor of wet grass and rotten wood spilled into the concrete room. "Our secret passageway!"

Clara saw the leaf-covered back stairs and the gray sky above. "There is a gate on the left that takes you out the side yard into the alley. From there you can go to your house, providing you have a back gate too."

"Done," said Daphne. "You weren't fooling when you said you weren't to have company." She looked at Clara hard. "Tell me, are the people here cruel to you?"

Clara's jaw dropped. "No! I'm very well treated."

"All right, then," she said. "Let's think ahead. You want to meet again, don't you?"

Clara nodded.

"Then I still have one visit left to come get the casserole," Daphne said. "But maybe we should save that for when we really need it."

Daphne was amazing, Clara thought. "Come over through the boiler room," she said. "But how will I let you know when it's safe?"

"I can see the upper story of your house from my father's study, but the curtains on that side of the house are always closed. Why don't you pull back a curtain when you want me, and I'll come here as soon as I can."

"Yes! And I'll leave the door unlocked for you," Clara said. "And if you want to leave me a note, you can always slip something under this door. No one ever ventures down here."

Daphne's eyes popped open wide, and she gave a little

jump. "I am so excited," she said. "And next time I come, if I start talking about myself, you poke me and tell me to stop. I want to learn about *you*. Do you hear?"

"I do," Clara said. She watched Daphne hop up the steps and out of sight, then locked the door behind her. She climbed the steps, shut the trapdoor, and stepped out of the closet only to hear her mother calling her name.

"Here, Mama," she called, wiping cobwebs out of her hair. She calmed herself and followed her mother's voice to the kitchen. If she also heard Mrs. Glendoveer's voice warning her against this ill-advised adventure, she did not listen. She felt too bright inside.

Chapter 7

For days, Ruby and Harriet sat with pen and paper, trying to figure the best way to spend the funds left them by the Glendoveer estate. They circled the house, making notes. Clara held her breath as she watched them descend the steps in the closet that led to the boiler. She was relieved to hear that this part of the house, at least, passed inspection and would require no workmen.

"I'll tell you what," Ruby said. "We're lucky the roof timbers are sound, what with those leaks in the attic. If you ask me, the shingles should be replaced. We've got more spells of hard rain coming."

Clara's mother agreed. "There's also glass to replace and doors too swollen to open. We can put our heads together and fix those ourselves."

"And what about me?" Clara asked. "May I help?"

Her mother put her hands on her hips. "Put your nose in a book. That's the best thing for you. We'll get back on firmer footing with your studies when Ruby and I are through with the repairs. In the meantime, we'll be too busy going in and out, gathering supplies, and raising a racket around here."

Clara nodded, having no objection to books. But what thrilled her most was seeing Ruby and her mother put on their cloaks. Both at once! That had never happened when Mrs. Glendoveer was here.

"We'll be going to the bank too, so we won't be back until well after noon," Clara's mother warned as she headed out to the street. "Do not answer the front door."

"I promise. No front door," she said, picturing immediately greeting Daphne at the door downstairs—for it was Saturday, and Daphne would be at home. At least Clara prayed she would.

There was a room across the hall from Mrs. Glendoveer's bedroom with windows that faced Daphne's house, but it had been locked as long as Clara had lived in the mansion.

"I'll get the key ring," she said to herself. She fetched the old round of iron from its nail in the pantry and examined the keys as she made her way upstairs. The three keys used most often were clean and shiny on the stem. The one for the aviary was the most distinctive, its bow carved to suggest outspread wings. The rest were for things Clara imagined were forgotten long ago.

One by one, she tested them in the door, twisting the keys left and right. Some gave promisingly, and then stopped at a half turn. Others merely wiggled stubbornly, seemingly stuck at the shoulders.

Her wrist weary, Clara held up the final key: the one for the aviary. All but certain that this last attempt would be futile, she pushed in the key and turned it to the right. It glided round in a perfect circle, the tumblers clicking with ease.

Clara gasped as the doorknob gave way and the hinges groaned against her push. She adjusted her eyes to the dark and saw that the room was filled with furniture. A built-in seat ran the length of the rear wall. The bank of heavily curtained windows above it must have once offered a cheerful view of the garden. She tiptoed in, then came to a halt and held her breath. A tinny melody was playing, muffled but distinct, and slowed to a stop. Was it "Here We Go Round the Mulberry Bush"?

Shaken, Clara said out loud, "Why, it's nothing but a music box. I must have jostled it."

Finally, she made her way through the furniture to a small west-facing window and pulled back a stiff and rotting drape, allowing a shaft of light to knife the room. She jumped! Two blue eyes gazed from the dark. Clara yanked the curtain now with all her strength and heard the rod clatter to the floor.

At once, everything in the room was revealed: two neat bed frames small enough for elves, a little desk with attached chalkboard easel, a bureau topped with a stuffed bear, a miniature wooden wagon, and a porcelain doll, staring with large blue glass eyes. Clara took in the scene and was puzzled. This didn't seem like a room for baby Elliot.

And there was more: a rocking horse made with real hide, a wooden crate piled with alphabet blocks, a white-painted wardrobe with a faded satin ribbon tied on the handle.

She ran her hand over the rocking horse's back. The desk and easel were much like the ones she used in Mrs. Glendoveer's room for her lessons. As she crept forward to take a closer look, she could make out chalk marks on the board under the years of dust.

She knelt down, blew the slate clean, and saw:

Helen will not steel biscits
Helen will not steel biscits
Helen will not steel biscits

Who was Helen? She saw in her mind's eye HELEN engraved on a plaque in the Glendoveer crypt.

Immediately, Clara wondered what Daphne would make of all this. Daphne! Well, as the curtains had fallen down entirely, Daphne would be sure to notice the change.

I won't lock the door, Clara decided. This way she could easily slip in and out to signal Daphne whenever she needed to. Also, with both the grown-ups gone, Clara could meet Daphne outside instead of braving the underground boiler room.

Clara passed the hall clock and noted with joy that it was only ten o'clock. She went to the kitchen, opened the back door a crack, sat on a stool, and waited, her heart in her throat. *Please be watching, Daphne. Please.* When she finally heard the creak of the side yard gate, she felt she might forget to breathe. She bolted from her stool and ran onto the grass as Daphne rounded the corner.

"You've come!" she shouted.

Before Daphne could call back, however, the birds in the aviary erupted in screams. Clara turned her head and saw that every bird had massed to one side of the cage like iron filings pulled to a magnet. The birds bobbed their heads in unison as if throbbing to the same heartbeat, their eyes fixed on Clara.

"Awwk awwk skwaaaaaaaaaaaaahhh!"

"Hush!" said Clara. "All of you!"

"Elliot!" cried the mynah.

Clara grabbed Daphne by the hand and dragged her inside.

"Elliot! *Statim!*"

Kicking the door shut behind her, Clara met Daphne's eyes, which were round as teacups. The room was silent.

"They've stopped," said Daphne. "What ghastly birds. Do they shriek at everyone like that?"

"Only me," said Clara.

"What were they shouting? Did one of them say 'Elliot'?"

Clara tried to explain that the birds hadn't always spoken. Something had recently set them off. "I do know that Elliot was the baby taken from Mrs. Glendoveer many years ago."

"How curious," said Daphne. "A stolen baby? Stolen by whom?"

"I don't know."

"Well, doesn't that rattle you?" Daphne asked.

"Oh, Daphne," breathed Clara, "that is not all. I've found more mysteries. We've got hours to poke around too."

"Please, then. Lead on!"

Clara showed Daphne up the stairs to the bedroom and pushed open the door. "I'd never been in here before today," she said. "It has always been locked."

Daphne stepped inside and gazed around. She leaned over and opened a bureau drawer. "Whose are these?" she asked, pulling out a stack of handkerchiefs.

Clara took one of them and held it up to the light. A white monogram was stitched in the corner. "F.G.," said Clara. "Why, I can't think who these might belong to."

"To a Glendoveer, I'd suppose," said Daphne.

"But the initials aren't familiar. And look over here. The chalkboard—there's a Helen mentioned. I've never heard of her, but that name *was* in the Glendoveer crypt. Where are these people now?"

"Hmmm." Daphne scratched her head. "You know, Clara, this is quite fascinating, but you must catch me up. The only information that I'm certain about is in the obituary for Mrs. Glendoveer. Everything else I've heard is chatter and hearsay."

Clara lowered her chin and gave Daphne a look. "What hearsay?"

Daphne's mouth hung open for a moment as if she realized she'd made a mistake. "Just talk. As I said, I know nothing, actually."

Clara felt odd. It didn't seem right that Daphne had heard tales of the Glendoveers while she herself lived here in ignorance. "Is it bad, what they say?" she asked.

Daphne swallowed and shook her curls. "It doesn't matter," she said. "There are such a lot of silly people in Lockhaven, don't you know that?"

"No," Clara said frankly. "I don't."

Daphne put her fist to her forehead and gave it a little smack. "Stupid me. I didn't come here to bring ugliness from the outside. I want to be part of *your* world. It's a deliverance to me. . . ."

"That is well and good," replied Clara, her voice rising, "but I am thoroughly sick of being in the center of this so-called world where no one tells me *anything!*" She was breathing hard now, and shaking.

Daphne spoke tenderly. "Of course you are, Clara. I should feel the same way. My object was never to upset you, but to know you. And now—"

"And now," Clara continued, "you shall tell me everything if you are to be my friend. You must promise never to hide anything from me, or I would just as soon have my solitude."

Daphne stepped back and surveyed her. "Forgive me, but I see that I've been mistaken about you."

"I disappoint you?"

"Not at all. I thought you were . . . delicate. I had no idea you had a temper. One *needs* a temper, I believe, and now I suspect we're more alike than I'd imagined." She raised her right hand. "You shall have my word," she said. "No more secrets. Unless they're ours together."

Clara closed her eyes and let out a breath. "At last," she said. "I cannot tell you. It is far more difficult *not* to know."

Daphne glanced around the room. "If I'm to speak to you, I'd feel better if we left this room. May we?"

Clara agreed, but first the girls managed to rehang the curtains in the window. Clara could simply pull them open as a signal now.

"You don't know how often I've looked up here from my house waiting for your signal," Daphne said. "I could scarcely believe my eyes this morning."

"And I was so fearful you wouldn't come," Clara said, leading Daphne to the kitchen. She sat on the bench and patted the space next to her. "I'm ready," she said. "Tell me everything."

Daphne knitted her brow and bowed her head. "I am afraid."

Clara gulped. "Why?"

"It's time for you to promise me something," she said. "Whatever I tell you, you must understand that it comes from the most ignorant and idle people. And though there's a grain of truth in every rumor, I've found that the worst gossip usually starts with something harmless."

"Indeed," Clara said.

"And you must consider your experience here with Mrs. Glendoveer and give it much more weight than anything I might say."

"Tell me," said Clara, holding steady.

"They say there were children here once," Daphne said. "And that they were murdered."

Clara's eyelids fluttered. The words barely penetrated. "Did you say . . . 'murdered'?"

"Yes," Daphne said.

"They must be thinking of baby Elliot. But he was taken, not killed."

"No," said Daphne. "The talk is of a group of children. The Glendoveers. I believe there were five or six of them. I can't recall."

Clara recoiled. "Who would murder them?" She saw Daphne tremble slightly, then recover.

"The rumor is . . . the parents killed them."

Clara gasped. "No! That is the most revolting— Never!"

Daphne grabbed Clara's hand. "I know. Remember, these are just old tales. Gossip no doubt embellished over the years."

Clara pictured Mrs. Glendoveer, bent over a picture book, tracing the words with her long ringed finger, her light and lovely laugh, and those deep, water-blue eyes that seemed to understand everything.

"Cenelia Glendoveer did not even know how to scold a child," Clara said. "She was the picture of loving patience.

73

The idea that anyone could even think that . . . It's not possible."

"I believe you," Daphne said. "I do."

And then, against her will, Clara felt a horrible weight in her head begin to dissolve. The old kitchen with its black stove and oilcloth-covered table and teacups on hooks grew wavery. Tears spilled over the edges of her eyes and down her cheeks. When she fell forward, Daphne caught her in her arms and held her.

"We will find out the truth, dear Clara," Daphne whispered. "We shall uncover it all."

And though Clara couldn't speak, she determined that she would no longer be aimless. Whatever wit or pluck she had would be used for one thing: clearing Mrs. Glendoveer's name.

Chapter 8

There was time left before Ruby and Clara's mother were due to arrive home, but Daphne's visit had to be cut short.

"I told my mother I'd be home for luncheon," Daphne said, "and I don't want to abuse the privilege of visiting here."

Clara wiped her eyes. "Tell me your mother hasn't heard these awful things about the Glendoveers."

"Not yet!" Daphne said. "I've heard everything from other children. It's a form of fun for them."

"But what if she does hear?"

Daphne thought. "She's open-minded. And fair. But she is a mother, so I don't know what she'd say."

"I understand," Clara said. "You should see my mother. Always protecting me from even the slightest excitement. No wonder she never told me anything about the Glendoveers."

"Ah. That explains it," Daphne said. "Why you seem so delicate at first. You've always been treated as if you were."

Despite her promise to share every secret, Clara didn't tell Daphne about her faulty heart. It was too gratifying to be recognized for her strength. Clara wanted to be the person that Daphne saw.

"I do have a question for you before you go," Clara said.

"Anything."

"When you told the children at school that you saw me in the window, what did they really say?"

"They said," Daphne replied, "that I must have seen a ghost."

"Me?"

"And that is what set me on my quest," Daphne told her. "Because I know what I saw, and the more I insisted, the more everyone tried to frighten me. And I was right, although I haven't told the little brutes at school. They'd only try to ruin everything."

As much as Clara did not want to speak ill of her mother, she felt the same way. "I know that if I say so much as a word about what we've uncovered, all the evidence will be swept away. Mama and Ruby are too efficient. So I'm keeping my mouth closed for the moment."

"Good," Daphne said. "And now I'm afraid I'm going to have to brave those birds again. I must go."

"They frighten you too?" said Clara. "I always tell myself that they can't possibly harm me. Did you see those iron bars? But I keep my distance nonetheless."

Clara hugged her friend and opened the back door. As Daphne stepped out into the calm of late morning, none of the birds stirred. But when Clara showed herself, the lot of them grew agitated, flying back and forth to one another's perches.

"It *is* you they want," Daphne said.

"*Statim!*" screeched the mynah. "*Statim!*"

Clara stamped her foot. "Oh, *statim* yourself, you nasty old bird!"

"That's telling him," said Daphne, applauding.

Clara waved goodbye, laughing, until Daphne slipped through the side gate. It was good having a friend like her. She felt not the slightest bit guilty about talking back to Mrs. Glendoveer's birds. Why should she let them frighten her?

The mynah continued to shout as Clara headed for the house. *It's always that oily bird,* she thought, *stirring up the rest.* She was opening the kitchen door when she heard a voice she did not recognize.

It was a sigh, soft and sad, and had nothing of the mynah's vehemence. She turned in time to see the cockatoo raising his wings to show his yellow underfeathers. Slowly pirouetting on his perch, he looked like a high priest performing a blessing. When he stopped, the birds also stood still. He lowered his wings, and the mynah bowed to him.

To Clara, this ceremony was more unsettling than the

birds' screams. She couldn't figure out if she was moved or frightened in a new way. She shut the door behind her with a firm click.

Standing there, Clara felt queasy. When she lifted her hands, she could not ignore the slight tremor in her fingers. She pushed past thoughts of her weakened heart and tried to find an immediate solution to her problem.

"It's hunger and excitement," she said to herself. "I need bread and butter and a glass of milk." And as she sliced the loaf and poked around in the icebox, it occurred to her just how many times she'd "cured" her weakness and trembling with nothing more than a snack from the kitchen. Knowing how to take care of herself helped Clara avoid complaining to her mother. The last thing she wanted was to add to that woman's worry.

"AWWWWWWK! KEE-yah kee-yah! SKEEEEEEE!"

The strangled shrieks of the aviary birds surprised Clara. They never screamed at her while she was in the kitchen. She held still and listened.

"Eee-owrr!" There was the unmistakable yowl of a cat.

In a flash, she was out in the yard, watching the birds dive toward the bottom of the cage.

"Rooooww-er—OW!"

At the bottom of the cage, dodging from corner to corner, was a small smoke-colored cat. The great-tailed grackle hovered over it, and the kiskadee dove down, nicking his ear. Clara rattled the cage door. "Stop it! Leave him alone!"

This time the birds ignored her, too intent on the

battle. When Clara bent down to look closely, she noted the bluish tinge to the kitten's coat. Why, could this be Daphne's cat? "Poor thing!" she shouted. "Hold on!"

Clara hurried to the mudroom, grabbed the heavy ring from its hook, and singled out the winged key for the aviary. When she returned to the cage, she thrust the key in the lock and sent the door swinging. Waving her arms, she shouted, "Bah! Enough! Or this'll be the end of you!" If she could have spit fire, she would.

"No!" said the mynah. "No, no!"

Clara felt claws on her scalp and was blinded by beating wings. She threw up her arms, planted her feet, and stood her ground.

"Back up, all of you," Clara commanded. Her own voice was a growl that she hardly recognized.

The fluttering slowed. The birds found their perches. And as Clara knelt down to pick up the kitten, she was sure she heard a low sob coming from somewhere above her.

The cat's ear was nicked. He lay with his back in a hump. As Clara lifted him, she saw the plump green honeycreeper lying with his eyes open.

"The end," said the mynah, his voice cracking.

Clara clamped the kitten under her arm and gently nudged the bird. One wing fluttered.

More sobbing sounds. The white cockatoo moved his head back and forth as if to say, "No! No!"

She blew the bird's feathers, and his legs twitched. "You're alive," she said, taking him in her cupped hand.

She moved backward, out the cage door, which she closed firmly with her foot, though the keys still dangled in the lock.

Inside, Clara shut the kitten in the mudroom while she attended to the bird, which she laid out on a towel on the kitchen table. The thing wasn't much bigger than an Easter chick, and as pale green as a pistachio. He had gone bald beneath his wings, so often had he sat in the upper corner of the aviary nervously pulling at his feathers.

"Of all of them," Clara said, "why should it be you?" She was sure he had lived a life of abject terror, locked away with creatures several times his size. Ruby had often remarked how lucky he was to be the only nectar feeder in the group, with a bottle all his own; otherwise, he might never get a thing to eat.

Clara thought she should try sugar water with him, but the honeycreeper was so weak, she was afraid to leave him. His breast heaved in and out. Gradually, the tiny bird stopped moving altogether.

"No, no," Clara said. She bent over him and stroked his breast. "Please come back." A tear rolled down her nose and splashed on his forehead. For a moment, Clara could have sworn she saw his eyes blink. Another tear touched down on his throat, and the honeycreeper's wings vibrated.

"Come on," urged Clara. "You can, I know you can. . . ."

His breast inflated, and the bird rolled to his feet.

"Oh, thank goodness!" Clara clapped her hands, feeling more grateful than she ever thought possible. It wasn't until the bird started to hop that she saw how one wing dragged. Unbalanced, the bird weaved raggedly toward the table's edge. She caught him just in time and cradled him in her hands. How relieved she was to hear Ruby's heavy tread in the hallway.

"Ruby!" she called. "Ruby, come here!"

Ruby came in still wearing her big coat, her windblown gray hair frizzing from her cap. "What you in a panic for?"

"That little green bird, the tiny one? A cat got at it."

Ruby covered her mouth. "Don't tell me—"

"He's alive, Ruby. But his wing drags. What shall we do?"

After she washed up, Ruby gave the honeycreeper a close inspection. "There are no punctures anywhere, so that is welcome news. We will have to bandage and isolate him for now. I'll need a regular canary's cage—something to keep him in indoors."

"I'll do anything to help," Clara said. "I feel horrible."

"The first thing I'm doing after we tend to the bird is check out the wire netting around the bottom of the cage. There must be a hole in it somewhere." She went to pull the big colander from the cupboard and placed it upside down over the honeycreeper like a cage. "That'll do for now."

The bird fluttered his good wing and bumped against the metal a few times before he quieted.

"If you think the bird's frightened, you should have

seen the cat. They had him cornered with their screeching and swooping and pecking. He's shut up in the mudroom."

"And *you*," said Ruby, incredulous. "You went in the aviary and got him?"

"I don't know what came over me. The keys are still in the lock. And here," said Clara, parting her hair, "one of them got *me*."

Ruby sucked in a breath between her teeth. "That's a nasty scratch. We'll have to get it washed immediately." She grabbed a bar of soap and bent Clara's head over the sink.

"Oooch!"

"Stings, does it?" Ruby worked cold water and soap into the wound. "I'm surprised, must say. In all the years I've ventured in that cage, not one of the old birds has come near me."

"They were wilder than ever this time, Ruby," Clara said.

"Because of the little one, I'll bet. They're a protective bunch. And smart. Do you know how long it took Mrs. Glendoveer to find an adequate lock for that cage? The cockatoo is a shy one, but clever as they come. He can pick a lock with his claw, but he never escaped. He likes puzzles, is all. Really, Clara, the whole flock of them are homebodies and prefer the cage. They make a show of it, but they're gentle at heart."

"They're always angry at me, though. You know how I've avoided them. To think I was in the midst of them!"

"Most of us have more courage than we know. Your maternal nature was roused." Ruby poured another pitcher of water over Clara's scalp and rubbed her with a towel. "Now let's see what we can do for the kitten."

Clara could hear the cat meow when Ruby entered the mudroom. The honeycreeper heard it too and circled madly in his makeshift cage. His call was thin and high-pitched.

"Tsip! Tsip!"

She put her hand on top of the colander and spoke calmly. "Don't worry. The cat won't get you. Ruby has him."

"Tsip! Tsip!"

"I'll keep you safe, all right? Or should I say, 'Tsip-tsip'?"

The bird stopped to look at Clara from one eye, then the other.

"*Tsip?*" she said again. "What a funny word. I wonder what you mean."

At once, Clara sensed someone behind her. Her mother stood with her arms folded.

"You're drenched, Clara. And would you mind telling me what has you talking to the pots and pans?"

"There's a bird in here," she said. "One of the Glendo-veer birds."

"No." Harriet peered in through the holes and turned wary. "He's wobbling. Am I seeing an injury?"

"A cat got in the cage."

"Merciful heavens!"

Clara thought her mother might collapse. "It wasn't anyone's fault."

"No, dear, I'm sure it wasn't."

When Ruby came in, she had the kitten wrapped tightly in a rag. "This is the little troublemaker," she said.

"Take him out, Ruby!" Harriet demanded.

"But he's injured, Mama," said Clara.

"Yes, he is," Ruby said. "And the dumb beast has no more sense than a flea. Can you imagine being a cat sneaking into a cage full of big, angry birds when you yourself have no claws to speak of?"

"No claws?" said Clara. "Then he *must* be Daphne's cat!"

Ruby pursed her lips as her mother raised an eyebrow. "And who would Daphne be?"

Clara gulped. "The . . . the girl two houses over. Her mother delivered the food, and . . ."

"Yes?"

"That's when she told me about the cat! That it was blue and had no claws!"

Ruby peeked into her bundle. "I declare. Why, the cat *is* blue." She folded back the rag and let the creature poke his head out. "And such beautiful golden eyes. What do you think of that?"

Seeing Ruby smile made Clara calm again. She reached over to where the cat nestled against Ruby's ample bosom and stroked his head. "I suppose we should take the cat back to his house?"

Ruby appeared ready to agree, and Clara was already picturing the triumphant moment when she showed Daphne the wound on her head.

"No," her mother said simply.

The word immobilized Clara.

"Now, Harriet, do be reasonable," Ruby said. "What harm can come of walking two houses over?"

"Yes, Mama! What harm?"

As Harriet drew herself up, Clara could feel herself shrink. Her mother had a way of inhaling half the air from the room and holding it quietly in her bones.

"Is this a mutiny? Ruby, you know how I love and appreciate you, but you may not enter into controversies between me and my daughter."

"Understood," Ruby said. Then with a curtsy: "*Ma'am.*"

Clara's mother flinched at the word. "I don't mean to be . . ." She looked quickly from Ruby to Clara. "You've obviously had a lot of excitement this morning already. I want you to rest and recover yourself. Please. Go and lie down now."

Clara tramped to her room, flung herself on the bed, and studied the water-stained ceiling. Clara loved her mother, and Ruby too. But she needed more. Not more love for herself, but more in life to love.

Maybe this was how Mrs. Glendoveer felt when she sneaked out to the tent shows and the theaters to watch the magicians and the traveling actors. She could imagine how young Cenelia's spirit expanded with fear and expectation as she waited outside George Glendoveer's door, wanting nothing more than to be taken away.

She also remembered Mrs. Glendoveer's warning: hold

your family close, or you will bring down upon yourself a lifetime of regret.

Did that mean that Clara should always mind her mother? Did it mean she was never to have a life of her own?

"Mrs. Glendoveer," she said, "I want to do as you asked." She tried to set her mind right. But it was her heart that struggled, and she had little idea how to master it.

Chapter 9

After an hour or two, Clara heard a quiet knock on her door.

"Are you receiving visitors?" her mother asked.

Clara was caught off guard by her mother's mild expression and the conciliation in her tone. "Of course, Mama," she said. "Come in."

Harriet entered, followed by Ruby carrying the most exquisite birdcage. It resembled a pagoda—or was it a Russian church? Wooden beads were strung on its golden filigrees, and ladders ran from one apartment to another. The entire structure was topped with a fantastic onion dome, from which hung a small wooden swing. Inside, the wounded honeycreeper confined himself to the ground floor, his celadon feathers shining like Chinese silk.

"It's something for a princess's room!" Clara said.

"Ruby says the Aspinals gave it as a reward for saving the kitten," said her mother. "Apparently, the cage was decorative and had a fern growing inside it, but when they heard about the honeycreeper, they insisted we take it."

"The Aspinals have fancy goods from all over the world," Ruby said. "Did you know her father has two large steamships? According to Mrs. Aspinal, he combs the world for pretty things. I suspect he's done well for his family, though he's hardly ever home."

"That's really none of our business, Ruby," Harriet told her. But Clara loved any glimpse into Daphne's life, and wished Ruby could say more.

"Plenty of room for the little greenie," Ruby said, patting the cage. "And see the red glass bottle and stopper? He can sip to his heart's content."

Clara peered down at the green bird. "Do you love it?" she asked.

As if to answer, the honeycreeper gazed up at her and chirped, "Tsip-tsip!"

Ruby and Clara and her mother all laughed. "I think *tsip-tsip* means 'yes,'" Clara said.

"He'll need a name, won't he?" said Ruby.

"I'll call him Gawain, after the man who fought King Arthur's Green Knight. He's a little bird who battled a much larger cat. I think he could use a heroic name."

"Very good," said her mother as she left the room. "I know you'll do well by him."

Ruby stayed behind and watched the bird with Clara. "He'll eat worms too," she said. "In fact, that should be a treat for him. Might strengthen him a bit."

"I'll dig them up for him," Clara said.

"Most important, though, is to bandage the wing. Your ma went through the Glendoveers' library and found that it's best to keep the broken wing still. I've trimmed some gauze, if you'd like to hold him for me."

Ruby showed her how to unfasten the roof from the cage, and Clara reached in to retrieve Gawain.

"We're going to make you better," Clara told him, and watched as he toddled directly into her hand.

"Well, knock me down," Ruby said.

Clara lifted him out and soothed him while Ruby wound the gauze over the broken wing, round the bird's body, and under the good wing. "Now, if Sir Gawain would be so kind as not to flutter, I'll bind this with my brass pin."

Gawain was motionless in Clara's palm. Not until he was returned to his cage did he test himself by hopping on one leg and then the other.

"I think he feels better with the bandage on," Clara said.

"We'll take it off in a week and see what he can do," said Ruby. She dusted off her hands and packed up her gauze. Clara couldn't let her go without a kiss on the cheek, but noticed that Ruby did not receive it with her usual bashful smile.

"I'm not done yet, little girl," she said. "Not until we've had a chat."

"Deary me. You have on your stern face, Ruby."

"Better you deal with me than with your ma. I know she said I'm not to interfere, but when I think what would get stirred up if I told her what I heard at the Aspinals'—"

"From whom?"

"From the missus herself!"

Clara, as frightened as she felt, was overjoyed that Daphne had said nothing.

"I hear that you had the little girl over to visit only this morning." Ruby scowled. "I could scarcely take it in. You've never been naughty before in your entire life, if you don't count your spitting out your mashed green beans when you weren't yet walking."

"But you didn't tell Mama," Clara said.

"So it is true." Ruby looked away and made her disapproving clucking sounds.

Clara leaned on Ruby's arm. "She is a wonderful girl, Ruby. We seemed to have an instant connection. When she came with the covered basket, I told her to please come back. Can you blame me?"

Ruby reached around and patted Clara's hand. "I think you know how I feel. But I'm not your mother."

"Are you going to tell?" Clara felt every muscle in her neck go tense. *Please, please don't,* she prayed.

"Not this time."

"Thank you, thank you!" Clara buried her head in Ruby's shoulder. "It means everything to me to have a friend."

"Clara," said Ruby, "I can't promise to do this again. Do you hear me? Try to be content with your new little bird friend, is my advice." With that, Ruby gave Clara a tap on the nose and left.

"Good old Ruby," Clara said, returning to Gawain's cage. "I do think she's the dearest, most capable woman in Lockhaven."

"Tsip-tsip!" said the bird.

"So you agree?"

"Tsip-tsip!"

"What a fine conversationalist you are. I feel fortunate to have made your acquaintance. You won't mind sharing a room, will you?"

"Tsip."

"Only one *tsip*? I'll take that as a no. You know, Gawain, perhaps I never properly understood you birds. To think it's taken us this long to get together."

"Tsip-tsip!"

He seemed to agree.

"You're a handsome fellow, though. I hope you like your name."

No chirp there.

"If you don't like it, we can change it," Clara said.

"Tsip-tsip!"

Clara had the most curious sensation. The game of

"yes" and "no" with the bird had been nothing but a lark. But now she wanted to try.

"Would you prefer another name?"

"Tsip-tsip!"

"You would? How about . . . Alfred?"

"Tsip!"

"Does that mean 'no'?"

"Tsip-tsip!"

The honeycreeper waited with what seemed to be complete concentration. Clara tried to keep her breathing steady, lest she break the spell.

"Are you . . . a girl?"

"Tsip-tsip!"

"Do you understand me?"

"Tsip-tsip!"

Clara exhaled. "Should I be afraid?"

The bird hopped to the edge of the cage and thrust out a thin, curved beak.

"TSIP!"

The single chirp was sharp and shrill. Clara sat for a moment in the silence, then covered her mouth with her hand. As she stared, the honeycreeper performed an astounding feat: she danced! Two hops to the right, then two to the left. Two hops forward and two hops back. She turned in a circle and started again.

"Extraordinary!" said Clara.

The bird stopped as if to acknowledge the compliment. As Clara leaned over the cage to get a better look, her locket clanked against the cage's golden bars. The sound set the bird off. She whirled and hopped like a dervish. But when Clara tucked the locket back inside her pinafore, the bird stopped.

"So it's the citrine you like?" Clara said, taking it out again. "It's almost the same color as your feathers."

"Tsip-tsip!"

"Then I will call you Citrine. It sounds like the perfect nickname for a sweet little girl. How do you like that?"

"Tsip-tsip!"

"All right, then. Citrine it is." But as soon as Clara tucked the locket out of sight, Citrine quieted and sat low on her claws.

"Will you talk to me some more?" Clara called the bird's name several times, but Citrine looked at her blankly.

"Now I don't know what to think," Clara said. The bird had wound down like the nightingale in the Hans Christian Andersen story.

Every hour until nine o'clock, Clara went in to check on Citrine. Always, she asked a question, hoping to get the bird to talk; but it wasn't until evening that the bird spoke again.

Clara had brought in the oil lamp, planning to read before going to sleep. She undid the strings on her pinafore and pulled her poplin dress over her head. She slid into her nightgown, then undid the clasp at the back of her neck and removed Mrs. Glendoveer's locket. As she lifted the necklace, Citrine burst into a chant.

"Tsip-tsip! Tsip-tsip! Tsip-tsip!"

Clara dropped the necklace on her bureau and went to the cage. The bird stopped.

"Oh! I wish I could figure you out, Citrine," she said. At last, Clara decided to retrace her steps. She moved backward to the bureau, reached on top, and pulled up the locket by its chain, swinging it in front of the cage.

"Tsip tsip tsip tsip tsip tsip!"

The bird began her dance again at such a pace that Clara feared for Citrine's health in her weakened condition.

"It's the locket, isn't it, Citrine?" she asked, once the necklace was safely coiled in her hand.

"Tsip-tsip!"

"There can be no doubt of it." Clara stared down into her palm. "But what am I to do?" She addressed the bird:

"You want something of me, yes?"

"Tsip-tsip!"

"Do *you* want the locket?"

"Tsip."

"Would you want me to do something with the locket?"

"Tsip-tsip!"

Citrine had a way of making her chirps communicate more than a simple yes or no. She could sound disappointed

94

or enthusiastic. This time, Clara could only describe the bird's attitude as forthright.

Keeping a close eye on Citrine, Clara clicked open the locket and shook the key loose. "Is this what you want? Do you want me to use this key? Do you want me to look in Mrs. Glendoveer's book? The one with the baby picture in it?"

"*Tsip-tsip!*"

"Yes?" To Clara, Citrine's voice had a hoarse edge, and she realized how strenuously the bird had been trying to alert her.

"You must think I'm very slow."

This time Citrine actually shook her head.

"*Tsip.*"

Clara put on her wrapper and pulled her slippers out from under the bed. Why would a bird want to see Mrs. Glendoveer's family album?

"Citrine . . . you aren't Mrs. Glendoveer, are you?"

The bird closed her eyes and gave a resounding "*TSIP!*"

"All right, all right," Clara said. "You must forgive me. I'm becoming too suggestible. The next thing you know, I'll be running around declaring that this whole house is enchanted."

Clara was only a few steps out of her room when she heard a crisp "*Tsip-tsip!*"

She was torn between retrieving the album and going to the library to find herself a sensible book to read. But

there were very few distractions in the Glendoveer mansion for a young girl alone, and the questions in Clara's
mind only grew more persistent.

"I must get Mrs. Glendoveer's book," she said at
last. "Now!"

Chapter 10

Clara headed upstairs to Mrs. Glendoveer's room. She almost did not want to open the door—she had avoided the room since the old woman had died. But now she counted to three, held up her lamp, turned the knob, and pushed the door open.

Clara inhaled. The room still smelled of dried lavender and was exceptionally cold. In the old days, the place had been the warmest room in the house, with its green enameled stove always stoked. Despite the room's familiarity, it took all of Clara's courage to shut the door behind her.

Now, where was Mrs. Glendoveer's alligator chest? It was still in the corner, but covered over with an embroidered shawl. Two candlesticks were arranged on top. It might have been a table in a Gypsy restaurant. Clara moved the candles and opened the box.

Empty?

She had seen that box full just days before Mrs. Glen-doveer died.

"This is impossible!" she said. Only her mother could have taken the locked album. What could it contain that it should have been confiscated so quickly? Clara had the key—surely Mrs. Glendoveer had wanted her to look inside.

She opened the drawers in the nightstand and the chif-forobe. Empty. The jewel box? Gone! The only thing that hadn't been cleaned out was Clara's old school desk.

She sank to the cold floor and leaned against the bed. "I'm so dim!" she said. "If I'd had an ounce of sense, I'd have been in this room two weeks ago." Daphne never would have hesitated, of that she was sure.

Clara sat, glum, until she felt a whoosh of cold air up her back as if somebody had opened the door. She ducked down instinctively, which was silly, considering that the lantern's glow alone would have given her away.

The view from under the bed proved that the door had remained closed. Clara almost laughed at herself until she saw the outline of something flat and rectangular on the floor near the footboard. Lying down, she stretched her arm and dragged the thing into the light.

It was a wooden frame, backed in brown paper. She turned it over and held it to the light. Beneath the glass was a kind of embroidered sampler. Weeping willows rendered in emerald silk draped from each corner of the picture. An angel, much like the weeping statues at the gate of Mount Repose, covered her face with her hands as her wings dragged on the grass. In front of her were five tombstones embroidered in glistening gray: HELEN, FRANCES, ARTHUR, PETER, GEORGE WM.

Clara recognized the names immediately. They were from the wall of the crypt where Mrs. Glendoveer lay. Her heart pounded as she read over the names again and again. Without a doubt, these must have been the Glendoveer children. Had Mrs. Glendoveer done the needlework herself?

And then Clara remembered: back when Mrs. Glendoveer could still get up and down the stairs, she had walked in on Ruby and her mother in the kitchen. Clara remembered because she was just beginning to read well enough to entertain her mother with short stories and tales as she and Ruby tended to baskets of mending.

"I know it's early, but I've come down to say good night to my birds," Mrs. Glendoveer had said. Glancing over Ruby's shoulder, she added, "Ah, Ruby, you do sew a fine seam. It's a shame, sometimes, when I think of all the hours I devoted to my needlework. And now I cannot."

"Do you miss it?" asked Ruby, looking up. "If you need someone to thread your needle, I'm sure Clara would be happy to do it for you."

"No," said Mrs. Glendoveer, growing solemn. "I put my needle down over forty years ago. I shall not take it up again."

"Of course, ma'am," Ruby said. She turned her eyes to her work, and nothing more was said.

It was an odd exchange. The mood of the room had

shifted, and Clara had asked her mother what Mrs. Glendoveer had meant.

"It's hard on the old people," was all she'd answer, "when they lose so much."

Clara went back to the embroidered picture and peered closely for dates on the stones. There were none—only a date sewn in the corner of the work: 1855 CNG.

"Cenelia Newsom Glendoveer," whispered Clara. Counting backward on her fingers, she determined that this piece must have been at least close to the last time Mrs. Glendoveer picked up a needle.

Clara noted some faded thread, light blue, running across the picture's bottom:

> Together always to the last,
> Our love shall hold each other fast.
> Delivered from the frost and foam,
> None shall fly till all come home.

The barely visible words were sewn into the waves of a creek or river flowing in the foreground. Clara put her finger to them, trying to absorb their meaning. And then she noticed something else: a darker blue rectangle had been sewn into the water. What was it meant to be? A raft? An underwater door?

And most perplexing, why was there no mention of baby Elliot?

If Clara thought she'd get answers by showing this work

of art to her mother or Ruby, she would have done so. As it was, she had to assume that this bit of evidence from Mrs. Glendoveer's past had been overlooked when her mother had cleaned out the room.

Clara dimmed the lantern, went back to her room, and looked for a place to hide her treasure. Between the mattresses, the glass might crack. And Clara's bed was too high to hide anything beneath it. There was just enough room for the sampler in her bottom drawer where her winter woolens were kept, and so she placed it brown paper side up and covered it with long underwear. Then she lifted the tea towel on Citrine's cage.

"Are you awake?"

The bird ruffled her feathers and opened her eyes.

"I want to tell you that I tried, Citrine. I went to Mrs. Glendoveer's room with the key and looked for the leather book. But it's gone. I'm sorry."

Citrine cocked her head as if she was trying to understand.

"Is it important that I find it?"

"Tsip-TSIP!" said the bird with emphasis. "Tsip-TSIP!"

"Then I shall keep looking," Clara said.

Citrine tucked her head back under her wing, and Clara went to bed.

"Lazybones, it's almost two."

Clara opened her eyes to see Ruby standing over her.

Sure enough, sun streamed through the windows and across the bed. "Why didn't Mama wake me?"

"She might have, but she's out to the lawyer's again. More business with the estate. I told her you must be growing, sleeping in until afternoon. . . ."

And staying up until quarter to four, thought Clara.

"I'm going to market soon, and I didn't want to leave you abed without something to eat." Ruby set down a tray with milk, shortbread biscuits, and jam. "We'll be back in time for early supper. All right?"

"Thank you, Ruby."

Just as she raised a biscuit to her lips, Clara felt a pang of guilt. Citrine's cage was still covered. She leapt from the bed and took off the towel. The little green bird hopped to the edge of the cage.

"You must think I'm an awful mother," she said. "Here the sun's overhead and you've nothing solid to eat. I should have been up digging worms before dawn."

Citrine said nothing.

"I fear you're angry with me." Clara went back to her tray and broke off a piece of shortbread. "Here, Citrine, would you like some biscuit?"

"Tsip-tsip! Tsip-tsip! Tsip-tsip!"

"Now you're dancing again," Clara said, crumbling the shortbread into the cage.

With every bite, Citrine chirped, twitched her tail feathers, and turned in a circle.

"You like sweets, don't you? I suppose that's why they call you a honeycreeper. I'll have to serve this more often."

"Tsip-tsip!"

"Clever bird. I can hardly wait to show you off to Daphne."

Clara dressed quickly and listened for Ruby's footsteps outside before running upstairs to signal Daphne. With the curtain pulled back, the crowded room appeared less forbidding. The shadows had been banished, and every object begged to be examined.

Clara's breath caught as she glimpsed her own reflection in a mirror inside the door of an armoire. Looking closer, she saw dresses hanging from a rod.

She pulled out one and then another. They were replicas of each other in different sizes—both in dark olive brocaded silk, one long and one short with pantaloons.

They were very old and brittle at the seams. Clara had not seen pantaloons in anything other than the old books in Mrs. Glendoveer's library. Curious, she put her shoulder to the door until the armoire stood wide open.

"Goodness." It was the same with all the dresses: one large, one small with pantaloons. Clara figured that the bigger articles of clothing would just about fit her.

At the bottom of the closet was a series of drawers that held stockings and petticoats, elaborately embroidered. These too were in small and large sizes. The stockings were particularly interesting, made of shimmering ivory silk. Clara and her mother wore nothing but cotton or wool, depending on the season. These appeared almost too precious to be owned in multiples, especially by a child.

She tucked one in her pocket and headed for the door,

clearing a narrow path before her. As she left, she noticed something stuck behind the door.

Clara bent down, pulled out a rolled-up parchment, and blew off the dust. She could hear the paper split along its creases as she opened it.

"REWARD! $25,000!!!" was blazoned along the top.

"FOR INFORMATION LEADING TO THE RE-COVERY OF MISSING CHILDREN!"

Below was printed an extraordinary photograph. A group of boys and girls stared back at Clara with direct, unsmiling faces. The caption named them in order of appearance:

Helen, age 4. (A small girl, the youngest of the group. She had mussed hair and leaned sleepily against her sister.)

Frances, age 12. (Intense black eyes in a face of fierce intelligence framed by black center-parted hair.)

Arthur, age 9. (Nearly Frances' double. The set of his jaw showed both confidence and perhaps a bit of stubbornness.)

Peter, age 6. (He was small and fair, and had a perplexed expression. He wore a brass-buttoned velvet jacket with a lace collar.)

George William, age 14. (He looked just like Mrs. Glendoveer! Transparent, wide-set, and dreamy eyes. Fine blond hair. A storybook prince.)

Elliot, age 5 mos. Not pictured.

They all were, at that moment, completely alive to

Clara's eyes and deeply familiar. It took a few moments for the crashing realization that they were all . . . dead.

Shaking with feeling, she read on. They were taken—all of them, not just Elliot—along with "Nelly Smith, age 22, nanny." On November 7, 1855.

Also missing—coins, jewelry, cash, and silver.

REWARD OFFERED BY
MR. WOODRUFF BOOTH!
203 Bellevue Avenue
Newport, Rhode Island

"Woodruff Booth?" Clara shook her head and tried to remember if she'd heard the name before. She tucked the poster under her arm and left the room, careful to shut the door firmly. Clara could only hope that Daphne had seen her signal. This picture of the living Glendoveers was too extraordinary to keep to herself.

Into the downstairs closet she went, through the trapdoor to the gray and musty room below. She nearly pounced on poor Daphne when she approached the back stairs.

"Aah . . . ," groaned Daphne, clasping her own throat. "Clara, you frightened me out of my skin!"

"Daphne, you angel. Come quickly, inside!"

Daphne followed. "Is someone at home?"

"Not yet," Clara said. "But I can't have you upstairs without knowing precisely when my mother is due back. We'll be safe down here."

"You look so anxious."

"Yes, I'm a bit beside myself right now. Thank goodness you are here." She placed the poster in Daphne's hands and watched her unroll it.

"Well, I'll be . . . ," she murmured.

Clara watched her friend's lips move silently as she read.

"Don't you see, Daphne? The children were kidnapped as part of a robbery. How anyone could say the Glendoveers had a hand in it is beyond me."

Daphne nodded, never taking her gaze from the children's faces. "Awful," she said. "Harebrained Lockhaven gossips . . ."

"It is hard to look away, isn't it?" Clara asked. "My heart aches for them."

"Of course," Daphne said. "Wouldn't you give anything to have known them? And what do you make of this Woodruff Booth?"

Clara took the poster back and examined it. "I know. A twenty-five-thousand-dollar reward!"

"It's a hefty sum. I think he's worth investigating, don't you?"

"Yes, but I have no idea how," admitted Clara.

"Neither do I. Maybe in an old newspaper? There has to be a way to—"

The sound of footsteps above made both girls hush.

"Oh!" breathed Clara. "Thank goodness we're down here. But whoever it is will be looking for me. I must go."

"Listen," said Daphne, "I'll leave anything I find out

about the Glendoveers or Mr. Woodruff Booth under the door here. So do check every day, won't you?"

Clara agreed. "I'm going up to distract whoever is there. Wait to leave until you hear some stamping on the floor. I don't want you running into anyone outdoors."

"Yes, yes. Be careful," Daphne replied.

Both girls waved silently to each other, and Clara climbed her way back into the dark.

Chapter 11

Clara had no opportunity to invite Daphne for the next week. Still, she checked the boiler room door for messages from her friend every day. At last, on a Friday, she was delighted to find a thick envelope, a little battered at the edges from the push under the door.

Darling Clara:

We need to meet! I have so much to say that my hand may fall off before I can write it all.

My mother gave a tea for the Lockhaven Ladies Club, and you wouldn't believe who was there! Frances Glendoveer's old teacher! (You remember—Frances is the oldest daughter.) Anyway, Miss Lentham is her name, and she is tiny and near blind and so doubled over with age, I wondered how she climbed the stairs to our front door!

It seems that Frances was serious and bright beyond her years. Miss Lentham says they shared a love of the classics and that she "saw herself in her." (That is, when she <u>could</u> see, poor dear. Oh, she is so old.)

She told me that the Glendoveers were the most famous people in Lockhaven and George was becoming fabulously wealthy. He was the first magician to "take the art from the streets to the theater." (She calls him always the <u>Great Glendoveer</u>.) Many have copied him since, though "they're common as lead pennies now," as Miss Lentham puts it.

The town and the entire seaboard were outraged when the children were taken. Miss Lentham remembers having to be sent home on the day the bodies were found. She fainted dead away!

Oh, and I should say that Mr. and Mrs. Glendoveer were on a tour of Europe at the time of the kidnapping. His fame had spread round the world. He was known for his Magic Closet, levitation of heavy objects, and his way with <u>birds</u>. He collected them from strange places. They were charming and would walk the aisle of the theater in a procession and bow for their own applause at the end of the show. So says Miss Lentham, who saw the Great Glendoveer perform many times.

Did I tell you they never found the baby? Elliot? Miss Lentham says that George always declared he would be found. And that . . . Well, I can't tell it all. Must see you, dear.

Now for my brilliant news: Woodruff Booth is still alive! He is old and lives in Newport. He traveled with the Glendoveers. They called him a mentalist or something. He made people fall asleep and do silly things. Miss Lentham says he was the Glendoveers' great defender and friend, and that's why he put up the reward.

What's more, Miss Lentham corresponds with him. Not regularly, but years ago he said he wanted her to keep him abreast of what went on with the Glendoveers. He still cares for them after all this time. She sent him the obituary you wrote, for the _Tribune_, and that's the last he's heard from her.

And now? I am going to write him, Clara. I am going to ask Woodruff Booth to tell me everything. He was in Berlin with the Glendoveers when the children were taken. Isn't that thrilling??? I only hope he still has his memory and all that, and doesn't hate children like some old folks.

Hoorah! Tomorrow is Saturday! Pull the curtain when you can!

Your spy in the wicked world,
DA

P.S. I'll post the Booth letter tomorrow morning.

Clara hugged the letter to her chest. "I knew it!" she said. There could be no doubt now that the Glendoveers had been smeared. How Clara yearned to speak to Miss Lentham herself. And now Daphne was going to correspond with the actual Woodruff Booth? Well, if anyone should do it, it should be Daphne, though Clara felt a stab of envy nonetheless.

After stashing Daphne's note with Mrs. Glendoveer's embroidered graveyard scene, Clara rested her arms on the bureau's top and gazed into Citrine's cage.

"Citrine, do you ever wish that you could fly? Freely, I mean."

The bird hopped to the edge of the cage. "Tsip-tsip!"

"I think it's time we remove the bandage and see what you can do."

Clara unhinged the top of the cage and lifted Citrine onto her bed. She unwrapped her gauze and cupped her hands around the bird's body.

"Careful now," she said. "Let's see if you can move the wing first."

Citrine seemed cautious and shrugged unevenly. When she attempted to flutter, one wing moved more fluidly than the other.

"At least there's some movement," said Clara. "That's a good sign. Mustn't try too hard, though." When she reached for the bird to return her to the cage, however, Citrine quickly hopped out of reach.

Clara understood. Without speaking, she watched as Citrine shook herself all over like a wet puppy, trying to get the injured wing to move. Her feathers fanned and ruffled as she hopped to the edge of the bed and back.

She wants to be healed so badly, thought Clara. But it seemed obvious that the bird was not ready to fly. After what must have been an exhausting effort, Citrine stopped and tucked her head beneath her wing. Clara imagined that this was Citrine's equivalent of a good cry.

"Citrine, sweet, would it help to tell you that I sympathize?"

Still, the bird would not look up.

"What if I brought you some biscuit?"

"Tsip-tsip!" was her muffled reply.

"Stay, then, and I'll fetch it for you." Clara lifted the bird back into the cage but did not attach the top. She was halfway down the hall when she heard something like the soft clapping of chalkboard erasers.

"Tsip-tsip! Tsip-tsip!"

Streaking past in a flurry of foam green was a most ecstatic honeycreeper.

"Tsip-tsip!"

Clara clapped her hands as Citrine zipped up and down the hall, then lighted on the lip of a hanging lamp.

"Citrine! You excellent bird!"

Citrine cocked a shining eye at Clara and—"Tsip-tsip!"—ahead she flew to the kitchen.

Now Clara began to feel uneasy. How was she ever to lure Citrine back to her cage? And if her mother should find the bird flying free, what would she have to say?

"Citrine? Citrine?" Clara tried to sound as sweet and

reasonable as she could. Luckily, neither her mother nor Ruby was in the kitchen. "Where are you, please?"

Clara investigated the ceiling, the curtain rods, anywhere a bird might perch. Was the door to the backyard firmly shut? She ran to rattle the knob but was distracted by a distinct, yet feeble, hammering sound.

T-t-t-t-t-t-t! T-t-t-t-t!

There, on the white biscuit tin, perched Citrine. She was knocking the lid with her beak like a woodpecker.

Clara had to laugh. "What? That didn't take you long to find."

The bird persisted until Clara lifted the lid and put half a biscuit out on the counter. There, Citrine proceeded to peck voraciously at the edge of it.

"I'll have one too," Clara said. "We'll celebrate together."

In the meantime, Clara's mother entered the kitchen bearing a wicker basket full of laundry.

"Uh-oh," Clara said.

"Uh-oh, indeed. What is the bird doing out of the cage?"

"She can fly, Mama."

"That's good news. But I don't think it's wise to have her flitting about. What if she were to find an open window?"

"Truthfully? I think that if she found an open window, I could easily lure her back with the sweet shortbread. She's mad for it. Look."

Her mother drew closer and watched as Citrine finished up the last crumbs. Clara held out her hand, and the bird hopped on.

"We have an understanding," said Clara. "Isn't it remarkable?"

Her mother chuckled. "You do have a way with her."

"I'll put her back now, so you won't be nervous."

"Thank you for that. But before you go, I'd like to ask you something." She dug into the laundry basket and produced a small ivory silk stocking. "Where did you get this? I found it in your pocket."

Clara stammered and was about to say she found it upstairs, but the bird in her hands trembled so violently that even Harriet was dismayed. Citrine stretched her neck and chanted her *tsips* so shrilly that Clara wanted to cover her ears.

"Perhaps Citrine wasn't ready for all that exertion," said her mother, dropping the sock back into the basket. "She seems distressed."

As suddenly as she started, Citrine stopped.

"You're right, Mama. I'll put her back."

"But first, Clara, what about the stocking?"

Clara thought quickly. "I was hoping you would tell me," she said. The look on her mother's face showed that she was not prepared with an answer.

"I want to know where *you* found it."

"In Mrs. Glendoveer's room. I sometimes go there

and sit at my old desk. We spent so much time together there."

Her mother pulled in her chin. "I never saw such a thing in her room. Are you sure?"

"Where else would I find it?" Clara asked. She waited while her mother considered.

"I suppose it's an antique of some sort," she said at last. "It's no matter, then."

"I'll take Citrine now," Clara said. As she walked away, she marveled at how easily she could fib to her mother. Only a few months before, she would have been mortified at the thought.

Clara held Citrine to eye level. "Do you think I'm a bad girl?"

"Tsip!"

"No?"

"Tsip!"

"I think you idealize me, Citrine. I hardly know who I am at times." At this, a cloud overtook Clara, and she felt horribly guilty.

She set the bird back in her elaborate cage and fastened down the dome. Citrine fluttered up to her swing for the first time. She lifted her tail up and down, shifting her weight until the swing began to move.

"Tsip! Tsip! Tsip! Tsip!"

It was a charming diversion, and Clara couldn't help but feel lighter.

"You're such a pretty clown, aren't you?"

"Tsip-tsip!" cried Citrine.

If only all the other birds were this delightful, thought Clara. And then, despite her best intentions, her thoughts turned toward tomorrow and the hope that Ruby and her mother would find some business to take them out of the house in the morning.

Chapter 12

Harriet and Ruby were surprised to see Clara awake and washed up, stoking the fire in the oven, before the sun rose.

"I'm making breakfast for you," she said. "I decided it's time I stopped being the baby of the family and helped out." In truth, Clara couldn't lie in bed any longer, so excited was she about the possibility of seeing Daphne. But she did think helping out was a good step forward in allowing her mother to see her less as a child.

"That is quite thoughtful of you," said her mother, "but I don't like you carrying in the wood. It's heavy. And may I warn you that you are *never* to chop wood?"

"Yes, Mama," Clara said.

"Because I know how it is. You're my daughter after all. It is tempting to overexert, but you don't have the luxury. You must take care."

Clara tried to hide her irritation. "Most people consider it a luxury to lay about with a book and listen to the clock tick—which I've done more days than I can count."

"It is a bit inside out," agreed Ruby.

"We bend to circumstance and necessity," said her mother. "Heaven forbid . . ." She trailed off. "Never mind."

Lately, Clara had been wandering up and down stairs more than ever before. The excitement of uncovering clues, scurrying, and then controlling her breathing so as not to betray her increased activity had actually increased her energy. If her heart pounded, it seemed to be from passion rather than a defect in that organ.

"Mama," Clara said as she set the table, "do you think it's time I saw a doctor?"

"Unless you feel particularly ill, I don't see why."

"Because I'm thinking that maybe my heart has healed. I'm rarely bothered by it. Maybe I had some childhood ailment I've outgrown."

Her mother crossed her arms. "Clara?"

"What? I think it's reasonable to ask. To wonder."

"The next thing you know, you'll be wanting to go to school," said her mother.

Clara handed her mother the teapot and did not speak for fear of losing her temper.

Ruby rubbed her hands together and put on a bright face. "Well, what shall we do today? I'm marketing this morning and have been thinking it's time for me to blow the dust off some of these elegant old cooking books."

Clara's mother appeared glad to change the subject. "Yes! Clara, would you like that? We could set the table in the dining room. Put a cloth on."

"I think there is still a silver candlestick or two left around here. We could be ladies for the evening," Ruby added.

The idea immediately appealed to Clara. "How long do you think it has been since that dining room was used?"

"Let's see," said her mother. "Mrs. Glendoveer used to take her dinner there when I first arrived, didn't she, Ruby?"

"She did, and for years before that. But I can't say she always enjoyed it. It was often she'd ask me to fix a meal and want to sit at the kitchen table."

"It's too lonely to eat by oneself," Clara said. "Especially at a long, grand table like that."

"I think she used to picture her family there. Truly, I do," said Ruby.

Clara watched her mother's smile disappear. "What family, Ruby?" she rushed to ask.

"Her childhood family, is what Ruby meant," said her mother, stepping forward. "Mrs. Glendoveer came from a large brood, a wealthy one—the Newsoms. And they weren't pleased with her running away with a person of the theater."

"They cut her off," said Ruby. "She used to grieve about it."

"They mustn't have been very nice people," Clara said.

"That's the way it was in those days," said her mother. "Magic shows were filled with riffraff, and pickpockets worked the crowd. The Newsoms couldn't accept that George Glendoveer was a different kind of entertainer. It was a disgrace to the family."

"I didn't know that," Clara said. "She told me she had regrets, but in a roundabout way." Clara was piecing together a fuller view of the depths of Mrs. Glendoveer's sadness.

"So, Harriet, after I make my shopping list, would you like to come with me?" asked Ruby.

"Hmm. I could use some seeds. I think that in the next week or two, it'll be safe to plant radishes . . ."

Clara did her best to hide her sublime excitement.

". . . but then, the ground could use preparing," her mother continued. "And it won't do to have seeds and no decent bed to plant them in."

Clara stirred herself to speak. "But it is so lovely this morning. We haven't had an early blue sky like this in ages."

"Which makes it a perfect day for gardening," her mother concluded.

Clara felt absolutely punctured. She stumbled over to the icebox, took out some eggs, and began cracking them into a bowl. It was all she could do not to start sobbing. But she kept a straight face and made eggs and toast. And when Ruby left and her mother was out shoveling earth, Clara went upstairs to further investigate the bedroom with all the Glendoveers' things.

But this time, the knob would not move.

She rattled it, and then shook the door.

Locked!

It could not be. Clara went over the last two days in her mind and wondered what had changed. Then she remembered: the stocking. That antique stocking had made her mother suspicious.

And what must her mother have thought when she found the door unlocked? No wonder she was reluctant to leave Clara alone today.

So this is how it is to be, Clara thought. No direct questioning or accusations, no punishments; just a silent tit for tat, like a chess game.

And so Clara determined that she would betray no disappointment today. Tonight at dinner, she would be as enthusiastic and gay as she could be. For if she showed any sign of indignation at being thwarted, her mother would make doubly sure there was nothing further to be discovered.

"I can be patient," she said to herself. And, smoothing her skirts, she headed downstairs to the library, where she would lose herself for hours, as expected, in the pages of a book.

・ ・ ・

By six o'clock, the Glendoveer household was fragrant with intoxicating aromas: roasting meat and buttery sauces, and baking bread had never smelled quite this heady before, and Clara knew she was in for something special. There had been much banging and hubbub with both women in the kitchen the whole day. Rooms all the way from the foyer to the dining room were bathed in the warm glow of fireplaces and candles—an unusual sight, for her mother was strict with her resources and usually lit and heated only the kitchen at night.

What's more, Harriet and Ruby insisted that Clara stay clear during their preparations, making this early-May occasion seem more like December 24 than a cloudless evening in spring.

An hour before dinner was to be served, Clara was called to her mother's room. Even that chamber had a changed aura. Harriet had laid out her few pieces of jewelry: jet beads and matching earrings. A cut-glass vase of mignonettes stood on her dressing table, giving off a spicy perfume.

"Ruby brought me the flowers," she said, almost embarrassed. "They're from a hothouse. I told her once how I loved the scent, long ago. And I do—but the *hothouse?*"

"I hope you didn't scold her," Clara said. "It's not like

Ruby to be extravagant. She only wanted to make you happy."

"No, dear, I thanked her. I know that the pleasure was hers as much as mine." Her mother smiled and opened her wardrobe, where hung, between worn gray gowns, a dress as white as a cloud. She took it from its hanger and held it up to Clara's shoulders. "It should fit, I think."

Clara sputtered. "It's a gown. A real gown." She took it and examined it front and back. There were finely sewn buttonholes for the twelve mother-of-pearl buttons. Lace insets were sewn at angles in the muslin above the ankle-length hem. And, most significantly, there was no pinafore to speak of.

"It's not quite a gown, but it is more grown-up. I found the pattern in *Godey's* and decided I must make it for you. I put in a tucked princess waist, so there's a shape to it. It will make a fine day dress for when the weather grows warm." Her mother hung back. "Well, are you going to try it on?"

Clara grasped her mother's hand. "I can't *wait!*"

Harriet helped Clara off with her old collared poplin and slipped the gown over her head. Watching the dress take shape as her mother did up the line of buttons along her back, Clara felt she was being transformed. She stood as her mother undid her braids and brushed.

"We could pin all this up at the neck," she said. "Would you like to try?"

"Please," Clara said.

When Harriet was done, she stood behind her daughter and lingered on their reflection in the mirror. "I see a young lady there," she said. "And a lovely one."

Clara saw it too, but her joy was not complete. The contrast of her mother's tired dress, her raw red hand on Clara's pristine sleeve, made her wish that she could perform the same transformation for her mother.

"If I could," she said, "I'd fill your entire room with mignonettes and tuberose and lilies of the Nile."

"All those flowers," her mother laughed, "and I'd have to be revived with spirits of ammonia." She thrust her hands in her hair. "Now off with you while I do what I can with this bird's nest."

Clara sat on the divan in the parlor as she waited for her mother and Ruby. This too was a room rarely used, but tonight the exquisite chandelier with the hanging crystals was lit. Each cup in the lamp showed shadows of women in Greek togas bearing jugs of water on their shoulders. The gilding on the ceiling shimmered, and the glass panels on the pocket doors glittered with their roundels in gemlike colors. It was easy to believe that this was a house where magic was practiced.

With the tinkling of a bell, Ruby summoned everyone to dinner. Clara saw the buffet laid out, capped on each end with towering vases of gladioli and calla lilies. The candelabrum was draped with ivy, and the china plates shimmered like pearl.

Ruby and Harriet came in with the final dishes and

urged Clara to have a seat. On a little placard near her plate, her mother had written out the menu in her fine hand:

Rockaway Oysters
Celery
Lobster à l'Américaine
Fricandeau with Sorrel
Barbe de Capucin Salad
Peach Pudding à la Richelieu
Swiss Cheese
Coffee

"Where am I?" Clara asked.

"You are dining at the Glendoveers', milady," said Ruby, who, Clara noticed, had tucked a lily into her chignon. "Unfortunately, the help have the night off, so we are forced to serve ourselves."

"We'll make do," said her mother. "In the meantime, I'll take the liberty of fetching my daughter a plate."

When the ladies were at their places, Harriet proposed a toast. "To Cenelia Glendoveer," she said, "and our great good fortune in having her as our patroness."

"Hear! Hear!" said Ruby, and the three raised their glasses in the air. As the crystal clinked, however, an extraordinary thing happened: the door to the kitchen swung open and shut on a gust of wind, and the candles blew out.

"Mercy," said Ruby. Clara looked to her mother, who sat still and composed.

"Shall we try again?" Harriet asked. She struck a match and relit the candles.

Clara knew that her mother, who wasn't easily rattled, was being deliberately calm. It took some minutes for them to resume normal conversation. But the delicious dishes soon won out and put everyone at her ease.

"This is the most savory veal roast I've ever tasted," said Harriet.

"Me too!" said Clara, who had never actually had veal roast but could easily believe her mother's sentiment.

Ruby stifled a grin, took up a napkin, and fanned herself, chuckling.

"Oh, Ruby," said Clara's mother, "what is it?"

"I'll tell you my secret," she said. And then, covering her face with her napkin, she chirped, "Madeira!"

"You didn't!"

"Oh yes, I did! A little for the veal, and a little for the cook!"

Clara marveled at Ruby, giggling into her napkin like a girl. And at her mother, trying to stare daggers at her but not succeeding.

"What's Madeira?" Clara asked.

"A group of islands off the coast of Morocco," said her mother, trying to reclaim a straight face.

"It's spirits, isn't it?" said Clara. "Oh, Ruby, you are wicked."

"And what do you know about spirits?"

"I started reading Thackeray once, and Mrs. Glendoveer confiscated it. But not before I read about Madeira," Clara said.

Her mother's eyes widened. "Well, we're all full of surprises tonight, aren't we?"

"Everyone but you, Harriet," said Ruby. "I've yet to hear a surprise out of you this evening."

"This dress was a surprise," Clara said. "It took my breath away."

"As was intended." Harriet set down her knife and fork. "But it just might be that I have another surprise in store."

"Another?" asked Clara.

Her mother folded her hands and placed them on the table. "I've been at Fitzmorris Blenney often of late, as you know. . . ."

"Ah! I knew it!" Ruby said, interrupting with a pound of her fist. "Mr. Clayton Merritt-Blenney. I've thought all along that he'd be a silly bachelor indeed if he didn't take notice of our Harriet. . . ."

Clara blanched. "Mama! You and Mr. Merritt-Blenney?"

"Hush, Ruby," her mother said, turning scarlet. "Absolutely not, Clara."

"Oops," said Ruby, covering over a gentle hiccup. "Sorry."

"If I may continue," said Harriet with dignity.

"Go on."

"I've learned that there is someone interested in the house. Mr. Merritt-Blenney has been approached by representatives."

"Representatives of who?" Ruby asked.

"We don't know. Someone who prefers to remain anonymous."

"Someone of means, you're saying?"

"Of ample means," said Harriet.

Clara did not know what she thought of this exchange. She was conscious only of growing cold and heavy in the limbs.

Ruby, cheeks aflame, fanned herself again. "And has an offer been made?"

"None that I've accepted," she said. "But this party is quite persistent."

Clara tried to speak, but her tongue was now stuck to the roof of her mouth.

"We couldn't possibly sell until our agreed time is up," said her mother.

Ruby stroked her chin. "Ah. But after that?"

Harriet shrugged. "I cannot rule it out," she said.

Now Clara's entire body went stiff. She was unable to flinch when the kitchen door swung open so hard that a glass vase on the buffet came down with a crash, sending the flowers jetting across the floor. Again the candles on the table blew out as a cold, sickly stream of air passed over.

In the lamplight, Clara could see the white smoke rise from the wicks and curl as if someone were trying to scribble on the air. Her mother found the candlesnuffer and suffocated the tapers one by one. But when she was done, the room was filled with such a singed, acrid odor they could no longer continue dining.

Ruby had to be helped out of her chair.

"On my life," she said as Clara and her mother each supported an arm, "we must go check the birds."

"Why the birds, Ruby?" Clara asked.

"It's burning feathers!" Ruby declared. "Can't you smell 'em? Burning feathers!"

Chapter 13

Clara stood numbly as her mother took a shambling Ruby out to the aviary. She heard the birds waking and chattering and the soothing sounds of her mother's voice assuring Ruby that no birds had been burned.

The leaden sensations in Clara's limbs had lifted, but her mind was clouded. She pressed her fingers to both sides of her temples, determined to think straight; but when she caught her reflection in the kitchen window, she jumped, sure that the girl with the pinned-up hair and the diaphanous white dress was a ghost!

It was all she could do to undress and take off her shoes. In bed she went over the evening's extraordinary events. If the house had been haunted before Cenelia Glendoveer's death, Clara had never felt it. But even sensible Harriet would have to realize that the incident with the candles was deeply unsettling.

In the morning, Ruby was not her usual talkative self. When Clara tried to engage her, Ruby would only say, "I'll not be going back to that dining room again. And that's that."

Her mother was no more forthcoming. She put all her attention on making sure the leftovers from last night's dinner would not go to waste. "Peach pudding for breakfast," she said, handing Clara a bowl. "There's enough food here for another half dozen, so please have seconds. And thirds, for that matter."

All Clara wanted to do was get to Daphne; but just as she feared, when she checked the mudroom, the winged key for the room upstairs had been taken from the ring.

Ruby must have it, Clara thought, *since it's for the aviary too.* After looking everywhere from under doormats to Ruby's cloak pockets, however, she concluded that the key might now always be carried on her person.

And so she waited for days, checking under the boiler room door when she could for news from her friend. Sometimes she took to her bedroom and talked to Citrine, allowing her to fly freely about.

"At least you're here inside with me, stretching your wings," she told the bird. "I can't suppose you miss that horrid old iron cage."

Citrine lit on the footboard and said, "Tsip-tsip!"

"You mean you *do* miss your iron cage?"

"Tsip-tsip!"

"Don't you like being here with me?"

"Tsip-tsip!"

"Oh, Citrine, I'm afraid I don't understand you," Clara said. At that, Citrine went to her little cage and turned her back as the church bell gonged three o'clock.

Leaving the bird to sulk, Clara decided to go outdoors and check under the boiler room door from the outside to see if this was the day that Daphne had left something for her.

The aviary erupted as soon as Clara entered the yard.

"Shhhh!" Clara said. "Please!"

To her surprise, the noise stopped. The shrill grackle shut his beak. The kiskadee sat still. The birds clung to the front of the bars as if magnetized. And then, in a marvelous display, the cockatoo spread his wings wide and fluffed the feathers out over his nose until his eyes were eclipsed. "Please?" he said.

Clara was sure that he said it, though he had never spoken before. His voice was soft and rich—nothing like the mynah's. She felt strangely moved.

"Did you speak to me?" she asked, taking a few cautious steps forward.

"Please," said the cockatoo in the same soothing tone.

"I . . . I like it when you say 'please,'" Clara said. "What can I do for you?" The cockatoo held her with his shining eyes. She was going to speak to him again, but the mynah, seeing Clara approach, could no longer contain himself and sprang forward, slapping and flapping.

"Elliot! *Statim!* Elliot!"

132

And then the grackle shrieked, setting off the kiskadee, who streaked from ceiling to floor.

"Skeeee! Skeee!"

They fluttered back and forth in their customary mayhem, and Clara covered her ears and retreated to the back stairs of the boiler room, muttering under her breath, "Oily bird."

Looking under the door, she saw no evidence of an envelope. Deflated, she proceeded to break off a twig from a bush and poked around beneath the door. When her stick met something solid, she worked furiously to bring out whatever lay there on the other side.

When she saw the lovely violet ink on the cream paper, she almost cried out. She could not get back to her room quickly enough. The letter was fat and contained yet another envelope. Clara read the return address:

MR. WOODRUFF BOOTH

"Ah! Good work, Daphne!" she said. First she opened the accompanying note from her friend.

Clara dear,

You do not send for me anymore, and I worry. Here I have the most remarkable reply from Mr. Booth. I can only hope that you receive this and are well. If you can, please find a way to let me know. Otherwise, I'll have to take desperate measures—

perhaps climb that old trellis to an open window? Do not make me try it!

> *Your faithful friend,*
> *DA*

Clara unfolded Mr. Booth's letter and found it covered all over in tightly spaced black type.

Dear Miss Aspinal:

I hope you will not be offended at the lack of a handwritten reply. I am arthritic and rely on my secretary. I found your letter charming and am happy to answer your questions regarding my esteemed friend and colleague, George Glendoveer.

First, George was an exceptionally talented and inventive man. I got on well with him, and he gave me a coveted place on his program. My "act," as they called it, was nothing magical, I can assure you. My specialty, neurypnology, is what the medical community now refers to as hypnotism. It was George who astounded us with his feats of the unexplainable. We were all in awe.

I suspect that he trusted me almost as much as his wife, Cenelia. A magician of that caliber is understandably jealous of his secrets—they are the fruit of his genius, and he has a right to them solely. But he did share a few with me.

Cenelia, I believe, was comforted that I, like she, came from a prominent family who disapproved of our taking to the stage. The difference between us was that my people eventually relented and took me back into the fold. Such a loss for her family that they did not do the same.

As for the children, it pains me even now to see their faces in my memory. The eldest, George William, resembled his mother in manner and his father in ability. I believe he would have been a distinguished inventor. He took apart clocks and disassembled doorbells when he was but knee-high. What a young gentleman he was and how mild-mannered, as well as exceedingly handsome.

His sister Frances was given free rein to read and say whatever she would—which she did often. She was a discriminating girl who had not time in her short life to learn the rewards that sweetness of temper and amiability might win her. But George adored her, and she was bright.

Arthur was noisy and high-spirited. He would not believe anything unless he found the sense in it himself. Cenelia worried about him burning through his meals so he could get himself outside. It was not uncommon to find him perched in a tree.

Peter was Arthur's little pet. He was also very pretty and knew it. He loved his velvets and his polished boots. It was difficult for him to keep up with Arthur and maintain the perfection of his appearance, so he was always changing clothes. He once asked for a tiny mahogany valet for Christmas!

Helen, in my opinion, was the dearest girl who ever lived. She wanted to be a dancer. She loved sweets. She was by turns shy and mischievous. A coquette, even at four.

And baby Elliot. He had yet to reveal himself to us. Such a great loss!

The story of what happened to them has now been repeated and exaggerated, and the trail leading back to the kidnappers grown cold. The nanny was thought to be involved. Some say only the nanny knew when the staff was to be off duty, where the various valuables were hidden, et cetera. Her disappearance with the children does seem suspicious, though she too was drowned in Lockhaven Bay when the boat carrying them off was dashed to pieces in a storm. When there were no demands for ransom, all of us were puzzled—until the bodies of the children were found. But none of the Glendoveers' stolen property was recovered, which made it hard on the family when some evil-tongued gentry speculated that George might have conceived of the kidnapping for his own gain.

This was a blow to George Glendoveer's career. Unscrupulous people spread the rumor that his European tour was failing and that theaters were going to be less than half full. This was a lie. As the Glendoveers' chosen spokesman, I told the papers so, but the rumor continued. Even the police theorized that the Great Glendoveer had originally planned the kidnapping as a prank to garner publicity, but with disastrous consequences.

In their grief and disgust, the Glendoveers shut themselves off from everyone, which only made the gossips bolder. Even I was discouraged from visiting, which still causes me much distress after all these years.

When I was informed of Cenelia's recent death, I could only hope that she found the peace that long evaded her and that she is in heaven reunited with her family. For what is more sacred, more comforting, than our bonds with our own blood kin?

When George left the stage, so did I. Since, I have been compensated with a virtuous wife (much my superior and now departed) and two fine sons of my own. It is for them alone that I live now. How Cenelia held on so long into old age is baffling to me.

So, Miss Aspinal, if you have the opportunity to set things right in Lockhaven, you will have done me a great service. Please use any information enclosed here. Do not let the scoundrels further blacken my friends' legacy, and surely you will be blessed.

With respect and gratitude for your efforts,

WOODRUFF T. BOOTH

Clara sat on the edge of her bed and read the letter through again. So the children had drowned. Picturing them helpless and flailing in the bay's cold gray water sent a tremor through her body.

Yet how lucky anyone would have been to have a friend like Woodruff Booth, she thought. If only Mrs. Glendoveer had had the strength to cling to his friendship, despite the memories it called up, she might have been a much less lonely person.

With the mystery of the Glendoveers explained, Clara wondered whether she shouldn't now confront her mother with what she knew. There was no longer any worry that the unsettling nature of the story would trouble Clara's heart. Perhaps even the restless soul of Mrs. Glendoveer would be soothed if the silence were broken in her home and the true story of her innocence were to be told?

"All we need around here, Citrine," Clara said, "is a little sunlight, and the shadows will retreat of themselves. When I think of the unnecessary misery this secrecy has caused us all . . ."

Citrine seemed to agree. She jumped from her swing and fluttered, singing without stopping. It was a cheering performance, for a while. But after a full minute of the racket, Clara grew concerned.

"Citrine, rest. You'll wear yourself out!" said Clara.

But Citrine remained agitated as ever. Clara bent over the cage until she was distracted by rapping on the window. Fully expecting to see her mother there with a rag and bucket, she turned around.

In spite of herself, Clara let out a scream, and then clamped her mouth shut. There, knocking on the pane with his sturdy black beak, was the white cockatoo, his sulfur-tinted head feathers raised high.

Mustering her nerve, Clara unlatched the window and

pulled it up, praying she would not frighten the bird away. But the cockatoo stood patiently until the sash was lifted, looked at Clara with his golden eyes, and pleaded in such a rich, melancholy voice that she was bound to him with all her sympathies:

"Please? Please? Oh, please?"

Chapter 14

Clara gestured to the bird to come in. He flitted past her, straight to the top of the bureau, where Citrine thrust out her beak at him and cried. As the honeycreeper seemingly poured out her cares to him, the cockatoo nodded in reply.

It occurred to Clara that the birds in the aviary had no idea about Citrine's fate until now. Had they been worrying all this time?

"I don't know how you escaped," Clara told the cockatoo, "but I must check if the other birds got out." She shut the two birds in her room and dashed to the aviary, dreading what she might find.

From afar, Clara counted the three remaining birds still inside: the grackle perched on a dead tree branch, the bright yellow kiskadee beside him, and the mynah on the floor, clawing at the pages of an old book. The aviary door was barely ajar, yet all the birds could have squeezed through and flown away if they had wanted. When Clara got close, she saw that a hard piece of straw had been jammed in the lock. The metal around the keyhole was crosshatched with scratches.

"The cockatoo!" Clara said, pulling the stick from the lock and closing the door. "He really is a genius."

The mynah, who had been watching her with interest, fluttered forward. "Genius," he repeated.

"That's what I said," replied Clara. "And I want to thank you, both for staying in your cage and for not screaming at me. Would you like to know how the honeycreeper is doing?"

The birds fluttered to the ground and stood rapt, waiting.

"She's fine. Very well," Clara said. "Her wing is healed at last."

The grackle gave a rusty laugh as the kiskadee darted around the cage. Only the mynah stayed silent.

"What do you think about that?" Clara asked him. "Aren't you happy?"

"Think, genius," said the mynah, growing irritable again. "Think, think, *think!*"

"Hmmm. It seems that you want me to think," Clara deadpanned. "Have I got it right?"

"THINK!" screamed the bird.

As Clara watched him leaping, flapping, and shredding

paper into confetti, she wondered if the bird was suffering from some form of insanity. Should she even try to make sense of what he said? "It doesn't help, you know," she told him. "I can't think any better or faster for your screaming at me. Goodbye!"

Her mind turned to the daunting task of luring the cockatoo back to his cage. So far, he hadn't been much of a wild thing, but his beak was sharp and his claws were strong. She did not know which bird had wounded her when she rescued the kitten, but in a contest of wills with the cockatoo, Clara would surely be the loser.

She hit upon the idea of luring him with food. Would the cockatoo like biscuits as much as Citrine did? It was worth a try. She went to the biscuit tin in the kitchen and took two—one for the cockatoo and one for Citrine, who would certainly be jealous if she were left out.

She eased open the door to her room and held a protective arm over her face, but the cockatoo did not stir from his place on the bureau next to Citrine. He didn't even look up at the biscuit when Clara waved it in front of him.

"Don't care for biscuits, do you?" she said.

But Citrine saw the shortbread and twirled in circles.

Clara broke off a crumb and dropped it in the cage. "I love watching you dance, darling thing. You'll have me stealing biscuits all the time just for the pleasure of—"

Oh my goodness.

She felt a tingle up both arms and dropped the entire

biscuit into the cage. Citrine was overjoyed, of course, but Clara felt she had been struck by lightning. In her mind's eye, she saw quite clearly the blackboard upstairs, its smeared-chalk sentences written in uneven letters, the lines sloping downward:

Helen will not steel biscits
Helen will not steel biscits
Helen will not steel biscits

Clara scrambled to her bed and picked up the letter from Mr. Woodruff Booth.

Helen, in my opinion, was the dearest girl who ever lived. She wanted to be a dancer. She loved sweets. She was by turns shy and mischievous. A coquette, even at four.

And George William:

I believe he would have been a distinguished inventor. He took apart clocks and disassembled doorbells when he was but knee-high.

Clara closed her eyes and drew a breath. When she opened them, the cockatoo was giving her that steady golden gaze. She cleared her throat and found her voice:

"Are you, by any chance, George William Glendoveer?"

The cockatoo spread his wings and bowed low like a courtier.

"Oh dear," she croaked. Fearing she might collapse, she placed a steadying hand on her dresser. When she was sure she could remain standing, she said, "And you, Citrine? Are . . . are you his sister Helen?"

The bird neglected the biscuit, flew directly up to her perch, and cried to the sky with a congratulatory cheer: "Tsip-tsip!"

Clara's lips quivered. She knew in her head that it could not be, yet felt sure in her heart that she had the Glendoveer children here beside her, in her room, in their old home.

"The biscuit tin. You knew where it was all along," she told the little bird. "And you've danced for me since the first day I brought you inside."

And to the cockatoo: "How could I not have seen how beautiful and elegant you are?"

She thought of these birds year after year in the iron cage, its roof either dripping rain or piled with snow or adrift with dead leaves of the old elm. Repetition. Desolation. Loneliness.

Yes, yes. This I know.

A sense of urgency overtook her. "We must go see the others. Now." Clara had only to raise her arm and the cockatoo perched upon it. She lifted the top off the honeycreeper's cage and took the little bird on her shoulder. The three went out to the aviary together.

The grackle, kiskadee, and mynah flew up and stood together on a perch as Clara opened the door. She stood in the middle of the cage and gazed up utterly without fear.

"Arthur?" she said.

The grackle swept down at her feet.

"Frances?"

The mynah circled the cage before lighting beside her brother.

Only the sleek yellow kiskadee remained aloft.

"Oh, Peter, you pretty boy, do come down!" Clara said.

The bird lifted his head. "BEE-tee-WEE!" he shouted before diving to greet her.

Clara sank to her knees, held out her arms, and let the birds take turns lighting on her outstretched hands.

"Arthur," she told the grackle, "you have always been the loudest. I thought you were angry. How could I know that you only wanted company?"

Arthur responded by jumping on Clara's shoulder and giving her his unmusical rusty shriek directly in her ear.

"*Silentium!*" barked the mynah as the grackle fluttered out of reach.

"It's all right," said Clara, wincing. "I know that Arthur is just high-spirited. And you, Helen," she said to the honeycreeper, "how am I going to call you anything but Citrine?"

"Tsip-tsip!" chirped Helen as she and Peter the Kiskadee fluttered between perches. They were engaged in some sort of acrobatic act, with the kiskadee sometimes pausing to dive for a stray fly that entered the cage. George, the suave cockatoo, perched in a high corner and swayed from foot to foot. Arthur the Grackle's squeaky exclamations could almost pass for laughter. The aviary radiated joy.

Clara felt it. Their mood was contagious—for everyone, that is, but the mynah.

"Frances?"

The mynah stood with her back against the wall in her torn nest of pages and regarded Clara with her masked red eyes.

"You're quiet."

Frances tilted her head, but would not reply. Clara tried to imagine what was bothering her. "You told me to think, didn't you?"

"Think, yes," said the mynah.

"I finally did, as you see," Clara explained. "I know you have been trying to talk to me, and I didn't understand."

"Think!" said the mynah again.

"All right." Clara rested her chin on her hand and struck a thinking pose. "Will this do?"

The mynah came forward and paced before Clara like an inspecting general, then stopped dead in front of her and piped up in a high-pitched voice: "STATIM YOURSELF, YOU NASTY OLD BIRD!"

Clara recognized her own voice immediately. "Oh dear."

"Oh *dear*," echoed the mynah with a decidedly sarcastic edge. "Oh dear, dear, *dear*."

The bird's feelings were hurt, Clara knew. But she also felt that humble apologies would not be in order either. This mynah, this *Frances*, rather, was not to be appealed to with sentiment.

"Frances, do you recall a Miss Lentham at the Lockhaven Public School?"

The mynah fluttered as if trying to summon her memory.

"Miss Lentham," said Clara. "I have a friend who has just spoken to her. She said that you shared a regard for the classics. Do you remember?"

Frances the Mynah appeared lost. Clara first thought she shook her head to say no. Or was it just a sorry shake of the head?

George the Cockatoo fluttered down to his sister Frances and made some tender whistling sounds. Helen the Honeycreeper circled them like a moth while Arthur the Grackle and his brother Peter the Kiskadee waited patiently above.

Clara crept over to join them in the mynah's corner. "I want to tell Frances that I will always try to understand when she speaks to me. I will never treat her with disrespect, because I know she has much to teach me."

The mynah shifted in her nest but would not face Clara . . . yet.

"You have told me to hurry. *Statim?* And I want to, with

all my heart. But I don't know what it is you want me to do!"

At this, the birds chattered among themselves, each in his or her own peculiar language, while the mynah listened.

"Tell me if you can, any one of you! Tell me what you need, and I will try to help!"

Frances the Mynah faced Clara, and the aviary went quiet.

"El-li-ot," stated the bird, enunciating every syllable.

Clara thought back to the first words the mynah had ever uttered to her. "It's what you've been trying to tell me all along, isn't it? Elliot. I know who he is. But what should I do?"

"Help," said the cockatoo.

"Find him, you mean?"

"Help," he said again.

"So none of you know where he is either?"

"Genius," said the mynah, though Clara knew she meant exactly the opposite.

"I wouldn't know how to begin," Clara said. "If the authorities couldn't find him, how do you suppose an eleven-year-old girl can succeed so many years later?"

At this, the birds all scattered and pecked at the ground distractedly, leaving Clara feeling confounded. And then she heard Ruby's voice coming from the kitchen door.

"Clara Dooley, I declare!"

"Uh, hello, Ruby," said Clara, waving weakly. She tried

to think of how to explain her presence in the cage as Ruby sprinted over.

"I never!" Ruby said. "What do you think you're doing?"

"I thought that Citrine might want to visit her old home?"

"Good enough," said Ruby. "But how did you get in? Your mother gave the aviary key to me days ago."

Clara's mind raced. "The cage was unlocked," she answered.

Ruby knitted her brows. "I locked up this morning, soon as I changed the newspaper, as sure as you're born." She bent close to the lock and had Clara come over. "Can you see any tampering? My up-close specs are in the sewing basket, and I'm helpless as beans."

Clara pretended to scrutinize the lock. "It looks perfectly fine to me. Perhaps you didn't turn the key far enough?"

Ruby didn't look convinced. "If that cockatoo has finally outwitted the locksmith on this one, we'll have to start wrapping this door in chains."

"No need. If he hasn't opened the door in years, I doubt he's caught on all of a sudden."

"You'd think so, wouldn't you? Especially seeing how old he is. How they do hang on. They should all be suffering from dementia by now. Or worse."

Clara cringed, embarrassed that this awful pronouncement had been voiced in the Glendoveers' presence, not to mention the other worrisome things that had been uttered unthinkingly for all of them to hear over these many years.

She exited the cage so Ruby could lock up. There were so many questions Clara had left unanswered, but of one thing she felt sure: the birds did not want to share their secret with her mother or Ruby. Otherwise, why did they speak only to Clara?

And yet, everything that occurred today was so sensationally odd and otherworldly, Clara simply could not keep it all to herself.

No. She would have to share what she had found with someone she could trust. And there was only one person who met that requirement: dear, indispensable Daphne Aspinal.

Chapter 15

While waiting for an opportunity to meet with Daphne, Clara had days to puzzle over everything she had learned about the Glendoveers.

One thing that she deduced on her own: Frances the Mynah retained a smattering of Latin, but her English words were few. After thinking back on her experience with both birds, Clara realized that the cockatoo seemed to learn English words after hearing them spoken—not by Ruby or Harriet but by Clara herself. The mynah, on the other hand, seemed to remember some words of her own, but also learned what she heard from Clara. This realization made Clara desperate to have time with the birds. For the more she spoke to them, the more they might be able to speak back.

But visiting the aviary undetected was not easy.

Occasionally, Clara would bring the honeycreeper back to her room for long "conversations." Piecing together what had happened to the Glendoveer children from Helen's *tsips* was a hit-or-miss process. But sometimes the questions bore interesting results. For example, it became clear that the Glendoveers' nanny, Nelly Smith, did take the children from their home when Cenelia and George were in Berlin. But Clara also found out that the nanny did not act alone.

"Was it a man with the nanny?" Clara asked. And when Helen replied yes, she went on. "Was it anyone you knew?"

"Tsip," said Helen.

"No? Was he ever found?"

"Tsip," said Helen again; and the thought chilled Clara that this man might still be alive.

Sometimes the results were more confusing and hard to follow up:

"Do you know what happened to Elliot?"

"Tsip!" said Helen. And then, "Tsip-tsip!"

"Yes *and* no?" Clara asked. "Oh, Helen, how I wish you could just speak."

Frequently, Helen would answer neither yes nor no. This made Clara wonder if Helen simply didn't know the answer, or if she was refusing to reply for some private reason of her own. After all, Clara reminded herself, Helen was just a little girl—and children wearied easily.

And so she collected all the information she could on

her own, sure that if Daphne were here to help, her friend would have cut to the quick of all these mysteries in half the time.

Therefore, it was with a sense of particular desperation that Clara watched Ruby and her mother leave unexpectedly late one Thursday afternoon for errands in town. It was nearly time for school to let out, and Daphne would be passing right by. She must speak to her! But their signal room was locked.

Clara checked the hall clock. She had ten minutes until the children passed, and the sound of the ticking clock taunted her. After pacing in front of the door and muttering to herself, she stopped.

"I'm going out!" she announced to the empty foyer. Clara marched to her mother's room and flung open the chifforobe. There hung her mother's winter cloak, which she put on, throwing up the hood.

"What a sight I must be," Clara said, "swimming in this unseasonable green tweed." But when she caught her reflection, she was satisfied with the shadow that the oversize hood made around her face. She was so well hidden, even the aviary birds did not scream as she made her way past them to the alley in back of the house.

As Clara closed the gate behind her and entered the alley, her perceptions felt weirdly off-kilter. She had seen the place where she now stood only from Mrs. Glendoveer's window upstairs; and now here she was in the great wide open. The blue infinity of the sky towered above her, making her fear that she might float away. A few steps ahead lay the street in full sunlight, and the sight terrified her.

Even when she had taken the carriage to Mrs. Glendoveer's funeral, she had not felt this shaken being outside. But she had been with her mother and Ruby, and was suffering from the shock of grief. And the crêpe veil! Wearing that dark funeral headdress had blunted the vastness of the unfamiliar view.

With her shoes now seemingly stuck to the ground, Clara reminded herself of all the days she had sat, shut up and yearning for adventure outside the walls of the Glendoveer mansion. "Get on with it," she told herself, and stumbled out onto the sidewalk just as the trolley came over the hill.

CLANG-CLANG-CLANG!

The sudden noise made her dizzy with fear. She felt the street vibrating beneath her feet and hugged the nearest lamppost to keep from fainting. She waited for the trolley to streak past and leave her in silence, but instead, she heard the squeal of the brakes and closed her eyes. *Great merciful heavens . . .*

"Step on, miss!"

Clara forced herself to peek. There was the conductor, leaning out of the cab, scowling. Behind the rows of windows, people sat and stood inside the car. Some had turned their faces, and Clara wanted to melt into the pavement.

"No, s-sir," she stammered. "I'm staying."

"Then what you standin' at the trolley stop for?" he growled, giving the bell a violent clang before driving off.

Clara looked up to see that, sure enough, she was standing beneath an enameled sign reading TROLLEY; and now the clock struck three. Her original idea had been to wait around the corner from the street where all the schoolchildren passed and to get Daphne's attention as she walked by. But now she began to have doubts. What would the other children make of her, this odd girl in winter clothing loitering on the corner when she should have been in school?

When at last the sound of footsteps and children's laughter came closer down the main street, Clara simply decided to plunge in.

Off she strode around the corner as the mob of children approached. Searching for Daphne, she deftly avoided two boys running in circles trying to steal each other's caps, a woman pushing a baby carriage, and a small dog on the loose. One older girl with braids crisscrossing her head looked into Clara's face and nudged a friend, but Clara did not slow down to see what followed.

When she spotted a knot of three girls giggling, she struggled hard to keep her composure. The one in the middle was wearing a red hat! Could it be? *Yes, yes, that's Daphne!*

With a sinking heart, Clara could see that Daphne was

not looking up. If only Clara could shout her name! Perspiring madly, she thrust her hands into the pocket of her cloak and grasped the only thing to be found there: an embroidered handkerchief.

Clara pulled it out and pretended to sneeze into it before letting it fall to the sidewalk directly in front of the preoccupied girls.

"Excuse me," said Clara in a strangled voice, bending over to retrieve the hankie. When she stood up, however, she was face to face with Daphne Aspinal. Seconds crawled by before she managed to pull a random question from her addled brain. "Where's the . . . cat and dog hospital?"

Daphne's mouth made a little O as the other two girls regarded her quizzically.

"My grandmother's cat," said Clara, feeling completely ridiculous. "It's sick. I am from, uh, another town."

The redheaded girl on Daphne's left put her hand on her hip. "I don't see a cat. Where you keeping it?"

"Keeping it?" Clara echoed dumbly.

Daphne, now recovered, smiled warmly. "I think she means she needs to pick it up for her grandmother. Am I right?"

Clara said, "Uh-huh," and felt Daphne tuck her arm in hers.

"You two go on," Daphne told the girls. "And I'll help our out-of-town visitor find her way."

"Are you sure?" asked the redheaded girl. "We can come with you."

"You have piano lessons, Gertie," Daphne said. "I'll be fine."

Gertie and her friend left, but not without glancing over their shoulders several times. Clara, on the other hand, clung to Daphne like an octopus.

"Don't dare let go of me," Clara said.

"You're going to have to let me look at you," said Daphne, taking Clara's hands in hers. She studied her face. "What's happened?"

"Nothing," Clara said. "No. Everything."

"Slow down," Daphne said, "and tell me."

Clara tried to obey. "My mother and Ruby left the house, but I couldn't signal for you because they've taken the key to the room upstairs."

"You mean they caught you nosing around up there?"

"Not caught, actually. It's more that they detected something amiss. But that's not the half of it." Clara peeked down the street. "Do you think we could go back to my house? I can't let myself be seen."

Daphne agreed to follow Clara at a distance and meet her near the aviary in Clara's backyard.

When the birds saw Clara coming, they fluttered from corner to corner.

"Hello!" Clara said.

"Hello, hello, hello!" said George the Cockatoo.

"I've got a guest coming," Clara told them. "I know you are all very secretive, but I can promise you that Daphne is most trustworthy. Do you mind?"

Hearing this, the birds flew up to the highest perch and sat shoulder to shoulder—all except Frances, who remained in her nest of newspaper, shaking her head from side to side.

"But she is really a lovely girl," Clara said. "And smart, like you, Frances. I do believe she can help."

But Frances was not moved. And when Daphne crept into the yard behind Clara, the birds remained stoic and watched from their heights.

"Gracious. Have you tamed them?" asked Daphne.

"Not in any way," said Clara.

"But they are awfully restrained. What's come over them?"

Clara bit her lip. "Would you believe me if I told you that they speak to me?"

Daphne considered. "I can believe it. I heard one of them say something in Latin to you, remember?"

"But, Daphne, it's more than that. They don't simply repeat words. They speak. Converse. Like people."

Daphne could not hide a gleam of alarm in her eyes.

"You must believe me," Clara said. "Watch." She wrapped her fingers around the iron bars and appealed to George. "Could you please say a word to my friend Daphne? She thinks I've gone mad."

George stared down, opened his beak, and let out a squawk.

"Is that what you're talking about?" asked Daphne.

"No! He speaks intelligently—although with a small vocabulary. And his sister here, the mynah—"

"His sister?" asked Daphne, incredulous.

"Yes," Clara insisted. "She speaks two languages—one rather better than the other. Isn't that right? Say something for Daphne. She's heard you before." ·

But the mynah just closed her eyes and dozed.

Daphne stepped forward and felt her friend's forehead. "Are you feeling all right?"

Clara took the hand firmly and removed it. "I am fine."

"Forgive me, Clara, but so much is out of order. First I see you floating down the street in a cloak like the grim reaper, and now you're telling me that you are having mystical experiences with animals." She put a hand to her own forehead now. "Don't tell me that's why you wanted to visit the dog and cat hospital!"

"Oh, honestly," said Clara. "That was just a ruse I came up with."

"I don't mean to be insulting, but how am I to know? Dear, I'm worried."

"Well, don't worry," said Clara, changing tone. "If you don't believe me, you don't have to. In fact, I insist you go home. My mother may be returning at any moment."

Daphne's eyes rounded. "I've made you angry? It's not my intention."

"Let me show you out."

"Please, Clara, wait—"

Clara grabbed Daphne's sleeve and took her out of sight to the alley gate. When Daphne began to protest, Clara softly covered her friend's mouth.

"Wait here," she whispered. "Don't make a sound, and listen. I'll get them to talk, you'll see. After, go around to the front door and we'll meet."

Daphne's worried eyebrows relaxed, and Clara knew she understood that her formerly cold manner was only for the birds' benefit. "Oh! All right," said Daphne. "Go on!"

Clara returned to the aviary and stood before the birds, who no longer regarded her in silence. Arthur the Grackle dressed her down from his corner with his rusty cackle while Peter the Kiskadee darted back and forth crowing his *bee-tee-WEE!* It almost seemed as if the two were laughing at her. They were so very much like real little boys in this, she could barely suppress a smile herself.

"Very funny," Clara said. "I suppose it amuses you to see me being made a fool. And you, George. I expected more from a gentleman. I hope you're a little sorry."

"Sorry," said George, bowing his head.

"I accept," said Clara.

"Little fool!" screamed Frances the Mynah.

"Who is the fool?" Clara asked. "George, me, or both?"

"Both!" said Frances.

"Now, please!" George pleaded.

"I only wanted to help," Clara said. "I promise to bring no one else to the aviary without your permission."

Frances strutted to the front of the cage and looked Clara in the face. "No one," she said.

"You have my word."

Then the mynah went back to her paper nest, and

Clara said goodbye to the other birds. "Goodbye!" said George as Helen chirped beside him.

Apparently nonchalant, Clara walked back to the kitchen. But once inside, she skidded across the slippery wood floors to the front door of the house. Daphne stood, breathless, on the step, turning her hat around in her hands.

"Well?" asked Clara, full of her own vindication.

"Astounding!" said Daphne. "Absolutely. My stars, Clara, I'll never doubt you again."

"I'm glad to hear that," said Clara, motioning her inside, "because if you can bear it, I have *so* much more!"

Chapter 16

After Clara returned her mother's cloak, she took Daphne safely down below the house into the boiler room and told her about the candle-dousing winds in the Glendoveer dining room.

"That raises bumps on my arms," said Daphne. "How do you sleep at night?"

"I do get frightened," Clara said, "but it isn't so bad if you believe, as I do, that it is Mrs. Glendoveer who still has a presence here. Mrs. Glendoveer was not a scary person."

"I think any kind of ghost is at least a little frightening," Daphne said. "But enough of that for now. Let me know about the birds!"

"Shh!" said Clara. "Let's make sure we keep our voices down. I already feel that I betrayed them, having you eavesdrop like that. . . ."

"I have pledged to you before and I'll pledge again," whispered Daphne, holding up her hand. "I am sworn to secrecy. To my dying day."

"Very good. Now all I need is for you to listen with an open mind."

"Definitely," said Daphne, leaning in close.

"I have reason to believe that these birds are . . . not just birds."

"Yes?"

Clara cleared her throat. "They are, to the best of my knowledge, *the actual Glendoveer children*." Clara waited for Daphne's response, which was slow in coming.

"Could you say that again?"

"I mean, of course, that the Glendoveer children used to be regular boys and girls. But somehow, they've come to inhabit the bodies of these birds."

"No," Daphne said. "How can that be?"

"I don't know how. But I do know that they respond to each of the Glendoveer children's names. And not only that, they match the character of each child described in Mr. Woodruff's letter. And when I asked them directly if they were the children, they said yes! The ones who can speak, that is. The honeycreeper, Helen, can only chirp true or false."

Daphne considered this information. "If I hadn't heard the creatures speak to you myself, I don't think I could believe you."

"But you do now, don't you?"

Daphne thought for a moment and then replied with absolute certainty. "Yes. I do."

Clara wanted to hug her. "You can't imagine how comforting it is to share all this strangeness with someone else who understands."

"I only barely understand," she said. "I have so many questions."

"Such as?"

"Such as, why are the birds talking now? Are you sure they've never spoken this way before?"

"I've thought this over," Clara said. "As far as I know, they've been here for nearly half a century and not spoken to anyone except me. So I know that I've set them off somehow."

"But you've lived here almost twelve years. Why haven't they said anything earlier?"

"Maybe because," said Clara, "I never spoke to them. The first time the mynah talked to me, I had spoken first. Since then, the birds have been learning to communicate at an alarming rate."

"Do you remember what the bird first said to you? I imagine whatever she told you must have been important to her."

"Yes. She said, 'Elliot.'"

"The youngest Glendoveer?" said Daphne. "And which bird is he?"

"There is no bird for Elliot. None of the others know where he is. And what's odd is, he is the only child

Mrs. Glendoveer ever talked about. It's as if he were the only one who existed for her."

"Interesting."

"And another thing," Clara said. "The birds want *me* to find him."

"Really? Don't they know by now that you're not allowed to leave the house?"

"I've tried to explain that they shouldn't expect such a thing from me. After all, if no one came forward with baby Elliot years ago when there was a huge reward offered, how could they expect me to find him as a grown man now?"

"It does seem an unlikely quest," Daphne said.

"Doesn't it? But stranger still—both George and Mrs. Glendoveer made provisions in their wills for this house to be kept up for at least fifty years after Elliot's disappearance. It seems that the Glendoveers never gave up hope that he would be returned. And his brothers and sisters haven't either."

As the clock struck four, the girls gave each other looks of desperation.

"My mother will be going out of her mind if I don't get home soon," said Daphne. "I am so frustrated with our arrangement, I cannot tell you."

"Imagine how I feel," Clara said. "At least you're free to come and go every day. I'll admit that I felt a touch of envy when you wrote to Mr. Booth. And meeting Miss Lentham! If I could speak to her now, the questions I'd ask."

"Then you should," Daphne said. "Ask her tomorrow, if you can."

Clara tried to decide whether she should laugh.

"I'm serious, Clara. Did you know that Miss Lentham volunteers at the Lockhaven Historical Society? She's there weekday mornings. I never mentioned it because I couldn't go, what with school. But now . . . why not you?"

"Do you suggest that I step out onto the street and hail a car?" Clara asked.

"The Historical Society is straight downhill nine blocks away. It's an old brick building with a captain's walk and black shutters. Keep your eyes open and you can't miss it."

Clara did not want to draw attention to her own cowardice. Instead, she said, "I could, certainly. But what happens if my mother finds out?"

"In normal circumstances, a parent might put you on restriction. But as you're already on restriction for life, what more can she do?"

Clara didn't have an answer. But the terror that had been built up inside Clara since she was a baby was formidable. "You don't understand. I can't disobey my mother like that."

"Clara?" said Daphne. "Shall we be honest?"

"Yes."

"You have been disobeying your mother for some time now."

Clara hung her head under the weight of this truth.

"It is no new thing," continued Daphne. "And I have encouraged you, I know. But is it wickedness? Think of those wretched birds! You've said it yourself that they are children and that they speak only to you. Who else has even come close to discovering their secrets? Who else will help them?"

"You have helped," Clara said. "And I am grateful. But you don't understand. I know you try, but you don't. My mother wants only to protect me."

"Then tell me everything. You have been clever and brave so far. What is so hazardous about a walk down the street? At the start, you told me that your mother wishes you always to keep still. But why? I have enough manners to know that you don't ask people about these things, but I can't help it. What ails you, Clara?"

Clara cast her eyes to the floor. She did not know why this question made her feel such burning shame. "Don't make me say, please," she said.

Daphne jammed her hands into her pockets. "No matter. You're alive, aren't you?"

"Yes."

"Well, guess what?" she said. "Life is for the *living*!" She made a fierce-comical face and held it—until she remembered that she really, truly had to leave. "The next time I see you," she said, "I hope you have something extraordinary to report!"

Clara knew that Daphne did not want to leave her with

the feeling that she'd been scolded, but as she stood alone in the half-light of the underground room, Clara did have the sensation that she'd been jolted into another frame of mind. She had been challenged, and, after the shock wore off, it had the effect of sharpening her focus on her surroundings.

"I am here and I am not locked in," she said. "I can come and I can go." She put a hand over her beating heart and noted how sturdy and regular it felt. All her life she had been cautioned not to trust it, that it was fickle, could fail and even kill her.

"I am going to give you a chance to prove yourself, heart," she declared, tapping herself on the chest. "You survived an outing among the living, and you'll do it again."

Clara spread her arms and was practically beaming with confidence when she felt a tickling over the top of her shoe. When she looked down, she spied a big, fat rat running circles around her ankles!

"Aaahhh!"

She yelped and hopped up on a small wooden crate. Her weight, however, proved too much for the box, and one leg crashed through. The rat skittered off into the shadows, but Clara was stuck. The heart she had just lectured now pumped furiously as she pulled at her knee to free her foot. Her hem ripped before her stocking foot came out—bootless! It was when she reached in the box to retrieve her boot that she also felt papers in a stack, but there was not enough light to see what was inside.

Clara stuck on her boot and dragged the box closer to the little window until she could make out a lithograph at the top of the pile, all red with black and white lettering. The section of the picture she saw showed a partial arm and a gloved hand stretched palm up with a black bird perched atop it. The cuff link was engraved with what looked like letter Gs linked back-to-back.

"George Glendoveer?"

Using all her strength, Clara pulled up the wooden boards that crossed the top of the box until she had made a hole large enough to see the entire picture.

The Great Glendoveer
World's Preeminent Magician
Featuring:
Prestidigitation!
Levitation!
And, most astoundingly,
THE TRANSMIGRATION OF SOULS!
Employing His Famed Phantastic Flock!

Clara could not believe her eyes. She thrust her hand into the box and pulled the handbill from the top of the pile, tearing it slightly down the center. At the bottom of the paper was mentioned in small print:

Assisted by his wife, Cenelia,
and the young Neurypnologist
Woodruff Booth!!!
<u>ENTRANCING</u> audiences
at home and abroad!

Clara immediately thought of showing this broadsheet to the birds. Presumably, the Glendoveer children had seen these advertisements when they were . . . alive. What would Frances say when she read it?

Anxious for more, Clara dug in again. There were several velvet jewel cases that she piled one on top of the other, a sheaf of posters featuring the missing Glendoveer children (just like the one Clara had found upstairs), and a large book of some kind. No, not a book but an album. Holding her breath, she turned it over and saw the lock.

It was here in her own hands: Mrs. Glendoveer's stamped leather album!

Clara pictured her mother rounding up everything she could find and hammering it into this crate. "I might never have found it," she said.

And now another problem presented itself to Clara: how to hide the damaged box from her mother.

Hastily, Clara tucked the jewel cases into the pockets of her pinafore and set aside the handbill and the precious album. There was no question of her repairing the box, so she turned it hole-side-down and dragged it back where she found it. She crept up the stairs, back into the closet, and listened with her ear on the door for signs that her mother and Ruby had returned. When she was satisfied, she tiptoed to her room and laid all the objects on the bed.

The first velvet box had a ribbon that resembled a military decoration, inscribed with HONORARY MEMBER OF THE COURT OF OLAV. Another was from a Leopold II of Belgium. Another held the key to the city of Lockhaven—which made Clara wonder if it was actually possible to open and close a city with a key.

The last box was stamped inside on the satin lining with the names Eicholt and Goessler, Lockhaven Jewelers. Beneath a folded paper were gleaming cuff links with the two letter Gs, exactly like the one in the handbill.

Clara took the paper and spread it out.

George—
    Glendoveer and Glendoveer, forever linked.
        With love, my darling!
        Your bride, Cenelia

Clara was about to take the links out of the box when she heard Ruby and her mother speaking animatedly somewhere in the house.

Gathering up everything from the bed, she wished she had opened Mrs. Glendoveer's album first. Now that discovery would have to wait as she tucked away her new finds in her bureau drawer, covered them with a pile of winter woolens, straightened her skirts, and went out to meet her mother.

Chapter 17

"Well, Harriet, I've lived in this city half my life, and I've never seen a crowd like that in Lockhaven on a Thursday afternoon," Ruby was saying as Clara entered the kitchen.

"Crowds?" asked Clara. "What for?"

"They're showing a moving picture downtown," Ruby told her. "They call it *The Great Train Robbery*. The old theater had lines around the block, and the trolleys are full!"

"Did you fear we were never coming home?" asked her mother.

"Oh, Mama," answered Clara, "but you always *do* come home."

Her mother seemed satisfied with this remark until something about Clara seemed to catch her eye. "Turn around," she said.

Clara did, once.

"Whatever has happened to your hem?" Her mother knelt behind Clara and picked up the edge of her dress. "There's a hole here big as a half-dollar."

"Is there?"

"Yes," she said. "Surely you heard it rip. How did you do it?"

Clara shrugged. "I can mend it myself."

"I'm not concerned about the mending," said her mother. "I'm concerned with how you managed to tear your clothing."

"I can't tell you how I did it," Clara said evenly, though she could feel the heat rise in her cheeks. Today had already been full of too much novelty, and in her tired state Clara believed she might betray some emotion she would later regret.

Her mother bit the inside of her mouth, considered, and rose. "All right," she said. "As long as you do mend it."

Clara looked at her hands and hid them. Her nails were dirty, and she felt the dust of the boiler room clinging to her skin.

"It's best you change out of those clothes before supper," her mother said, looking her up and down. "And I think you could do with a bath as well."

The days had lengthened enough to provide a dreamy, lingering twilight, and Clara loved delaying the lighting of lamps. Through the clerestory window above the tub, she saw the sky turning dusky blue, then soft purple. It seemed like a good time to talk to Cenelia Glendoveer.

"Mrs. Glendoveer, I'm going to open your album tonight. I hope that's all right, seeing that you did trust me with your locket and the key. I'm trying to help your children. Do you understand?"

No sign manifested from the departed, which made Clara feel a little silly. The world had so changed for her that she could find herself chatting up the air one moment and wondering about her sanity the next. However, no news was better than "no" itself, and Clara took extra candles to her room that evening, intent on poring over Cenelia Glendoveer's secret book.

With some difficulty, she managed to work the tiny key in the album's lock. When she lifted it to read, a litter of crushed blossoms crumbled onto her lap. Whatever these flowers were part of—a wedding bouquet, perhaps?—must have been important to Mrs. Glendoveer.

Carefully, Clara lifted her nightgown, gathered the dried stuff in a pile, placed it in a neat heap, and tied it in a hankie. On returning, she found the album had opened where it would—on the photograph of baby Elliot that Mrs. Glendoveer herself had shown her.

She could not resist tracing the child's face with her finger. Everything about him was round—his eyes, his nostrils, and his little rosebud mouth. It was impossible for Clara to imagine him as a man.

On the next pages she found a watercolor of a train

engine spouting steam by young George William, a certificate of scholastic merit for Frances, a list for Santa from Arthur specifying a bow and arrow, tracings of Peter's hands decorated as Thanksgiving turkeys, and a lock of Helen's soft pale hair clasped in a pink ribbon.

"*When you and Father come home,*" read one postcard, "*you will get a good report from Nanny on everyone but Arthur. He rolled his hoop in the parler and broke your Stafordshire spaniel, but now he regrets it and wants to buy one new before you return. He asks or would you rather have his dimes from Xmas?*

"*Arthur's seckretary, GEORGE.*"

The items were little things that mothers collect and cherish—bits from the everyday life of a happy household full of children. Clara was glad to be able to see these relics from the past and appreciate them for what they were, but she saw nothing that one might feel it necessary to hide. What could be the cause of Mrs. Glendoveer's secrecy?

The last remaining item was substantial: a square green cardboard envelope with twine-and-button enclosures stuffed full. Opening it, she found a pile of yellow paper that she supposed might be correspondence. The edges of the paper were ragged as if ripped from a ledger. Attached to the front with a straight pin was a note.

At George's request, I have destroyed all descriptions of his original work, their sketches, and detailed directions.

He insisted that no one be privy to the secrets of his trade, not only because he was their legal proprietor but also because he did not wish to encourage young people who might try to follow in his footsteps. It may be said that he no longer believed in magic, but I think it is more precise to say he no longer felt satisfaction in producing amazements for crowds of strangers. Strangers had not been kind to him, and whatever magic he was able to practice was nothing compared to what had been taken from him.

What remains here are his private thoughts, significant for me and perhaps for an heir who might be restored to us. We live in hope.

           Cenelia Newsom Glendoveer

The following page was dated November 29, 1855.

We have had one week at home, although I do not recognize it as the same place, for it has never been so silent. I cannot comfort Cenelia, who tears at my sleeve if I attempt to touch her shoulder. She blames me utterly, and I cannot con-

vince her that the suspicions she has harbored for so long are delusions.

She has insisted that Woodruff never set foot in our house at Lockhaven again. I asked her, "What reason shall I give him? He has been steadfast as a brother to me during this nightmare. His readiness to be of assistance with the newspapers, to organize searches—even to offer a most substantial reward for our children's return—has not moved her.

I could not, in my current state, have battled the rumors that came thick and fast when the children disappeared. Many assumed that because I made my living by "tricks," I would not be above staging the stealing of my children to draw attention to myself. Some said I did so in order to save the European tour—as if we weren't already adding appearances and turning audiences away. Why people invent these theories is beyond me, but Woodruff answered them, point for point.

Yet Cenelia still insists that he does not have our best interests at heart. And now that the worst is known, she takes this as a confirmation of his iniquity.

I wonder, how did I arrive at this

place? My house is now a tomb. My sweet wife (whose sympathies were once unfailing) now growls such odious words in her misery. And always with me are the images: our children's bodies discovered and brought home in a wagon; their mother laying a hand on the sheet covering her son's face. I was not the only one to hear her say:

"I hope I live to see _him_ dead."

The sergeant's face went white, and the people with their coats buttoned over their nightclothes, standing on their toes to witness the horror, already started to whisper.

I could not bring myself to tell them all that she was cursing Woodruff Booth. My wife had gone out of her mind with grief. Little did I know that through my silence, the infamy we had suffered would only deepen and spread.

The words, now distorted, come back to us in scrawled anonymous letters, in poisonous questions from investigators. Witnesses have sworn they heard Cenelia declare: "I hoped to live to see them dead"—as if these vile murders were a fulfillment of a mother's wish.

These were our children, whom we loved beyond measure! It defies logic. And the accusations! My dabbling in black magic? Blood sacrifices to demons? The people who used to flock to see my magic have now let blossom every vile superstition and turned on us in an instant.

I have no one living to console me or to console. Oh, that I were able to be with my own children, even if it required keeping company with the dead. . . .

GG

Clara took in every scene as George Glendoveer described it. Imagining Mrs. Glendoveer in anguish, viewing her children's dead bodies while onlookers gossiped, was almost too painful to contemplate. But now to get a glimpse of George's broken spirit as well? She wished she had been there to take his hand. Why had Mrs. Glendoveer cut her husband off from his closest friend and confidant? And how unfortunate for Woodruff Booth to be so vilified. Maybe, Clara thought, George Glendoveer was right: there are some sorrows so heavy, they make people come undone.

There were other entries where George wrote for pages without punctuation, trying to capture all the impressions of his children before they slipped from memory. Some of the writing was difficult to decipher. In places, it was splashed with tears. As time went on, the record showed that he did his best to be patient with his distraught wife. When George stated that he was relieved to see his wife distracting herself with needlework during the sleepless nights, Clara felt the prickle of recognition:

> Like the women in her family who came before her, Cenelia has dedicated herself to embroidering a mourning picture to memorialize our children. I am happy to see her employed in something that always gave her pleasure, but she has told me that when the picture is finished, she will lay down her needle forever.
>
> I asked her to remember that until we have proof to the contrary, we can always hope that Elliot will be returned to us. "If Elliot returns," she said, "I will take him from this house and never let him leave the safety of my arms." She said this, I thought, with bitterness toward me, but when I attempted once more to reach out my hand to her, she startled me by grabbing it and covering it with kisses. I knelt and held her. I do not know how long we lingered, clutching each other, shaking with tears. . . .

The embroidered picture of the Glendoveers' tombstones still lay hidden in Clara's drawer. She took it out and saw it with new eyes. The blue rectangle under the water might be Mrs. Glendoveer's way of leaving room for baby Elliot. Apparently, she did not know whether to include him with the dead.

Clara thought about the birds outside sleeping in the moonlight. Even after their parents' deaths, they held the hope of finding their baby brother. But what perplexed Clara was, why were these trapped souls still pursuing the quest to recover him? What could result from it? The family had been torn apart, betrayed. Nothing could be put back where it was, with George and Cenelia Glendoveer now in the crypt.

The birds' urgency made Clara weary and sad. The time had long passed for mending, and she wondered how the Glendoveer children would ever find peace.

Chapter 18

The next day, whenever Clara could steal a minute to herself, she would return to the green envelope with George Glendoveer's writings. Because most of the pages were neither numbered nor dated, she couldn't determine how large a portion of the diary Mrs. Glendoveer had destroyed.

George mentioned at times his absorption in study, but his notes were cryptic, referring to some text known only as *The Book of H*. On several pages, he had drawn out pictures in neat rows with SPELL FROM THE PAHERI TOMB written beneath. Clara could make out several birds and the figure of a reclining man, but many of the drawings looked merely like scribbles.

She started to feel she would need the assistance of a scholar to get even an inkling of what George Glendoveer meant. And then she found this page:

It is done. My forty-nine days have expired, and the souls can no longer be called back. As for the incantations, even if I were to consult every document available to me in the West, I wouldn't know if the translations of The Book of H are faulty. I can only decipher the pictograms in English as they are presented to me.

Have I succeeded in mastering actual magic? Until now, I have been an artist, a performer, a craftsman. I am a rationalist—or at least I was. Now afternoons find me sitting outside the aviary on my folding chair, waiting for the birds to give me a sign.

On occasion, I think I glimpse my Frances. Of them all, she is most likely to show a spark, and I am borne up by what I imagine are attempts to speak. Her facility with languages was impressive, and the stirrings in her throat are such an odd mixture of vowels, such as I never heard from a bird.

If I have saved the children in time, I hope also to save them for time. The soul of my youngest does not return, and I cannot fathom whether it is through some fault of mine in summoning him, *or whether he still lives. I must impress upon Cenelia that the birds are to be cared for without stinting. She has put my words in a place where she shall not lose them. I've done my utmost, and as fervently as I desire our reunion, I cannot expect it. We shall see what comes of my work, or what does not come.*

Together always to the last,
Our love shall hold each other fast.
Delivered from the frost and foam,
None shall fly till all come home.
GG

Of everything George Glendoveer revealed, Clara was most surprised by the fact that he never knew whether or not his children's souls inhabited the birds. If he intended to gather his family together again, he must have died a disappointed man.

And Mrs. Glendoveer? Clara could still see the shock on her face when she learned that the mynah had finally spoken. If she had lived just a bit longer, perhaps she could have heard Frances speak herself.

Her eyes returned to George Glendoveer's poem—or was it an incantation? It was the same inscription Mrs. Glendoveer had included in her mourning picture. Clara figured that the frost and foam must refer to the chilly waters of Lockhaven Bay, for that is where the children were drowned. But it was the final line that added to her understanding of the birds' quest.

"None shall fly till all come home," repeated Clara. "All of them, even Elliot, must come home." But then what? Where would the birds fly, and what would become of Elliot?

Clara got out her own paper and began making a list of things in George Glendoveer's notes that needed investigation.

The Book of H
Spell from the Paheri tomb
Pictograms—aren't they Egyptian?

Who on earth could read pictograms? Was there a chance that Miss Lentham, expert in Greek and Latin, might also know something about Egyptian texts?

She copied George Glendoveer's tiny jottings as well as she could.

"I'm ready!" Clara stated. And she was in no mood to wait. She would find her way to the Lockhaven Historical Society and beg for Miss Lentham's help.

Friday morning was a likely time for Harriet to go into town for provisions, so Clara was happy to find her mother singing to herself as she stood in front of the glass:

"To market, to market, to buy a fat hog . . ." She placed

her straw hat on her head and fastened it with a long pin before spotting Clara in the mirror behind her.

"Ah! There you are. Do you know what day it is?"

Clara considered. "I almost forgot! It's Ruby's birthday. Are you going to make a cake?"

"I thought that might be nice. And maybe some salmon and potato hash. We don't often have it, and it's her favorite."

"Where's Ruby?"

"She's got her feet up in the kitchen. I told her not to stir today."

"And that's the way it should be," Clara said.

"I'll try to be back by twelve-thirty," said her mother. "In the meantime, I trust you'll treat her like a queen."

Clara watched her mother leave and made a beeline to Ruby, who was feasting on strawberries and confectioners' sugar. "Happy birthday, dear!" she said. "And what will you do today after you've enjoyed breakfast?"

"Don't know," she said. "I'm so seldom left to my own devices, I'm stymied."

Clara slowly dusted the table with her hand. "Really? I'd supposed you'd be off to those moving pictures."

Ruby lit up, then stopped herself. "Oh now, couldn't do that. The lines are so long, I'd be gone half a day."

But Clara could tell by the dreamy way Ruby licked stray sugar from her upper lip that she was entertaining the idea. All she needed was a little push.

"But it's your birthday. . . . Why, it's a once-a-year op-portunity!"

Ruby pondered this last statement, then planted her feet on the floor. "Not even once a year. Did I go out on my last birthday, or the one before?"

"Never, that I recall."

She threw down her napkin. "That settles it, then. I want to see *The Great Train Robbery*, and I can't imagine it'll harm anyone if I do."

"I only wish I could go with you," Clara said. "Please see it, come back, and tell me everything!"

Ruby jumped up and patted her temples. "Dear me. Must get some combs in my hair. And my coin purse. Ah, what time is it?"

It tickled Clara to see Ruby so full of excitement. If she had sent her out of the house, at least she had done so in the service of Ruby's happy birthday.

Clara tried not to pay attention to the sudden trembling of her own hands as she wrapped a shawl around her head and shoulders. On her way out, she stopped by the aviary to speak with the birds, who greeted her with riotous whistling.

"Hello, all of you. Sorry I have to hurry. I'm off on a special mission for you."

"Elliot!" said George.

"Frances," Clara said, "I'm going to talk to your teacher Miss Lentham."

The mynah studied her as if waiting for more.

"She knows so much about your family. And I have so many questions. I'm hoping she can help."

"Go," said Frances curtly.

Clara tried not to take Frances's manner to heart, but she wondered what she would have to do to win her favor. "Goodbye to you all," Clara said, waving. She felt a bit as though she were about to walk the plank, but she managed a smile anyway.

Stepping from the alley to the street wasn't quite as forbidding as the last time Clara tried it. The weather had turned chilly and the clouds were misting, so not many people were about. She tucked her hands inside her sleeves and walked downhill, carefully counting the blocks.

The farther she went, wooden homes gave way to brick row houses. Each entrance had stone steps leading up to a different style of door. Some were painted dragon red or deep green. Others had little beveled windows or were elaborately carved. The one with the lacquered black door had a ship's bell above the threshold and an engraved brass sign:

Lockhaven Historical Society
Est. 1831
Maintained by Lockhaven Women's Club

Clara knocked, but no one answered. She screwed up her nerve and turned the knob. Open!

"Hello?" she said, and stepped inside.

Chapter 19

Clara recognized the soft smell of paper and old leather. In the front room, there was a cool marble floor and an unoccupied mahogany counter with chairs and green-shaded reading lamps. To her right was a glassed-in room with displays of old anchors, ships' wheels, and knotted rope. Down the hall, she could see a stoop-shouldered lady in a plain gray dress pushing a cart. When the old woman drew near, Clara noticed that her glasses were so thick, they almost flattened her nose.

"May I help you?" the woman asked in a voice as dry as sand.

"Yes, please," Clara answered. "I'm hoping you are Miss Lentham."

The lady squinted and leaned in very close. "And who are you?"

"I'm a friend of Daphne Aspinal's. Clara's my name. I heard you have information on the Glendoveer family you might be willing to share."

"A friend of the little girl?" Miss Lentham unhooked her cane from the cart and leaned upon it. "I wondered if anyone would come. Follow me."

Behind Miss Lentham's desk was a file box, which she indicated with her cane. "It's all in there. You may look at it as long as you like, but put everything back *exactly*. These are my personal clippings, which I have lent to the society."

Clara saw that Miss Lentham was not going anywhere, but stood close as she went through the newspaper clippings. Each item was dated and placed in order of publication. The headlines were in bold type:

Magician's Children Missing!
Nanny Suspect

Five Glendoveer Children and Nanny
Dragged from Bay
Stolen Items Still Missing

Great Glendoveer?
Public Sympathy Turns to
Public Suspicion

"I've often wondered," said Miss Lentham, "why the young people today don't want to know more about the

Glendoveers. This is the only event of note our city has seen, and it was a global sensation."

"Perhaps they don't want the truth," Clara said, echoing Ruby's theory. "Maybe the stories they tell are more interesting."

"I can't see how that could be," Miss Lentham said. "To think it shall someday fade from all memory. And what brings you here to investigate?"

"Daphne got me interested," said Clara, pulling a clipping from the file. "She's corresponded with Mr. Woodruff Booth, you know."

Miss Lentham looked up to the heavens. "Mr. Booth! Such a gentleman. I had no doubt he'd reply to her."

"He spoke of the children," said Clara, "and gave descriptions of each one of them. But I thought you might be able to tell me more about Frances Glendoveer. I know she studied here often."

"Frances was a brilliant child. I do believe she found in me a compatible intellect."

"You spoke often with her, then?"

Miss Lentham's cloudy eyes looked over her spectacles. "Not in a personal way."

Clara believed Miss Lentham sensed her disappointment.

"Twice a week after school, I tutored her in her study of Greek and Roman literature—both of which are my specialties. She could read for hours. Not like the children today with the attention spans of houseflies."

At once, Clara dug into her pocket and pulled out her notes. "Speaking of ancient civilizations, you've reminded me, Miss Lentham," she said. "Have you by chance heard of something called . . . *The Book of H?* It apparently has pictograms in it."

"And the *H* stands for what? You'll have to be more specific about the title."

"I don't know, I'm afraid," said Clara. "Then how about the Paheri tomb? Have you heard of that?"

"Never. My word," said Miss Lentham, "have we already tired of the Glendoveers?"

"Not at all," said Clara. "It's only that I've heard the tomb was of interest to Mr. Glendoveer. I don't know where it is, but it has a poem written on it." She reached into her pocket and pulled out her paper. "Do you read pictographs?"

"You mean hieroglyphs?" Miss Lentham eyed her and, with sudden irritation, added, "Now, *why* would you bring me something like that? Am I an Egyptologist?"

Chastened, Clara stuffed the paper back in her pocket, hoping to recover her footing with the old woman. But as she did, Miss Lentham burst out with a frustrated sigh.

"Are you *not* going to show it to me now?" she asked.

"But you said you weren't an Egyptologist."

"And I am not. But after years of wide-ranging study in ancient civilizations," she said, peering over her spectacles, "I do know a thing or two."

"Of course," Clara said. "I didn't mean to—"

Miss Lentham took the note, fetched her heavy magnifying glass from her desk drawer, bent close, and squinted.

"Look here," she said, stabbing the page with her finger.

Clara read over her shoulder. "Do you know what those wavy lines are?"

"Yes. As it happens, I do recognize a few of the symbols. This one is water. Oh! And here—this cup-shaped object? That's a tomb. A tomb under the water, it seems."

Clara held her breath as Miss Lentham continued.

"I do think that this figure here—the little man on his side? That's a corpse." She tapped the page. "And it appears that the corpse lives among the birds. Or is it that the corpse becomes a bird? Strange. I couldn't tell you much more. That's about all I can make out."

"But it's uncanny!"

Miss Lentham put down her glass. "In what way?"

"There's so much of the Glendoveers in it," Clara said.

"On the contrary, I see nothing of the Glendoveers in it."

There was no way, Clara realized, that she could explain to Miss Lentham the significance of souls assuming the form of birds, or that this might be part of an incantation used by the Great Glendoveer himself. "I meant, well, the water and the tomb and the corpses," she said.

Miss Lentham regarded her with distaste. "How perfectly morbid," she said. "As much as I wish to impart historical information pertaining to the Glendoveer family, I do not approve of sensation seekers."

"I'm sorry, Miss Lentham," Clara said. "I'd be happy to go back to our conversation about Frances."

"Frances," said Miss Lentham, "would be a good example for you. In fact . . ." She returned to the Glendoveer files and retrieved a book. "I have something for you."

Clara took the volume from her. VIRGIL POEMS was imprinted in gold on the spine.

"This old book's backing is broken from use. It was a favorite of Frances Glendoveer's. You might study it. Improve yourself. Now, if you'll excuse me . . ."

Before Miss Lentham could start off, Clara grasped at one last opportunity to keep her talking. "I was so hoping to learn a bit more about Mr. Booth. Obviously, there is no one who would know him better than you, Miss Lentham."

"Indeed, there is not," she said. "Certainly not in Lockhaven."

"He said in his letter that he came from a distinguished family."

"Quite distinguished," she said. "From one of the first families of Rhode Island."

"He also said that they did not approve of his taking the stage. So perhaps you can tell me how he joined Mr. Glendoveer's traveling show?"

A smile played at Miss Lentham's lips. "Very well. It is an anecdote that I'm sure few know. As you can imagine, a man with Mr. Booth's pedigree would be expected to go to university and then abroad, but he had an artist's temperament. A . . . sensitive nature. Do you know he published a book of poetry for distribution only among his friends, to avoid exposing himself to raw, public criticism? And he did almost complete his studies at Yale—that is, until he was overtaken by a series of ailments."

"Was he quite ill?" Clara asked.

"Yes. In his way." She lifted an eyebrow above the rim of her spectacles. "These were nervous ailments. Sudden fears. He agonized before entering a room full of people, for instance, and would often just return home. Or he would become paralyzed at the prospect of crossing a bridge. The worst of his terrors, however, involved birds. He became housebound, deathly afraid of crows, gulls, or purple martins flying overhead. He felt they might attack him."

"Do you know why?"

"I suspect he was too highly refined, just as thoroughbred horses are often the most skittish. In any case, he went to take a cure in Switzerland, where he not only underwent hypnosis but also learned the art himself. He came away quite cured, and that is when he joined the Great Glendoveer."

"Wasn't he afraid of Mr. Glendoveer's birds?"

"Yes, terribly," stated Miss Lentham. "That is how they met. Mr. Booth considered it the ultimate test of his Swiss cure to sit in a closed theater with birds flying over the crowd. So he went to see the Great Glendoveer and was enchanted by the spectacle. And since he now had mesmerizing powers of his own, he asked if he might try his luck on the stage. And, of course, Mr. Booth was a stellar addition to the bill, even though he never quite conquered his ornithophobia."

"Ornithophobia," repeated Clara. "Is that a fear of birds?"

"Exactly. He told me he had to perform self-hypnosis for at least an hour before every show." Miss Lentham patted her hair. "It is one thing to be a man afraid, and quite another to conquer that fear day after day. I daresay Mr. Booth was a man of great courage after all."

Clara nodded in agreement. "I know he was a close friend of George Glendoveer's. But do you know how he got along with Cenelia Glendoveer?"

Miss Lentham's voice grew sharp. "The *wife?*"

"Yes. Mrs. Glendoveer."

"That Cenelia . . ." Miss Lentham shook her head. "I mustn't blame her, and I try to be sympathetic because who knows how any of us might behave in the midst of such horror."

"Of course," said Clara. "But what did she do?"

"Mrs. Glendoveer let it be known that she believed Mr. Booth had spread rumors about her family. I heard she even tried to alert the press. No one printed anything against Mr. Booth, of course. They considered the woman's condition and thought better of it."

"What rumors did she think he spread?"

"Every time the paper quoted someone anonymously, Cenelia supposed it was actually Mr. Booth. And there were some awful rumors about the Glendoveers' motives, to which I myself strenuously objected." Miss Lentham sniffed. "You won't find two better defenders of that family than Mr. Booth and myself."

Clara felt there certainly could be no more passionate defender of Mr. Booth than Miss Lentham. "Pardon me if I don't understand," Clara said, "but surely George Glendoveer would be able to help his wife see reason? That is, if Mr. Booth truly had been such a help . . ."

"Mr. Booth is beyond reproach," stated Miss Lentham.

"I'm sure he is," Clara said soothingly, "but why would anyone suspect him, especially Mrs. Glendoveer, who knew him so well?"

Miss Lentham leaned on her cane. "I know only what Mr. Booth confided to me. The Booth family had disowned him at the time, and Cenelia came to the conclusion that he was in dire need of cash. Which makes no sense, if you consider the ample reward he offered for the children's return. If you ask me, it was Mrs. Glendoveer spreading rumors about Mr. Booth and not the other way round."

Clara had no idea how to reply. The idea of Mrs. Glendoveer spreading rumors, attempting to ruin a good friend's reputation, was unbelievable.

Miss Lentham lifted her chin. "It has been an inestimable honor to have been of assistance to Mr. Booth since he left Lockhaven. If the authorities had been inclined to listen to the ravings of Cenelia Glendoveer, he might have found himself wrongfully imprisoned. Because of my interest in the Glendoveers and my expertise on the matter of the kidnapping, I told him I'd report to him any significant news, gossip, or threat that I perceived against him. And in return, he has given me his friendship."

With difficulty, Clara kept her anger at bay. "But, Miss Lentham," she said, "surely there can't be anything more about which to inform Mr. Booth."

"On the contrary," said Miss Lentham. "As long as that woman was alive, Mr. Booth had no idea whether she would turn against him again. An angry old woman with diminished faculties—who knows what evidence she had secreted up there in that old house, either circumstantial or manufactured?"

Clara could no longer keep the vehemence out of her voice. "Manufactured, you say? You think Mrs. Glendoveer would invent false evidence?"

Miss Lentham banged her cane on the floor. "I say what I mean."

"And so do I!" said Clara. "You have called me morbid. What shall I call you who would malign a deceased woman this way?"

At this, Miss Lentham stood at attention, quivering with suspicion like a deer that has heard a twig snap in the woods. Her lip crawled up, exposing her ivory teeth. Slowly, she pushed her glasses up on her nose and bent so far forward Clara feared she'd pitch over.

"All right, my dear," she rasped. "Who are you *really*?" Her withered hand reached out to snatch Clara's arm.

Horrified, Clara leapt back.

"Who sent you?" Miss Lentham demanded.

"No one; I'm no one!" Clara escaped the building as fast as she could, clutching the book of poems to her chest. The rows of houses blurred past, and she did not pause until a stitch in her side stopped her three blocks up the street. She put one hand to her ribs and kept climbing the hill.

"Home," she panted. "Oh, let me be home!"

Chapter 20

Clara, head reeling with new questions about Woodruff Booth, was still clutching the volume of *Virgil Poems* when she crept up the alley to the back of her house. She wondered how Frances would react, hearing about the threatening behavior of Miss Lentham. But before she would ask anything of the mynah, Clara planned to slip the book into the aviary, hoping the sight of this favorite volume of poetry would be a cheerful surprise for her. However, she was stopped in her tracks by the sound of someone behind her throwing open the kitchen window.

"Clara. Elizabeth. Dooley."

Her mother's voice was still and even—which was how she always sounded at her most outraged. Clara hunched her shoulders, afraid to look around.

"In the house. Now."

Dragging her feet, Clara went up the back stairs, past

the mudroom, and into the kitchen, where her mother stood. On the table beside her mother was a picture in a frame—Mrs. Glendoveer's mourning picture. Rolled up on top of that was the poster with the picture of the Glendoveer children. George Glendoveer's papers lay nearby with Mrs. Glendoveer's scrapbook, as well as the velvet jewel boxes Clara had found in the boiler room.

"You've been in my drawer," said Clara.

"Yes," she said. "And where have you been?"

There was no use lying. "I've been to the Lockhaven Historical Society."

Harriet took the book from Clara's hands and leafed through it. "Latin poetry?"

"A lady there gave this to me. It was a favorite of Frances Glendoveer's. I left the house to find out more about *them*," Clara said, pointing to the table.

She watched her mother sink into a chair.

"Why are you so afraid of my finding out about them? Why is Mrs. Glendoveer's family such a secret? I want to do as you ask—always. But I don't understand why."

"You don't need to understand," said her mother. "I have your best interests at heart. You must trust me."

"But I've tried, Mama. I've struggled."

"You are not the only one who has struggled!" her mother said, gaining color. "With the exception of the people living in this house, I am alone in the world. Do you think I've chosen this life for my own selfish motives? Don't you know that *you* are what is most precious to me?"

"I know that's what you say," Clara answered. "But then

I see the ways you keep me in the dark and lock me away from everyone and everything, and I—"

Clara broke off, but as her mother regarded her sternly, she felt a weight inside her shift—as if she were forcing aside something heavy. "I have to wonder if you *do* love me."

Her mother's eyes grew soft and round, the way a child's might during a harsh scolding.

"Don't say that."

But Clara could not stop the words that were now coming in a rush. "You won't tell me about my father, and so I am forced to wonder if you are hiding that he was a bad man. Other times, I wonder if it is *you* who are hiding from something terrible, and then I fear that I may not know you at all—"

"Clara!"

"And you tell me I'm weak, though I don't feel it in my body. But I have to believe it because you say so! And so I do grow weak—inside. If I want truth, I have to skulk and pry to find it. Oh, Mama, don't you see? I no longer trust or believe you. It is a horrible thing!"

Her mother stood. "Enough!" she shouted. "No more of this. We're finished." She pointed to Clara's room, refusing to look her in the face.

Clara stood in the quiet, waiting for her mother to acknowledge her once more. When it became apparent that she would not, Clara turned on her heel.

"Poof," she said, just loud enough for her mother to hear. "She disappears."

In her room, Clara kept thinking that when she came out, her freedom would be even more stifled. She would never be left alone again, and then what would she do?

The sun's light moved the shadows across the wall. Clara heard Ruby come in chattering, and then heard a sudden change in her voice. What would Ruby make of Clara now, knowing how deceitful she had become?

She lay back on the coverlet and did not cry. Instead, she thought of how far apart she and her mother had grown. Clara berated her mother for hiding the truth, but Clara had secrets too. Even if she hadn't promised the Glendoveer children her silence, she could not imagine her mother believing the true identity of the birds.

Clara fell asleep and didn't dream. When she awakened, the sun had set and the dark shape of her mother stood over her.

"Mama?"

"Yes, dear," she said.

"How long have you been here?"

. "A long time. I've been doing some serious thinking." She lit the lamp, and Clara could see that her mother had been crying. She moved closer, sat on the bed, and smoothed Clara's hair. "Now," she said softly, "shall I tell you about your father?"

Clara sat up and pulled her knees to her chest. She guessed that Ruby had had a part in her mother's new willingness to talk. Not wanting to miss a word, she listened intently.

Her mother took a handkerchief from her sleeve and smoothed it on her lap. "I want to start by saying he was not a bad man. That is so important for you to know."

"I'm glad you told me," Clara said.

"Nevan Dooley was his name. I met him when he was in the hospital down the coast. I was a nurse's assistant, and he was a carpenter. He'd fallen from a rafter and broken his leg."

Though she knew nothing about him yet, Clara cringed at the thought of her father being hurt. "It's good you were there, then," she said.

Her mother smiled vaguely. "That's what we both thought. Nevan and I grew fond of each other. He was nothing like me, you see. He was very soft, Clara. And sweet. The type who picks a spider up on a newspaper and takes it outdoors."

Clara had seen her mother deal rather mercilessly with spiders, and this bit of news charmed her. "You fell in love while he was in the hospital?"

Her mother looked at her hands and found she had twisted her handkerchief round and round. "I was alone, forced to work as my parents were both gone. And his own childhood had been so bleak and full of cruelty. He had run away from his father and spent his life traveling and working, never settling down."

"What about his mother?"

"He remembered her as kind, but she died when he was five."

206

"What awful luck!"

"Yes. It was awful luck all around, and we wanted to change it. We thought, why should we both be alone? We can make our own family." She glanced at Clara. "When young and in love, we are wishful people."

"But you did make a family for a while. That's why I'm here."

"Yes, that's why. And we were happy. He was a good deal older than I was, but he was strong and a hard worker. We had a snug cottage that he repaired from the floor to the roof, and I thought that when you came, our happiness would be complete."

Clara saw her mother falter, and she worried what might come next. "And then I came," she said, "and what happened?"

Harriet took Clara's hands in hers. "Nevan was excited about having a child, but it was also a strain on him. He started having dreams with odd glimpses of his past, or so he believed. Shortly after you were born, he saw an old advertisement for the Great Glendoveer's traveling show— something tacked up in a shed somewhere. And that's when he became convinced that, somehow, he was the missing Glendoveer baby."

"My father thought he was Elliot?" Clara asked. "Why?"

She shrugged helplessly. "Oh, something about cuff links. He said he remembered seeing the distinctive cuff links on the poster when he was a boy. . . ."

Clara squeezed her mother's hands. "George Glendoveer's cuff links! The double Gs. I know them. They were given to him by Mrs. Glendoveer. Didn't you see them in the jewel box?"

"Darling, of course I know. But Nevan said they were in a box his father dug up from under a tree, of all things. And apparently he was severely beaten when his father found him looking through the box. But he was certain he could go back to his childhood home and find proof. If not the cuff links, then something else connecting him to the Glendoveers."

Clara considered this. "Did he ever get to speak to Mrs. Glendoveer?"

"No. Nevan sent me here with you while he went to search for proof that he was Elliot. He didn't even want me to know where he was headed. Nevan feared his father, and it was an obsession with him that you always be protected."

"He loved me, then?" Clara asked.

"As much as I do."

"But he never returned. Why?"

"I don't know. Everything he did, he believed was right. I found him utterly convincing for so long. But now I've come to the sad conclusion that he was unable to discern the truth from his own imaginings."

Clara studied her mother's face. "Why are you sure he isn't Elliot? What did Mrs. Glendoveer say when you came here?"

Her mother wiped the back of her hand across her forehead. "This is the worst part of the story," she said. "When I began to see that I'd made an awful mistake. I told Ruby that my husband believed he was Elliot Glendoveer. And she looked at me, standing there in the fog with my bundle, and said, 'Good gravy, we've got another one.'"

"What did she mean?"

"You know Ruby. She is very frank. She brought me in for tea and explained that they had lots of visitors ringing the bell and letters and telegrams from all over from people convinced they were the missing Glendoveer. She said the number had dropped off in recent years, but invariably the claims were proved false."

"But Mrs. Glendoveer must have had her own opinion."

"She was as kind as she could be. I described Nevan to her, but of course it wasn't enough to match him up with baby Elliot. As for the cuff links, she said George liked the ones she gave him so much, he had copies made. A pair could have been stolen when the children were taken. But they hadn't been missed. And your father did not return."

"And yet here we are still, in the Glendoveer house," Clara said. "Perhaps she did believe he was Elliot."

"Mrs. Glendoveer never said as much. Seeing that I had you, she took pity on us, and, as it happened, she had a position for me. Yet, if I am honest, I'd say we both hoped your father's story was true. It kept me here much longer than I might have stayed, certainly."

Clara sat, going over the details of her mother's story in

her mind. Almost everything fit, but questions remained for her.

"Didn't you look for my father?"

"Clara, I told you, he wouldn't let me know where he was going. He feared his father enough not to want me to follow. . . . I suspect he might have gone out to one of the Pincushion Islands far out in the bay, but there are so many of them! They're an untraceable lot, those people out there."

Clara had heard of the Pincushions from Mrs. Glendoveer. They had odd names like Skull's Head, Grindstone, Double X, and Tick's Mouth. "Good places for scofflaws, sailors jumping ship," Mrs. Glendoveer told her.

"But, Mama," Clara said, "doesn't it hurt to know that he might be out there somewhere? What if he suffers?"

"Of course it hurts," she said. "Not knowing has made the years here quite difficult for me. No matter what passes, for good or ill, it is always better to know."

On hearing this, Clara's eyes filled with tears. "I am glad to hear you say that," she said. "It is exactly what I tried to tell you today. It *is* better to know, Mama."

Her mother dropped her chin and stared at her handkerchief.

Clara wiped her eyes. "And now you must tell me why you have shut me away."

Her mother's gaze met Clara's. "Because I am afraid."

"Of what?"

"Shall I name the fears one by one?" her mother asked.

"All right, then. First, I promised your father to keep you safe. He believed the man who raised him was an outlaw, after all, someone who might seek to silence him and us. And as he hasn't returned . . . it's possible that danger was real.

"Also, Mrs. Glendoveer convinced me that any children living in this house would be better off hidden—at least until they were no longer children."

"But you know why she said that," Clara said. "She spoke from her own experience."

"Yes. Her experience was horrifying." Harriet shuddered. "But beyond that, she convinced me that there were evil enough people around who might want to reenact a Glendoveer kidnapping. I already told you about all the false Elliots who came to her door. Well, there were also strange letters from people claiming to be the nanny's accomplice, and worse. So Mrs. Glendoveer begged me to keep you inside, and I saw the sense in it."

"But you told me I was ill!" said Clara with a pound of her fist. "I loved Mrs. Glendoveer, but wouldn't it have been better to go away somewhere no one knew us? Then I could have lived like a normal girl and gone out in the world, and had friends and gone to school!"

Her mother's eyes glittered in the candlelight. "You are a normal girl," she said. "I believe this now with all my heart. But, darling . . . I didn't always know."

"You mean you thought there really was something wrong with my heart?"

"I kept you close," said her mother, "because I wanted to make sure you hadn't inherited anything . . . bad from your father." Her shoulders began to shake, and she held her handkerchief to her mouth to stop the noise.

"But, Mother, surely you don't think that I am mad!" Clara protested, which only made her mother sob harder.

"I have seen it run in families—more than once," she said.

Clara felt helpless, seeing her mother broken like this. "But I'm fine," she said, trying to be tender. "You've said so yourself. You don't need to worry anymore."

"I see only his goodness in you, but you don't know how guilty I've felt. Who did I think I was, marrying a man with a secret past who had only roamed from one place to the next to escape his misery? And before he left, he was wild with the idea of being the surviving child. Not sleeping, not eating."

"You loved him."

"It wasn't enough, Clara," she said.

Clara dared to touch her mother once more. "You do love me, don't you?"

"More than myself," she said. "Darling, I needed an excuse to keep you hidden. If only I were cleverer, I might have thought of something better. Clara, if I haven't done anything right so far, I mean to make it up to you. We're going to change the way we do things around here. Do you believe me?"

Clara clung to her mother, believing.

She might have been content to go on even longer if not for her stomach, which was quite empty. "Did you fix Ruby her birthday dinner? I hope she doesn't think we have forgotten her."

Her mother straightened up and, finding her handkerchief soaked through, wiped her face with the back of her sleeve. "Not yet. If you help me, we can get ready twice as fast."

But Ruby was already at the sink peeling potatoes when Clara and her mother entered the kitchen with their arms circling each other's waists.

"How horrid, Ruby," Clara said. "Forced to make your own birthday dinner."

Ruby, though, dropped her paring knife, crossed the floor, and flung her arms around the two of them. "No, this is the best present," she said. "Are we all right, all of us now?"

"Much better," said Harriet, accepting the stout woman's kiss on her cheek. "More than we have been in such a long time. Oh, Ruby."

Chapter 21

The best part about Ruby's birthday supper was the new openness the three of them shared.

"It was Clara's idea that I see *The Great Train Robbery*," Ruby said with a mock frown. "I thought she wanted to see me off to a good time. But now I know she only wanted to see me off."

"But I did want you to have a good time, Ruby," Clara said. "I just had to get to the Historical Society. Mama knows all about it now."

"Too much idle time," said Ruby. "I've said it before, but a girl needs a playmate. Didn't I say that, Harriet?"

Clara looked at Ruby with wonder.

Clara's mother dabbed at her lips with a napkin. "Yes. You said it this evening, as I remember."

"And what?" said Clara. "Mama, did you agree with Ruby?"

Harriet took a long drink of water. "Who is the little girl two houses over?"

"Daphne?"

She put down her napkin. "I've forgotten her last name."

"Aspinal," said Clara. "Oh, please, Mama, tell me, are you going to let me have Daphne over to visit?"

"I'm considering it. If you would consent to have Daphne and no others for the present, I think we could try."

Clara threw her arms in the air. "Hooray! I feel it's my birthday too, Ruby."

"I don't mind sharing," she replied. "The more, the merrier."

After dinner, Clara remembered her copy of *Virgil Poems* from Miss Lentham and went to the mudroom to fetch a lantern.

"Where you going?" Ruby asked.

"I'm taking this book out to the aviary," Clara said. "It's an old one, and I don't read Latin. Besides, you know how the mynah loves her pages."

"You've come round with those birds, haven't you? I suppose we can thank Citrine for that."

"Citrine was easy. I'm trying to make friends with the mynah now."

"That old bird's the toughest one," Ruby said. "Good luck!"

When the birds spotted Clara, they greeted her with their customary excitement.

"Hello, my friends! Hello, George, Helen, Peter, Arthur! And you, Frances, I've brought something for you."

Frances flitted over and Clara knelt down, shining her light so that the book's gold lettering glinted in the dark.

"Can't you see it? It's a book from Miss Lentham, Frances."

The mynah studied the volume without a word.

"I imagine you're anxious to read it by yourself," Clara said. She slid the book between the bars and let it fall open for Frances to examine. The bird bobbed her head, placed one claw on the edge of a page, and then withdrew it. "Can't read," said the bird. Her voice was uncharacteristically soft.

"Do you need more light?"

Again the mynah touched the page with her claw, ran it along a line of type, and stopped. "Can't. No more."

"But, Frances, you've always loved scratching around in your pages of words. I thought that's why you wanted the papers brought to you."

"Can't," whispered Frances. "No."

Clara thought she'd rather have more of Frances's sharp tongue than to see her withdrawn with her beak to her breast. "Should I take the book?"

Instead of answering, the mynah threw her head back and let loose a piercing cry unlike any noise Clara had ever heard her make. Three times she wailed to the roof, and the other birds shook their bodies as if they were deeply disturbed.

"I'm sorry. Let me know what you want. Do you want me to go? Please tell me!"

Frances flapped her glossy black wings. "Let me go! Let me go!" she said, in a voice so hoarse with desperation that Clara realized she had given the mynah words she had been searching for.

"I can't let you go from the aviary, Frances," Clara said. "These aren't my words. Your father has said you must stay."

"Elliot!" said Frances.

"Find Elliot," said George from his perch on high. "Let me go too."

"Tsip-tsip! Tsip-tsip!" chirped Helen.

Arthur and Peter took up a rhythmic cry, whereupon the entire cage erupted in squeaks and shrieks.

Clara stood, absorbing all the sound until it resonated in her bones. In her mind, the bits and pieces of everything she had gleaned about the Glendoveers' story held together. She had a picture now! The blue embroidered poem, barely perceptible at the bottom of Mrs. Glendoveer's mourning picture.

None shall fly till all come home. . . .

Thrusting her hand through the bars, Clara reached toward the mynah. "I need to know," she said. "When I find Elliot at last, will he break the spell?"

"Yes," said Frances.

"But then what?" Clara asked. "What shall happen to all of you?"

"Fly!" cried Frances.

"Let us go," pleaded George.

"Go where?"

The mynah twisted her head back and forth. "Father!" she said.

"Father!" echoed George.

"And Mother?" Clara asked.

"Ma-MA!" squealed Frances, and the rest of the birds responded with such a racket that Ruby ran outdoors. "Mercy!" she said. "How did you get them so stirred up? If I didn't know any better, I'd think you were pulling out their feathers."

"It's all right, Ruby," Clara said. "I'll try to calm them down."

Ruby appeared doubtful. "Do you think you can?"

"Let me try. I promise, I won't be long."

The birds fluttered to their various perches, and Ruby went back inside. When the kitchen door closed behind her, Clara knelt again to face Frances. "It's just as well that you all know, I have extraordinary news," she said.

Frances cocked her head and waited.

Clara lowered her voice. "I have been told, just this evening, that my father believed he was Elliot Glendoveer. I don't know what to think, Frances."

The mynah looked up at George the Cockatoo, and they nodded at each other.

"Do you believe this might be true?"

Frances fixed Clara with a red eye. "I believe."

"I believe," echoed George.

"Tsip-tsip!" said Citrine as Arthur and Peter circled the cage.

Clara didn't know whether to laugh or to cry. She looked up to the stars. "I want to believe too!" she said. But before she could trust this affirmation from the birds, she had to find out more.

"But how do you know?" Clara asked. "Is there a resemblance? Can you see him in me?"

"In your words," stated Frances.

"You can't mean I sound like him, do you?"

"Your words. Break spell."

"I broke the spell?"

"Need WORDS," said Frances with a little of her old impatience. "Words from you!"

Clara knew her earlier guess had been right: the more she spoke to Frances, the more words Frances had to speak for herself. George was the same, only slower. "Have you begun to speak because there is a bit of Elliot in me?"

"Yes, *genius*," Frances said. "At last."

Clara lit up inside. "If I have Elliot inside me, then I must be his daughter. This is just the proof I've wanted!"

"Yes," said Frances. "NOW MORE WORDS."

Feeling dull-witted, Clara was about to ask where to find more words until it became suddenly obvious. "I could read to you, couldn't I?"

"Yes!" Frances said, exultant.

Clara bit a nail and thought about which books might

be best. "All right. There are so many here in your own library. My goodness, if anyone can enlarge your vocabulary it must.be our beloved Mr. Dickens. Or maybe I can start with Mother Goose for the young ones. George can learn more words, and Helen and Peter and Arthur can listen. Would you like that?"

The three youngest Glendoveers gabbled excitedly among themselves.

"Yes," said George. "Thank you."

Clara curtsied to him. "You are quite welcome."

"Start now," said Frances. "Read."

"Yes. Read, please," said George.

"Let's see. I can do a nursery rhyme from memory." Clara paced until she thought of one, then stood and recited:

> Girls and boys, come out to play.
> The moon is shining as bright as day.
> Leave your supper, and leave your sleep,
> And come with your playfellows into the street.
> Come with a whoop, come with a call,
> Come with a good will or not at all.
> Up the ladder and down the wall,
> A halfpenny roll will serve us all.
> You find milk, and I'll find flour,
> And we'll have pudding in half an hour.

The birds chattered their approval. "More, please!" said George.

Clara went through "Hickory Dickory Dock," "Three

Blind Mice," "Miss Muffet," and "Bobby Shaftoe," becoming bolder and more theatrical with each recitation.

"Don't stop now," said Frances.

"All right. One more," Clara assented. She opened her arms like an opera singer and declaimed:

> *Three children sliding on the ice*
> *Upon a summer's day,*
> *As it fell out, they all fell in,*
> *The rest they ran away.*
>
> *Now, had these children been at home . . .*

Here Clara faltered, realizing that she was about to make a grave mistake. "Let's not do this one," she said. "I have better rhymes."

"More!" said Frances.

"But I can't. I don't want to offend any of you."

"MORE!" repeated Frances.

Clara closed her eyes and felt her throat grow dry.

> *Now, had these children been at home*
> *Or sliding on dry ground,*
> *Ten thousand pounds to one penny*
> *They had not all been . . . drowned.*

Oh, the awkwardness! She opened an eye and found all the birds absorbed and waiting.

"More?" asked Frances.

221

"A little," said Clara. And she rushed through the rest.

> You parents all that children have,
> And you that have got none,
> If you would have them safe abroad,
> Pray keep them safe at home.

The birds didn't chirp or cheer. They might have been appalled, for all Clara knew. It was Frances who started in with a long, low chuckle.

"Upon a summer's day?" she laughed.

George tittered from above.

"Sliding on dry ground," said Frances, giggling.

"PRAY KEEP THEM SAFE AT HOME!" said George to Helen in a booming bass voice. She chattered until her "tsip-tsip" sounded more like hiccups.

"Baaaaaaaaaaaaaaaahp!" Arthur let out what had to be a mock belch, and Peter hung upside down, swinging on his perch.

"It *is* a ridiculous poem," Clara said. "I'm glad you found the humor in it."

"A ridiculous poem!" Frances repeated. "Thank you, Clara."

Thank you? Clara felt a smile spread across her face. "My pleasure, Frances."

"Thank you!" said George as the others twittered.

"I am surprised the drowning part didn't make you sad. It has to be a painful memory, I would think."

"We are here," said the mynah. "SAFE AT HOME," she added in a mocking voice.

"Safe at home," said George with a sigh.

Clara wanted to ask them what they meant, but she heard her mother calling her in and had one more important question. "Do any of you know if my father is alive?" She automatically crossed her fingers and waited for a reply.

"We believe," said Frances.

"Then I believe as well," said Clara.

Her mother called for Clara again.

"Good night," said Frances.

"Good night, Frances. Good night, George. Good night, my friends!"

As Clara passed her mother in the kitchen, she wished she could tell her what she had learned from the birds. How satisfying to be able to say, "Mama, my father was right all along. He *is* Elliot Glendoveer!"

Not until she retired to her bedroom and blew out her candle did a fact occur to Clara: if Elliot was her father, then Mrs. Glendoveer was . . .

"Grandmother!" she cried.

In front of Clara's eyes, the extinguished candle lit up again.

"You're here," Clara said, looking around. Quickly, she blew out the candle and watched it light once more by itself. The feeling in the room was nothing like the cold, sickly air that had descended on the dining room the evening of their fancy dinner. The candle's flame was large and steady and bathed the walls in yellow light.

"I wonder if you knew all along that I was yours?" Clara said. "I suppose in one way, it doesn't matter. We had such good times together, and you gave my mother and me so much."

She rested her arms upon her bureau and looked deep into the flame. Although this was a single candle, Clara felt it give off a penetrating warmth that was almost as comforting as Mrs. Glendoveer's embrace.

"I will always love you," she said. "You must know that."

The candle's flame deepened to a gorgeous orange, and Clara thought she would gladly stay here with Mrs. Glendoveer until all the wax had melted away.

"Mrs. Glendoveer—I mean, Grandmother," said Clara, "I am only beginning to understand what has happened in our family. I have unearthed the Great Glendoveer's diary, and I have spoken to Frances and George. They want me to find Elliot, and I want to, but I don't know how."

The candle burned steadily.

"If only you were here to answer my questions. The children try to help, but I fear there is much they may not know. And then there is the question of Mr. Booth. I have a letter from him, you know—"

The flame went pale, and shuddered and smoked.

"He says that you and he were friends, once."

The candle's flame shrank as the smoke grew sooty enough to sting Clara's eyes.

"I know you think he was responsible for taking the

children," Clara said. "It makes me wonder if . . . if he might set me on the right path to find Elliot?"

Clara watched the flame leap up and tremble as if with rage, then plunge down, leaving nothing but an ember on the wick and that awful smell of scorched feathers saturating the room.

"Come back!" said Clara. "Don't go yet!" But the candle did not relight, and she was forced to throw open the windows for fresh air. The moon was half-full, pale and serene behind the new-leafed branches.

Hundreds of miles down the coast in Newport, Mr. Woodruff Booth was enjoying the same moon, the same spring evening. How in the world could Clara get to him? And when she did, what could make him tell her the truth?

Chapter 22

Clara had so many things to do, she had trouble figuring out which task to perform first. She pulled *The Fairy Tales of Hans Christian Andersen* from the library shelf to read to the birds. The morning was still chilly and the light was thin, but the birds were happy to see her.

"Read now!" said George.

"I will. I mean not to waste time," she said. "If I rise early and read each morning, and again in the evening, you shall be speaking as well as I in no time at all." Clara leafed through the book and found the tale "The Wild Swans."

"Say, would you like to hear a story about children who were turned into birds?" she asked.

"We know it," said Frances flatly.

"Yes, I suppose you do," Clara said, and turned the page. "How about 'The Emperor and the Nightingale'?"

"Tsip!" Helen called out.

"No?"

"No thank you," said George.

"No birds!" said Frances.

Clara understood what the Glendoveer children wanted from a story: to be taken away. She had always felt the same about books. If she had been forced to read about a young shut-in with a weak heart, she might never have picked up another novel.

"I have just the thing," Clara said. "It's about a foolish king who parades down the street naked."

Arthur the Grackle nearly pushed Peter the Kiskadee from his perch, flapping his wings and laughing with his raucous "Chaa! Chaaa! Chaa!"

"Thought you'd like that," said Clara.

She finished the tale about the emperor and another about magic galoshes that made wishes come true, and made it halfway through the book on Sunday. When the clock struck eight on Monday, however, she excused herself and quickly made her way inside the house. She planned to stand at the front door and peek at the passing schoolchildren to get a glimpse of Daphne. To her surprise, no children passed by at all. "And here it is a school day," she said. "Where could they all be?"

She ran back to the aviary to continue reading and heard a noise on the other side of the gate. "Who's there?" she asked.

The answer came in the form of a sharp whisper. "It's Daphne!"

"Daphne?" Clara exclaimed. "I'm here! I'm here!" She lifted the latch and flung open the gate.

Daphne, bareheaded today with her curls in blue ribbons, stepped back and stifled her giggles. "Careful, Clara. You almost flattened me! I take it there is no one home?"

"Actually, *everyone* is home." Clara pulled Daphne into the yard. "We don't need to hide. My mother said I may have you over, and when I saw no one on the street this morning, I was so disappointed."

"We're out of school for the summer," said Daphne. "So I thought I'd try to catch you alone out here."

"May I tell you how happy I am that you tried? To know that you'll be free the whole summer is almost too much for me. And I can see you without all the sneaking."

Daphne groaned. "I wish I'd known you could see me! We're going to the shops in half an hour. So hurry and tell me why your mother changed her mind."

"I will," Clara said. "But first, would you like to meet her?"

"Delighted," Daphne said, extending her hand.

Arm in arm, the girls skipped inside. Clara's mother, who was pulling a sopping pile of laundry from a copper tub, promptly dropped the bundle and pushed back the stray hair that had fallen over her eyes.

"It's Daphne Aspinal, Mother," said Clara. "Isn't she the loveliest girl you've ever seen?"

"Clara, really," said Daphne.

"She is quite lovely," said her mother, out of breath. "I'm glad to meet you, Daphne. It has been Clara's greatest wish to have you as her guest."

"She can't stay long," Clara said. "But I'd like to have Daphne over tomorrow."

Her mother wrung her apron with her hands, and Clara knew she was ill at ease. "In the morning would be all right," she said. "I will be gone later in the afternoon."

"Thank you, Mrs. Dooley," Daphne said. "I hope I can return the favor and have Clara over to my house sometime."

"How exciting!" Clara said. "Mama, you must let me go."

"We shall see," said Harriet.

Clara smiled. "I'd like to show Daphne my room."

"All right. Run along," said her mother. "And, uh, have fun."

Clara nudged Daphne as soon as her mother was out of sight. "She has never told me to have fun. I feel as if I've woken up in a new world."

"What happened?"

"I took a walk to see Miss Lentham," Clara said with a touch of pride, "and I got caught!"

"You naughty, daring girl," Daphne said, giving Clara's braid a playful yank. "You went, and the sky didn't fall. I knew it would be all right."

"You don't know the half of it." Clara told Daphne the story of her parents and how her father was convinced he was Elliot Glendoveer. She also confided why her mother had kept her in the house.

"See," Daphne said, "if you hadn't gone out and been caught, you'd never have learned about your father. Now if only we could prove that he truly was Elliot."

"Or *is* Elliot," Clara said. "The birds believe he is still alive, and they're also convinced he's my father. They want me to find him because, somehow, finding him will break the spell. At least that's what Frances said."

Daphne put her fingers to her temples. "This is all too much for my little head. What do you mean by 'breaking the spell'?"

Clara had Daphne take a seat on the bed and told her at length all she had learned from George Glendoveer's diaries. "I don't have the whole story, but I believe that George Glendoveer had some sort of ancient book of incantations he used to transfer the souls of his children and keep them in these birds. I showed Miss Lentham some of the hieroglyphics, and she helped a little."

Daphne wrinkled her nose. "What did you make of Miss Lentham?"

Clara folded her arms. "From your description, I expected someone a little more pleasant."

"But she's so enthusiastic about the Glendoveers. Did she help?"

"She did help at first." Clara shuddered. "I did not make a good impression. In fact, we ended up quite angry with each other."

"You, brawling with Miss Lentham? I'm trying to imagine it."

"I couldn't help it. Miss Lentham said terrible things about Mrs. Glendoveer. And what's worse, she practically worships Woodruff Booth and takes him at his word about everything, when I'm convinced that he is a liar!"

"Our nice Mr. Booth? Are you sure?"

"He says in his letter how Mrs. Glendoveer was fond of him, but I know from George's diaries that it isn't true. Why would he say that unless he had something to hide?"

Daphne crossed her eyes. "Clara, you are making me crazy. You hold on to this shocking news until I have no more time to listen. Now I must go."

Clara smiled. "But we have tomorrow, Daphne. All morning long. Isn't that miraculous?"

"It is going to be my favorite summer," Daphne stated. "I know it already. Walk me to the gate, will you?"

Clara walked with Daphne, and said goodbye. On her way back to the house, she felt the sun on her shoulders and in her heart. Mrs. Glendoveer's favorite yellow roses were in bloom and spicing the air. In celebration of her first morning as a free girl, she decided to enter at the front door.

From the front yard she could look out at Lockhaven Bay sparkling in rare sapphire blue under the cloudless sky and the Pincushion Islands glowing an exuberant green. When she faced the house, however, all its flaws were revealed by the dazzling sunlight.

Clara had never examined the front of her home at leisure. The moss from the rainy season had left splotches like dead seaweed on the shingles. The splintered windowsills needed scraping, and the awning over the front steps had drizzled rust for so long that the marble below was stained orange.

It hurt to say so, but Clara's first thought was *How hideous it is!* She remembered Daphne and her mother standing here with their basket of food on the day of Mrs. Glendoveer's funeral and wondered how Mrs. Aspinal ever consented to let her daughter come over and play. The memory made her hurry inside.

In the foyer, the bright sun shone through the chinks in the shutters like swords piercing the darkness. The carved wooden panels on the wall with their flowers, boughs, and birds made Clara sad, because she knew the love that had once imbued this house with beauty.

She roused herself with the conviction that she was the one who had been chosen to bring it back.

"Clara!" cried Ruby from over the banister. "Tell your mother that the tub upstairs is leaking and I need help bringing the linens down to the line. I'd do it myself but I'm dripping at the hem like a thundercloud."

"Yes, Ruby," Clara said, startled out of her reverie. When she confronted her frazzled mother looking up from the washboard, face misted over with steam, she almost couldn't bear to tell her.

"Mama, Ruby says the tub is leaking—"

"Leaking?" her mother asked. "Onto the floor?"

"I think so. She said her hem was soaking and that she needed help bringing the linens down."

Her mother pinched the bridge of her nose with a wet hand, and Clara felt sorry. "Let me help her," Clara said. "You have too much to do right here."

"There is always too much to do," her mother said. "And I don't say this because I'm not up to the work. . . ."

"I know, Mama," Clara said.

"But if this wretched house would only stop breaking down, we might make improvements instead of constantly staving off emergencies."

Clara brought a chair over to her mother and had her sit. "I'm making you tea. You're exhausted, and you can afford to put your feet up for a moment while I help Ruby."

"No, Clara, I cannot afford it," she said, hopping up. "We are going upstairs with a mop and bucket, carrying down the bed linens, and hanging them on the line, and then you and Ruby and I will sit and talk."

"Yes, Mama," Clara said. The old Mama was back—the one with two deep lines between her eyes and a set jaw.

Ruby and Clara gave the sheets a final rinse while Harriet dealt with the water upstairs. The three of them stretched the wet linens over the line and were waterlogged by the time they were finished.

"Look at us," said Ruby. "Three drowned rats."

"Let's each take a garden chair into the sunshine," said Harriet, "and have a chat while we dry out."

In view of the aviary, Ruby wrung out her hem and sat, spreading her skirt wide. Clara shucked her damp boots and rested her stocking feet on the grass. Her mother examined the puckered skin on her fingers, looked up, and said simply, "We can't go on like this."

"I agree," said Ruby. "We should send the wash out—the household linens at least. Why not? Give ourselves a bit of a break. Goodness knows there are projects enough around this old place to keep us on our toes until the last trumpet."

Clara placed her hand on Ruby's arm. "I don't think that is what Mama means." And then, "What do you mean, Mama?"

"What do I mean?" Her mother gave in to a rueful laugh. "I'm such a mule. You know that, Ruby."

"Indeed, I do," Ruby said. "A mule bred from a blinkered workhorse, is what I'd say. Stubborn and—"

"Yes, and all the rest of it," she said. "That's why it took me so long to figure it out. Life here for us is, and will remain, impossible. Providence has finally got through to me."

Clara frowned. "You don't think God made the upstairs tub leak, do you?"

"No," her mother said, shaking her head. "It was that little girl. Daphne."

Clara felt a surge of dread. "What did Daphne do? You said yourself she was lovely."

"She is a perfect picture. But perhaps you didn't notice

the look on her face when she saw me bent over the wash-tub in my old poplin? Because I did."

Clara did not know where her mother was leading. "I think you must have misread her."

"No, Clara. She has probably never seen her mother at such work. Would you agree, Ruby?"

"Harriet is right," Ruby said. "The Aspinals probably have a laundress and a cook and a hired girl or two to do the cleaning. Not to mention a gardener—"

"What does that matter?" Clara demanded. "Do you think Daphne cares about such things? Why, if she did, she never would have climbed our front steps to seek me out."

Her mother looked pained. "It isn't Daphne, dear. It's this place. Maids of all work don't run their own mansions. The house and grounds are quite unmanageable for a staff of two. We don't have the skill to repair the place ourselves, and we don't have the funds to hire out."

Harriet took a breath. "And if you are now to go out in public, Clara, it is proper that I also go out and make myself known in the community as your mother. As it stands now, I miss church every Sunday. So you were quite right last night when you suggested that we might have gone on to live someplace where we would fit in. We cannot fit in here."

"But this is our home," Clara said. "It belongs to us."

"Not for three weeks," said Ruby.

"And even then we won't have the enormous amount

of money required to fix the house. But if we sold it, we could buy our own small home—something lovely for the three of us. We could start over in a new place where you could go to school and make appropriate friends."

Clara knew that there could be no more suitable friend for her than Daphne Aspinal. But when she saw Ruby nodding in agreement, she held her tongue.

"Ah!" said Ruby. "The buyer. You've heard from him again?"

"I have. He won't be discouraged. It's rather incredible the lengths he has gone to, trying to acquire this place."

"Is he offering more money?" Ruby asked.

"Not only that," Harriet said, "but he is also offering to buy everything in the house, as is. 'From cellar to attic,' is how Mr. Merritt-Blenney put it."

"Who is it?" Clara asked. "Who wants to buy?"

"I don't know, Clara. He insists on anonymity."

"But surely you've heard something. Has he sent you a letter? Where is he from?"

"I've no idea." She shrugged. "All the correspondence comes through the gentleman's lawyer in Rhode Island."

Clara felt as though she had been slapped awake. "Oh no!" she said. "Mama, you cannot sell. I know the man! It must be Woodruff Booth!"

At the sound of the name, the birds in the aviary darted from perch to perch, squawking.

"Woodruff Booth?" said Ruby. "I think I remember Mrs. Glendoveer mentioning him long ago."

"She despised him, is why," said Clara, her voice rising. "Mrs. Glendoveer believed he was responsible for the deaths of her children!"

Arthur the Grackle sounded his ear-splitting cry, and the others responded in a chorus of gabbling.

Her mother drew back. "Clara, how do you know about Mr. Booth? And why do you imagine he's the buyer?"

"Miss Lentham keeps him informed about the Glendoveers, and she sent him word of Mrs. Glendoveer's passing. And he lives in Rhode Island. Plus, I read about him in George Glendoveer's diaries. Mrs. Glendoveer would never have sold him this house. She banned him from it! I beg you. Promise you won't sell."

Ruby came over and drew Clara to her. "Now, now. Nobody's selling nothing yet, little girl. Am I right, Harriet?"

"I can't accept offers until we've passed the deadline in the will," she said. "But after that, it may be in our best interest—"

"But what about the birds? Where shall they stay?"

Her mother lowered her voice. "I can't answer anything until I've met with the man's representative. He's offered to meet with both Ruby and me on the nineteenth, and I intend to ask him all my questions then."

"You aren't going to sell them with the house, are you?" Clara cried. "You can't! Ruby, don't let her."

"But, Clara—"

Clara slipped from Ruby's grasp and ran across the damp lawn to the aviary, snagging her stocking on a twig and falling forward on her elbows. She wanted only to see the birds and reassure them. But when Ruby caught up to her and lifted her from the ground, she saw that her sleeve was torn and streaked with blood. As she was led back to the house, Clara turned and saw the Glendoveer children lined up on the big bare branch, and swore she would set them free before they would ever be the captives of Mr. Woodruff Booth.

Chapter 23

That evening, Clara showed her mother George Glendoveer's diary in hopes of convincing her that selling the
home to Woodruff Booth would be against Cenelia's wishes.
But Clara's mother saw things differently.

"It appears that Mr. Glendoveer was quite fond of Mr.
Booth," Harriet said. "Look here: he says that he believes
his wife has wrongly accused him."

"But that isn't the whole story."

"From what I read, the Glendoveers agreed to disagree
about him. And Mr. Booth offered a reward for the children's return. If anything, I feel for George Glendoveer,
losing his best friend at a time when friends were in short
supply."

"But why would Mr. Booth then lie in his letter to
Daphne and say they were all great friends?"

"Perhaps he wants to dwell on happier memories of their association. He seems most forgiving."

Clara stiffened, frustrated by her inability to make her mother understand. "I have more proof," she said. "But I don't think you'll listen to that either."

"I'll listen to any proof you have," her mother said. "I'm not averse to facts."

Facts, Clara knew, were not her strong suit in this matter, and her mother was not going to like where the conversation was going. Yet she felt she had no choice.

"Ruby," Clara asked, "do you remember the evening when Mama first brought up selling the house? Our night in the dining room?"

Ruby, who had been absorbed in mending a pillowcase, stitched more slowly. "I do."

"The candles blew out," Clara said. "Not once, but twice. It was quite remarkable."

Ruby dropped her mending in her lap and looked warily at Harriet. "She's right, you know; it was after you spoke about selling. I've never got that evening out of my head, though some of the details are, er, blurry."

"I'm sure they are," murmured Harriet.

"So tell me honestly," continued Clara. "Don't you believe it was Mrs. Glendoveer, Ruby? Giving us a sign?"

"For goodness' sake," Ruby said, letting out a breath. "And all this time I've been frightened to go back in that room for fear of something evil. Who knows what might haunt that room where the family gathered, what with all the tragedy that befell them. But if it is Mrs. Glendoveer? Clara, you have eased my mind."

"You aren't suggesting that Mrs. Glendoveer lurks here as a ghost," said Clara's mother.

"I don't see why not," Ruby answered, puffing out her chest. "Elderly people hang on, don't they? It's common knowledge where I come from. Especially if they have unfinished business."

"You see, Mama?" cried Clara. "Ruby agrees, and she's completely sound."

"Well, I'm certainly not barmy," said Ruby, her finger circling her temple, "if that's what you're getting at."

Harriet caught Clara's eye and blushed. "It isn't *that* I'm worried about. I simply will not listen to either of you if you go on about the spirits. It's pure nonsense."

"I don't tell you that you're full of nonsense," Ruby mumbled, obviously hurt.

"Forgive me," Harriet said. "I should have said that you have a gift for the fanciful. I am not similarly gifted. Is that better?"

"Not much," said Ruby.

While Harriet gathered up the Glendoveers' things, she came across Clara's hankie tied in a wad. "Clara, what is this, I ask you?" she said, dangling the bundle.

"It's only the bits left over from some flowers Mrs. Glendoveer had pressed inside. I didn't want to throw them away, because I thought they must have meant something to her. I'll take them."

Her mother placed the filled hankie on the table. "Very well," she said. "But I'm storing the rest in my own cedar chest—out of sight, out of mind, one hopes."

Clara kept quiet until she was sure her mother couldn't hear. "Ruby!" she burst out. "You believe."

"It's nothing more than common sense," Ruby said.

"Then perhaps I can also convince you to reconsider selling the house to Woodruff Booth. Mama can't sell without your consent, can she?"

"Don't get ahead of yourself, little girl. We don't even know it's him who wants it."

"I do," Clara said. "Who else in the small state of Rhode Island would be so intensely interested in getting hold of this old place? Who would even know it was possibly for sale? Why would anyone offer to buy it all, down to the boxes in the boiler room?"

Ruby paused and considered, then quickly held up her hands as if to push this subject away. "Clara, the disposition of the house is a legal thing with all sorts of papers filled with mumbo jumbo. Harriet has handled it all, and that is fine with me."

"But, Ruby dear, this has nothing to do with the law. It has to do with . . . Oh, how can I say this?" Clara searched for a word until she found one. "It has to do with *loyalty*."

As Ruby thought this over, Clara could see she'd made an impression.

"I'd say," continued Clara, "that turning over Mrs. Glendoveer's home and everything in it to the man she feels betrayed her family is the worst sort of disloyalty. So let's make Mrs. Glendoveer a promise."

She cleared her throat and aimed her words at the ceiling. "Mrs. Glendoveer, I hereby promise to do everything in my power to prevent Mr. Woodruff Booth from taking possession of your house or anything in it. So help me God."

Ruby clutched at her chest. "No, no, Clara. You shouldn'ta done that."

"Now your turn, Ruby."

"I can only say this: I promise to help Clara Dooley, poor fool that she is for making such a promise. And may Mrs. Glendoveer treat her lightly if she should fail."

"Good enough," said Clara. "Thank you, Ruby. I'm sure Mrs. Glendoveer is pleased anyway."

"Pshaw," answered Ruby. "The dead who hang about are rarely pleased. That's why they stay. And it is fine to have the dear old lady still with us, but I told you not to make an oath. Did I tell you not to make an oath?"

Clara gasped and pointed to the little milk-glass vase with three yellow rosebuds on the table.

"Glory," Ruby said. "In all my days . . ."

One at a time, the buds opened their petals until they were full as cabbages. Their scent intensified as Ruby took Clara's hand.

"If that isn't Mrs. Glendoveer giving us her blessing," whispered Clara, "what else could it be?"

Ruby stared at the flowers, awestruck.

"Are you all right?"

"I'm fine," Ruby said softly. "But please, if you don't mind, I'd like to sit here alone for a while. Let it settle, if you will."

"I understand," Clara told her, for she had already been drawn into the supernatural realm of the Glendoveers by degrees.

Clara felt grateful that Ruby was not as bound to the concrete world as her mother was. With Ruby's help, she might tip the balance in the fight against Mr. Woodruff Booth. As far as finding her father was concerned, though, she would have to work on that herself.

So she took up a lantern and went out to the aviary with her books to read to the birds, but they were so concerned about her injuries that she spent most of her time pulling up her sleeves, showing them her elbows with the iodine on them.

"See? They're scratched, is all. I was clumsy."

She tried distracting them with several stories from her Hans Christian Andersen book before bidding them good night. Frances, however, was too clever to be kept in the dark.

"Mr. Booth," Frances said.

"Why, yes," Clara said. "I supposed you would ask about him."

"Don't like Mr. Booth," said George. Arthur cackled his agreement and lit next to Frances while Peter and Helen huddled together in the shadows and listened.

"I think your mother had reason to suspect him. What do you know about him?"

"Mother suspected Booth," Frances said. "But not the *girl*."

"Until too late!" said George sadly. "Too late."

"The girl," repeated Clara. "You mean the nanny? Oh, what was her name . . . ? Nelly?"

"Nel-ly," said Frances. "Nel-ly." Then, shaking her head sadly, "Cold."

"Co-o-o-old," said George, drawing out the word. "Cold eyes."

The description made Clara shiver. "Do you know why Mrs. Glendoveer hired her? I would have thought she was a good judge of character. . . ."

"It was Mr. Booth!" Frances said. "Mother didn't know."

"I don't understand," Clara said. "Unless you're saying that Nelly was working with Mr. Booth."

"Tsip-tsip!" cried Helen, jostling her brother.

"Mother didn't know," said George. "And Nelly didn't know."

"Nelly didn't know!" repeated Frances. "*He* made her sleep. *He* made her eyes cold. I won't forget her eyes. *I* saw her white, white petticoat around her face in the cold water. Falling . . ."

Clara felt sick in the pit of her stomach at this vivid picture of Nelly's drowning. The birds' heads drooped. But how could Mr. Booth make her eyes cold? "Did . . . did

Mr. Booth hypnotize her? Before he and your mother and father went to Berlin?"

"Yes," George said.

"He killed Nelly!" stated Frances. "He made her cold!" And above her, George began to make a low huffing sound as he swayed side to side.

"Huh-huh-huh . . ."

Clara recognized the sound; it was a soft sob. Helen, Peter, and Arthur flew to George's perch and rubbed their heads against his snowy feathers.

"Please don't cry, George," Clara pleaded.

"The boat broke," said Frances. "We all fell. A shoe dropped past me. Peter's shoe."

"Skee!" shrieked Peter.

"And Helen fell past me. The weeds got her. . . ."

"Tsip-tsip . . ."

"Arthur and George. Their boots kicking above me. I saw them by lightning. Then my eyes went out."

Frances stared straight ahead when she had finished, but George continued to weep on Arthur's shoulder.

"My darlings," said Clara, too shocked to cry. "You remember it all so vividly. It's too much to bear."

"I broke the boat," said George. "Me!"

"Stop!" said Frances. "You tried."

"My fault!" he replied.

"Frances," Clara said, "tell me what he means."

"The man with Nelly," Frances said. "Oh, George bit him deep in the hand! George, red in the teeth. I shoved with my boots. The oar? He dropped it in the storm. We hit rocks."

Clara grasped the bars. "Who was the man? Tell me who it was."

Frances extended her wings and shook her shoulders. "Young, tall, skin and bones. Mean. Chipped tooth. Big knife."

"Did you know him?"

"No! But the poor crying baby . . ." Frances trailed off as Arthur and Peter keened near the roof. Helen looked as if she had shrunk to half her size, and George sat with his eyes shut.

"What happened to Elliot?" Clara asked softly. "Can you tell me?"

Frances cocked her head as if listening for the memory. "Tied with linen under the heavy coat. Tied to the man's chest. Shivering. Poor cold baby . . ."

"Oh, Frances!"

"Too cold! The baby cried until the man tied him under his coat! With a storm coming on. And Nelly asleep with her eyes open. She did not dress us warm. She stopped nothing."

Clara could see it all in her mind. George, the eldest, turning on the man in the boat as the summer storm threw its lightning on the water. The children huddled with the hollow-eyed nanny, who sat in eerie calm; the boat dashing in the foam, hurling the children in odd directions—with only Arthur and George able to tread water.

"But the man," Clara said. "Do you think he survived with Elliot?"

"George says he floated on a box. Floated with Elliot, and let us all go under."

Clara leaned her forehead against the bars. "Why did it take you so long to tell me the whole story?"

"Little by little, we remember," said Frances, her slash of yellow mask shining in the lamplight. "Slow. Because of you, every day we have more words, more memories."

George, who had gone silent, raised his sulfur-colored crown and lifted a claw. "But we need Elliot," he stated.

"Please tell me, where were Nelly and the man taking you on the boat? Did they say?"

"Islands . . . ," said Frances. "To hide."

"The Pincushions? Do you know which one?"

"No," said George. "No, but—"

"He lives!" exclaimed Frances, and the birds warbled their assent. "We believe! Do you?"

Clara stretched her arm inside the cage and reached out to all of them. "I do believe my father lives. And I shall bring him back somehow. I need him too!"

She gazed up at the brothers and sisters perched together, crying back at her. And Helen flew to Clara's open hand, dancing and bowing in what could only be a heart-felt show of gratitude.

Chapter 24

Clara hoped that if her mother saw more of Daphne, she might understand what a good influence she was. That morning, she brought strawberries from her garden as a gift and would not retire to Clara's room to share secrets until she had chatted politely with her mother and Ruby.

When Clara finally did get Daphne alone, her mother's desire to move was the first thing she told her about. Daphne's fishbowl-blue eyes immediately dampened, even as her manner became more determined.

"It won't happen if I can stop it," Daphne said. "And if we are parted, I can write as well as you, and we could insist on trading off, spending summers together. I won't let you go."

"My feelings exactly," said Clara. "Though there is

more to my predicament than simply selling the house. I haven't told you who is trying to buy."

"Who?"

"Woodruff Booth!"

"The villain!" Daphne exclaimed. Then, uncertainly, "He *is* a villain, isn't he?"

Clara grimaced. "I am convinced of it. Now that the birds have spoken."

When Clara had finished telling Daphne all her suspicions in detail, including Miss Lentham's hint that Mr. Booth feared there might be incriminating evidence stored in the house, Daphne bit her thumb and brooded.

"This is serious, Clara. If it was he who plotted to rob the Glendoveers, the man is no one to be trifled with."

"That is true," said Clara. "My knees shake when I think of meeting him face to face. But he is the only one who might know the fate of baby Elliot. . . . And, Daphne, this you won't believe—"

"My dear, I think I've already demonstrated that I believe anything you say," Daphne told her.

"Well, it seems that Elliot *is* most probably my father."

Daphne grabbed her friend's hand. "Clara, are you sure?"

When Clara laid out all that she had heard from her mother and the birds, Daphne was convinced as well.

"Where would Mr. Booth be keeping your father all these years? And for what purpose?"

"I don't know," Clara said. "But I not only have the

story from the birds; I also have had indications from Mrs. Glendoveer—"

"Indications? Has she spoken to you?"

"Not in words. But she does send signs. I told you about the dining room candles—and now I've had another experience with my bedroom candle the other night. It is obvious that Mrs. Glendoveer is convinced Mr. Booth is an enemy to the family. And when I tried to get information on whether she thinks he knows of Elliot's whereabouts, the candle extinguished itself with lots of black smoke."

Daphne pursed her lips. "But you haven't got a yes or no, have you? Black smoke could simply be Mrs. Glendoveer showing anger. We really know nothing about Elliot from that."

"But we have good reason to suspect that Elliot is alive somewhere—otherwise, he would have come back to inhabit the body of a bird along with the others. And even if Mr. Booth was in Berlin when the boat crashed with the children, would he not know what happened to the baby if he set up the plot himself?"

Daphne lowered her eyes. "I don't know."

"Well, I know that time is running out for finding my father. If Mother sells the house, how can he return? And if he does not return home, the Glendoveer children will live on without release."

"Do you mean they will not die, even of old age?"

"From what I understand, they won't. Ruby has told me

that cockatoos can live longer than many people; but the rest of the birds should be long dead by now. We say that they thrive on her excellent care, yet I know they are weary of their life as birds. If you had only heard Frances cry the other day, begging to have the spell broken."

Daphne placed a hand on her heart. "What was the Great Glendoveer thinking when he did this to his children? It is cruelty, plain and simple."

Clara sighed. "There is nothing plain and simple about any of it. It is all good intentions and disastrous consequences. Poor Mr. Glendoveer cast a spell to save his children from death, to call back their souls. But he never knew the outcome of his dabbling in magic. In fact, he was never sure that the spell had worked!"

"Then it is a tragedy, all of it," Daphne said. "A sad story that doesn't end."

"And now everything is urgent. It would be such a help to have some sign from Mrs. Glendoveer that her Elliot is definitely alive and that Mr. Booth knows where he is."

"Ask her," Daphne said.

"Right now?"

"Yes. If you'd rather try it alone, I'll understand."

"No. Please stay," Clara said.

Daphne sat with her hands knotted in her lap while Clara looked up at the ceiling. "Mrs. Glendoveer? My friend Daphne is here with me. We want to find Elliot. Do you think Mr. Booth knows where he is?"

The girls waited in silence. Not even a curtain stirred.

"Maybe you should light a candle," suggested Daphne.

"We could try." Clara opened the top drawer in which she kept her matches, stood on tiptoe, and looked in. The handkerchief that had held Mrs. Glendoveer's faded blossoms had opened and spilled. For a moment, the blood rushed so quickly from Clara's head, she saw spots. "It's her. She's been here."

"What is it?" said Daphne. "Show me."

Clara moved out of the way so that Daphne could see: an almost empty drawer littered with crushed petals. And written in their dust?

"'Yes'!" said Daphne. "She wrote 'yes'!"

"We asked for a sign, and she gave it," Clara said.

Clara watched her friend reel over to the bed and plop down. "Gracious," Daphne said. "I'm used to you telling me the most fantastical things, but seeing it for myself . . ."

"Are you scared?"

Daphne sat up and set her jaw. "Only a little."

Clara sat beside her. "Good. Then we must figure out what comes next. If Mr. Booth knows where Elliot is, then we must find a way to make him tell us. You will help me, won't you?"

"You don't need to ask," Daphne told her. "I'm already thinking."

After only an hour or so in Clara's room, the girls were putting the finishing touches on a letter to Mr. Booth.

"I'll have to go home and write this on my own

stationery," Daphne said, looking the paper over, "but I'm almost ashamed. I sound like such an awful pill."

Clara laughed. "Read it out loud!"

Dear Mr. Booth:

Please forgive me when I confess that I first wrote you out of mere curiosity. After reading your moving reply, I felt rather small. It was obvious that the Glendoveers are as near to your heart now as they were when they were alive. And when you asked me to help prevent any further "blackening" of their family legacy, I felt absolutely chastened and vowed to be your advocate wherever I could.

However, today I write you with urgent news. It is your own legacy now being threatened, sir. I have it from the daughter of Mrs. Glendoveer's servant that the family has a document in which the old woman accuses you of the most unspeakable crimes. She lays the deaths of her children at your feet and claims that you plotted to kill them!

It hurts me even to write such a thing, but I cannot remain silent. This revelation must wound you, to have your extraordinary kindness repaid with such treachery.

For myself, I refused to believe such "evidence" existed until the girl, Clara, showed it to me. The girl says that both her mother and the cook plan to sell it to a magazine of the lowest reputation for their own gain.

Clara is pious and shy. I've convinced her of your

innocence and good intentions, and told her that to stain your reputation with these lies would be a grave sin, whereupon she was reduced to penitent tears.

She tells me now that she would gladly turn the paper over to you—but <u>only</u> to you personally. She is most fearful of having the document fall into the wrong hands. I assured her I would write you at once!

The girl is seldom left alone. However, I have learned that both her mother and the cook are to meet with attorneys on June 19 to discuss the sale of Mrs. Glendoveer's home. If you are able to travel and meet me at the house in the morning, I will be happy to introduce you and assist in recovering the document.

For her own safety, the girl does not want neighbors to see a car or carriage parked out front when you visit. If word gets back to her mother that she has let people in the house, she shall be beaten. Please arrange to have a car drop you off and then drive away or she will not answer the door. (I'm sorry, but it is the best accommodation I could make with her.)

I have not informed my own parents of our possible meeting. They would surely forbid me, and then what would become of you? Please write back and let me know whether you can come to Lockhaven and at what time I should meet you. But do not be explicit! My mother reads all my mail.

Do write as soon as possible, as it is barely two weeks' time before the 19th.

Bless you, Mr. Booth. I shall not fail you!

Sincerely,

Daphne Aspinal

The two girls shared a wordless moment before Daphne said, "We don't have to send this if you aren't completely sure."

"No, Daphne. I'm sure."

"Do you think he'll actually come?"

"We'll know when he answers the letter," Clara said. "I just hope he minds the part where we warn him to come alone."

Daphne held the letter to her chin. "There's no reason for him not to mind it. He knows we're just two little girls. He also knows that your mother will indeed be gone, seeing that she is meeting with his own representatives."

"Miss Lentham says he's easily frightened. Or that he used to be. In any case, let's hope he hasn't overcome his ornithophobia."

Daphne covered her mouth and giggled. "I'm sorry. Something about that word. It sounds like a cross between a lisp and a sneeze. ORNITHOPHOBIA!" she exclaimed, sneezing the word into her pinafore.

"Gesundheit," said Clara with a nod. "Now, don't you think you should hurry? The postman comes at noon!"

Clara walked her friend to the foyer, where the two embraced. Simultaneously, each gave the other a smart pat on the back for courage. But when the door closed, Clara leaned against it and felt a trickle of fear.

She knew she must keep moving or she might lose her resolve. So she went to the aviary, sat in the grass beside it, and began enlisting the help of her friends for the work ahead.

Chapter 25

The reply from Mr. Booth was not long in coming. When Daphne arrived, breathless, waving the torn envelope, Clara surmised that he must have written back the same afternoon he received their letter.

"He's an anxious one," Daphne said. "And crafty. Look!"

> Dear Miss Aspinal:
>
> Your recent interest in the Glendoveer family history has had a most fortunate side effect! It has prompted Miss Lentham to arrange a tea for some of Lockhaven's elder residents. These are people I knew years ago and have not forgotten. Apparently, they have not forgotten me either, for they wish

me to attend so we might reacquaint ourselves.

Although I do not travel often, I am delighted to attend. I arrive on the morning
of the nineteenth at 10:00 a.m. and will
have time for a look around before the
tea. I am interested to see how the town
has changed and how it has remained the
same.

We old people lose such a great number of
our loved ones that renewing past friend-
ships is much like rediscovering lost treasure. I only wish that Miss Lentham and I
had put our heads together sooner.

I remain yours,

With gratitude,

Woodruff Booth

P.S. I invite you to write to me anytime. It
is a tonic for me to hear from youngsters
like you. Take care, dear girl.

"Do you think there's really a tea?" asked Clara.

"No. He's telling us in code that he'll be here at ten.
Duplicitous old man. And he wants me to confirm that
I've received his letter."

Clara rubbed her moist palms together. "He's really
coming. It's all just as we hoped! So why am I having trouble catching my breath?"

Daphne gave her a smile. "May I tell you something? At my last school, I was put in the corner once with a sign around my neck. 'POLRUMPTIOUS!' it said."

"Never heard the word."

"It means 'bumptious' and 'overconfident.' It was one of Mrs. Carthill's favorite terms and not meant to be a compliment. But I think it's just the attitude our situation calls for."

"Then go ahead and be polrumptious. I shan't hang a sign on you."

"I'm not joking. If one of us goes wobbly, we'll infect the other. From now on, we don't do anything but show our polrumptious side to each other. Agreed?" Daphne flared her nostrils and did her best to appear imperious.

"If it will help us keep our wits about us, I will do it," declared Clara.

"Then let us shake hands like men."

The friends shook so firmly and so hard that Clara's shoulder twinged, though she was careful not to show it.

Daphne wrote back to Mr. Booth at once on a postcard. "That should do it," she said. "I've confirmed the time and the place for him. Now all we have to do is make sure our plan is foolproof. We must anticipate every single thing that might go wrong and arm ourselves beforehand."

"And I'll ask the birds. They're all clever, and I'm sure they can contribute at least as much as I can."

"We certainly can't do it without them," agreed Daphne.

The girls wrote a list of preparations.

"First, we must write some statement from Mrs. Glendoveer about Mr. Booth. If we make it look like a deathbed declaration, I can forge her signature."

"You can do that," Daphne said. "And you also must get the aviary key."

"I've got it," said Clara. "Mama put it back on the ring. It's hanging in the mudroom."

"Do you think the birds will speak if we need them? I'm hoping that if we get into trouble, one of them can fetch help."

"I'll ask Frances," Clara said. "She knows that we are only working on her behalf, so how could she refuse?"

Daphne cleared her throat. "And now, in regard to weapons—"

Clara dropped her list and sat with her mouth agape.

"Polrumptious!" prodded Daphne.

"Yes," Clara said, resuming a firm grip on her pencil. "What in regard to . . . weapons?"

"Isn't it best to have some form of self-defense? In case of emergency. Think."

"Um, we have a scythe in the garden shed."

"Is it very heavy?" Daphne asked. "Because if it's something cumbersome, it can easily be taken and turned against us. I read that in a Rover Boys book." She gave Clara a sly look, then snapped her fingers. "I must go back and read more! They defeat several criminals in every volume. Write that down. They'll know how to trap a rat!"

"What *about* rattraps?" Clara asked. "We *have* had rats down in the boiler room, actually. I'll ask Mama to get some."

"Brilliant. We could set up a nest of traps somewhere and lead him into it unawares if he threatens us with a pistol."

"But, Daphne, even if he's covered with rattraps, he'd still be able to fire on us."

"True, but then we could always put up our hands and apologize and act terribly sorry and cry 'boohoo!' while we draw close enough to paralyze him with a kick. Pardon me, but anyone who points a pistol at two little girls deserves nothing less."

"I should say so," agreed Clara.

Daphne drummed her fingers. "The more I think about it, I'm sure we shouldn't let Mr. Booth into the house."

"Won't he find that peculiar?"

"Let's lead him to the boiler room through the back-yard door. I think that if we let him in and he intends to do us ill, he'll find more things to use against us. Fire pokers, kitchen utensils. You never know."

Clara wished to present a courageous front, but

Daphne's constant references to their physical peril were making her stomach upset. "If you don't mind, I need to talk to the birds and let them know that Mr. Booth will be here. The sooner, the better."

Daphne agreed. The girls decided that they would prepare the house for Mr. Booth the day before his visit. Until then, Daphne would scour Rover Boys books for ideas, and Clara would ask the birds.

"I'd never have thought in a million years that I, Clara Dooley, would lead an intrepid life. But here I am," she said aloud to give herself courage. But secretly, she wondered if there weren't something important she hadn't taken into account.

"What news?" asked Frances as Clara approached.

"Mr. Booth is coming. We've had an answer from him."

The birds did not celebrate this information, and their gravity made Clara wonder if they weren't also a little afraid.

"We will be ready," Frances said.

"You will be our first defense."

"We know," George said. "Look." He stretched out the talons on his left foot, which were indeed impressive.

"I could use any ideas you have." Clara told them of the plans so far. "Are there other traps we could set up?"

Arthur and Peter fluttered and squawked to Frances.

"They say find powdered lye. Put it in glass jars in the rafters," she told Clara.

Arthur cackled again.

"Without the lids on, he says," added Frances.

"Thank you, boys," Clara said. "You're both quite diabolical." To which they laughed uproariously.

Helen tsipped for attention next.

"She says glue the floors! Use great, deep puddles!"

"Good idea," Clara told her. "And what about you, Frances? Any other secret weapons?"

The mynah hopped over. "Doctor," she said. "In the blue bottle."

"What?"

"Go to the medicine cabinet and get the blue bottle."

Clara went upstairs to the bathroom. She climbed on the little stool beside the basin and opened the mirrored cabinet. Glass containers of old patent medicines with yellowing labels had sat there for years. Mother's Remedy, Pink Quartz Brain Tonic, Stomach Bitters, Epsom Salt . . . *There!*

On the cobalt-blue bottle was a picture of a man with bushy side-whiskers. Above him was written "DR. PINCUS'S CHLORAL SEDATIVE." Below him, in smaller script: "The Sandman's Friend."

"Good for insomnia, restlessness, nervous complaints, extraction of teeth and minor surgery, female ailments, cough, catarrh, and neuralgia. One teaspoon dissolved in cold water . . ." Clara took the bottle in hand and went down to show Frances.

"Yes!" Frances said. "For Mr. Booth. Nighty-night. Sleep tight!"

"Will it put him out completely?"

"Double the dose," Frances said, "and doubt not."

"Getting him to drink it might be a problem. But I'm glad to have it on hand just in case."

"Don't worry." Frances drew her claws quickly through a page of newspaper. "We can persuade him."

"I see," Clara said, surveying the shreds. "I also have a request for you and George."

"Ask," George said.

"If things don't go as we plan, and Daphne and I are in danger, we'll need you to get help. And it has to be either one of you, because you both speak. Would you be willing?"

"I will!" declared George.

"He will *not*," said the mynah.

Clara began to wonder why she ever thought she could rely on Frances's cooperation, when the bird added, "*I* will go."

"Frances, how courageous of you."

"No!" George interrupted. "Not Frances. I'm stronger."

Frances peered up over her shoulder at him. "Look at you: Bright white! A yellow crown! Some brat will sling-shot you. No one will notice me."

"You have a point, Frances. I think you'll be safer than George would be," Clara said. "And goodness, you speak so well now, you could converse with anyone, should we get in trouble."

"Have Arthur go with you," George said. "Please, Frances."

Arthur raised a fuss until Frances consented. "It would be practical. Arthur can come too."

Immediately, George fluttered down from his perch, lowered his head, and clicked his bill against the mynah's. Clara thought it was one of the sweetest displays of brotherly love she could imagine.

"Enough now," Frances said briskly. She hopped forward. "Clara?"

"Yes, Frances?"

"You are not stupid."

"Hmm," Clara said. "It is good to be recognized as not stupid, so thank you."

"You are a brave girl and a smart one. Like me."

Clara bowed to Frances, deeply touched by the compliment. "That is because I am a Glendoveer," she said.

"Unmistakably so," Frances said. "Agreed?"

"A Glendoveer," said George.

"Tsip-tsip!" said Helen, joining Peter and Arthur in a crazy song.

It was enough to make Clara's heart swell. She didn't dare tell them all how much she loved them for fear of offending Frances with mush.

"Let me go find a story for us to read," she said. "Something for a summer afternoon."

"Yes!" said George. "Let's read!"

"Bee-tee-wee! Wee tee!" chirped Peter.

"He asked you to make sure it's funny," Frances said. "And as for me, you know."

"I do," said Clara, reluctantly thinking of the day that they might fly away forever. "No birds, Frances. *No birds.*"

Chapter 26

It was Clara's task to falsify a document to present to Mr. Booth. She found some old monogrammed stationery and, by candlelight, wrote out a list of charges against him:

> I, Cenelia Glendoveer, of sound mind and failing health, do charge my house-keeper, Harriet Dooley, with recording the following:
>
> It is my contention that Mr. Woodruff Booth hypnotized our nanny, Nelly Smith, and engineered the kid-napping of our children for the purpose of extorting ransom money from my husband, his employer....

Every few minutes, she'd check the candle to see if Mrs. Glendoveer had any opinions on her actions, but the flame burned steadily until her work was finished. When Clara came to the end of the document, she dated it, signed a shaky facsimile of Mrs. Glendoveer's signature, and examined it.

"Hope that's all right," she said. The candle blazed a warm orange, so Clara felt Mrs. Glendoveer approved.

When the day before Mr. Booth's arrival came, Clara was prepared. She had so well convinced Ruby that the house was overrun with rats that there were now dozens of traps upstairs and down. She'd had quite a job of it, setting them off with a stick so that they could be brought safely down into the boiler room and reset.

She was placing a bottle of Royal Glue she had plucked from the mudroom in a corner when Daphne knocked on the doorframe.

"Already hard at work, are you?"

"I don't think I could keep still even if I tried," she said. Clara gave her friend a tour of the variety of weapons she had stashed around the room. Daphne picked up the umbrella and held it against her shoulder like a soldier.

"This is a good one. You can leave it out in the open. He'll never suspect its purpose." She dug into her pocket and produced a box. "Look what I brought."

"Tacks," said Clara.

"I say we find an old chair and place these beneath the upholstery. When he sits down . . ."

"Ouch. Suppose he asks us to take a seat instead?"

"Never thought of that," Daphne said.

"But look at these," Clara said, pointing to a row of glass jars she'd lined up on a box. "Arthur says to fill them with lye and put them in the rafters!"

"And bomb Mr. Booth? That's the best idea yet."

"I haven't brought the lye down yet, though. There's always a chance that this will be the day Ruby decides to make soap. I can't risk her missing it."

"And don't forget to open a little window. In case we need the birds to get help."

"Done."

"Well, then . . ."

Clara thought she read something in Daphne's expression that was not completely polrumptious. "Is there anything else?"

"Yes. I'll understand if you say no, but I would be assured—not that I'm *not* assured now—but still, if I could know that the birds are fully enlisted in our cause, it would be helpful to me."

"You want to speak to them?"

"Actually, I'd like them to speak to *me*. The success of our plans depends so much upon them. Do you think you can arrange it?"

Clara understood Daphne's jitters. If their situations were reversed, how confident would Clara be feeling right now? "Wait here," she said, and proceeded to the aviary.

The birds flapped their wings and chattered as they saw her approach.

"Tomorrow," said George, "is our day!"

"A day for the Glendoveers!" Frances said. "A long time coming."

"It is," Clara said. "It is our day. But you know, don't you, that there is someone else here who has helped make that day possible. Someone without whom I never would have found Mr. Booth—"

Here, she was interrupted by rusty squawks. Peter was poking Arthur under the wing in a most annoying manner.

"Arthur thinks she's pretty," Frances said grimly. "The little towhead girl."

Arthur leaned down to shriek his protest, but Clara could see right away that he was merely embarrassed.

"Arthur's right," Clara said. "Daphne is pretty. And she's taking a risk for all of us. What did we do to deserve such generosity from a stranger? Isn't she remarkable?"

All the birds except one gave their loud approval. It was George who asked Frances, "Don't you think we should thank her?"

"I'll thank her later." She sat down in her nest to show she was through discussing it.

Clara leaned forward and propped her hands on her knees. "Frances? I think it would help Daphne to hear from you. It would shore up her loyalty to feel part of our family."

"Please, Frances . . . ," said George.

"Ohhhhh," Frances said, still sounding irascible.

Clara brought Daphne back around in a flash and took her inside the cage.

Frances flew up out of her nest, and the other birds backed up on their perch to make way for her. Clara could feel her friend trembling and pulled her in close beside her.

"This is Daphne Aspinal, my best friend," Clara announced. "She has a very important part to play in our plan. Tomorrow she will be the first to greet Mr. Booth and lead him to our trap. We rely on her courage and quick thinking! Therefore—"

"Does she talk?" Frances asked sharply.

"Why, yes, I do," Daphne said. "Very well, thank you."

"Oh?" said Frances. "Because it's hard to tell with you standing there breathing through your mouth."

"Frances, be kind!" commanded George, and the others began scolding their rude elder sister.

"Ah, it's fine for the towhead to come gawking, trying to get *me* to speak!" said Frances. "But should I ask her to talk, why it's a positive insult!"

Clara clapped her hands for their attention. "If we cannot give Daphne an assurance that we are all behind her and grateful, I don't know that we deserve her help."

"Daphne," said George, "I thank you very much."

"Tsip-tsip!" said Helen, flying down to alight on Daphne's shoulder.

"I'm happy to help," Daphne told them. "And proud to know you."

Peter sat on Daphne's head and chirped. Frances flew down and paced at the girls' feet. But Arthur put his head under his wing and extracted a shiny black feather, which he dropped down for Daphne to catch.

"For good luck!" Daphne said. "I'll keep it in my pocket."

"Me too," said George. And he pulled a downy white feather for Daphne.

Peter reached around and caught a bright yellow tail feather, and Helen plucked a tuft of green fuzz from her breast.

"What a lovely *voluntary* gesture," Clara said, training her sights on Frances.

"Who, me?"

The birds chattered at her until she twisted around, bit a feather from her left wing, and placed it on the toe of Daphne's shoe. "Here. You are an honorary bird."

"Much obliged," Daphne said.

"Don't be silly," Frances said. "No one *wants* to be a bird—not anyone who has once been a child. It's a start, though. When we recover Elliot, *then* I'll make you a Glendoveer."

"Fair enough," Daphne said. "You've given me something to strive for."

Clara appreciated that Daphne was not being sarcastic. As brusque as Frances was, one got the impression that she was also deeply honorable. If suffering had made her cross, who could fault her?

"We are all in this together," Clara said. "Thank you, all of you."

"Until tomorrow!" said George.

Arthur crooned goodbye, trying to sound as suave as his brother George, and his voice broke embarrassingly, causing Peter to twitter and tease him. So Daphne blew Arthur a kiss, and the aviary went wild. Frances, however, scratched at her nest and said, "Hmmph!"

"Clara, that was magical," Daphne said. "They are all so vivid and childlike."

"It was a little like presenting someone at court," Clara told her. "You can ignore Frances's moods, by the way. Arthur the Grackle is smitten with you, and she's jealous."

"I will win her over," Daphne said. "You'll see. I want to be an honorary Glendoveer!"

"As far as I'm concerned, you already are," Clara told her.

"Then you are an Aspinal," said Daphne, "though there's no magic in it—just sisterhood."

There was much Clara wished to say to Daphne, but she didn't want to become sentimental. Opening a doorway to that feeling might lead to another softening, and before she knew it, she'd be swamped with second thoughts.

"As if sisterhood weren't enough for me!" teased Clara. "Now come, let me show you the document I made up from Mrs. Glendoveer."

Chapter 27

Before bed, Clara went to Ruby's room and made her promise to do everything in her power tomorrow at the attorney's office to delay the sale of the house.

"Ask every question you can think of. And remember that even if Mama signs something, you don't have to."

"I've thought of that already," Ruby said, tucking her frizz into her nightcap. "You realize that you are asking me to talk my way around two practitioners of the law and the most willful woman since Eve. What makes you think I'm a match for the three of 'em? I might just run out of words."

"Then collapse, like this," Clara said. She put the back of her hand to her forehead, rolled her eyes, dropped to the floor in a mock faint, and then peeked. "See? You can stay down indefinitely."

"Or as long as it takes them to get the spirits of

ammonia," Ruby grumbled. "Give me strength, is all I've got to say."

That phrase echoed in Clara's mind as she tried to sleep. Cares always increase after the lights go out, and this night was especially unnerving. Yet as soon as the sun made its appearance, Clara awoke surging with energy. Everything about her surroundings down to the old, worn kitchen chairs seemed steeped in history and meaning. And when she saw the women off at the door, Clara found herself memorizing details like the buttons on her mother's coat and the smell of freshly ironed starch discernible when she hugged her neck.

"Goodbye, Mother! Goodbye, Ruby!" she said as they descended the front steps. "Remember Mrs. Glendoveer!"

"As if we could forget," Ruby cried over her shoulder.

Then Clara was off to the boiler room with a stepladder and lye. Wobbling, she placed the jars on the largest ceiling beams. She set the rattraps and dumped the glue. The forged document with Mrs. Glendoveer's signature she put in an envelope and stashed in an unfinished wall behind a two-by-four. Finally, Clara got the key and opened the aviary.

All the birds flapped wordlessly from the cage. Arthur tested his wings by soaring straight up to the height of the treetops and swooping inches from the ground.

When all the birds had assembled near the basement door, Clara warned them, "There are traps and snares throughout the room. You will need to be exceedingly careful where you light."

"We understand," said George.

Inside the room, the birds fluttered up and took their places in the rafters. Frances noted the small open window where she and Arthur would escape if need be.

"Do you think that we're ready for him?" Clara asked.

"Yes!" said George, setting the rest of them off into whistles. "Ready!"

"Onward, Clara," said Frances. "Onward, my girl!"

Clara gave them all a last look and shut the door to the boiler room. Once outside, she proceeded to the kitchen door. On the counter she had left her bottle of Dr. Pincus's Chloral Sedative. She pulled out the glass stopper, measured the crystals into a small pitcher, and filled it with water. Although Clara doubted she would have any opportunity to use the potion, she thought it best to have it on hand—especially since Frances had recommended it. So she placed the pitcher in the icebox and wandered down the hall to have a look at the clock.

Nine-thirty-seven. Clara didn't know how she was going to stand the wait. Where was Daphne? She was turning the question over in her mind when she heard a door opening at the back of the house. Instinctively, she flattened herself against the parlor wall and held her breath as footsteps approached.

"Clara? Clara!"

Thank goodness it's her! thought Clara. But when she whirled around into the hallway, she startled Daphne so badly that both she and her friend leapt away from each other and screamed!

As Clara stood panting, Daphne merely shook her head. "Look at us," she said. "And the old fellow isn't even here yet."

"Maybe it's good we got that out of our systems," Clara said.

"Did you sleep well last night? I had such dreams!" Daphne shook herself. "In any case, Mr. Booth should be joining us soon. I will wait for him out front as we discussed."

"And I will keep an eye out. There's a place on the side of the house where I can see through the shrubbery to the front."

Daphne inhaled deeply. "All right, Clara. Today is the day we find your father."

Clara nodded. "I will see you soon."

They did not embrace. Instead, they turned their backs smartly on each other and parted.

Waiting in the shrubbery, Clara kept her ears pricked for the sound of a car, as she could not see all the way to the street. When she did hear a car come to a stop, she listened for a man's voice but could not hear over the rattle of the motor. As the vehicle finally pulled away, she could hear Daphne chattering as if to herself.

Slowly, very slowly, the old man came into view. Clara felt a pang. Mr. Booth was so stooped, he was shaped like the letter S. One of his crooked hands grasped his cane, and the other clutched Daphne's arm for support.

Running to take her place inside the kitchen door,

Clara felt close to tears. The old gentleman had dressed for the occasion in spats and a waistcoat and watch chain. He had a tremor and dark spots on his wrinkled forehead. The thought of her hidden rattraps and lye shamed her. Fragile Mr. Booth could be toppled with no more than the jab of an index finger.

She chewed her nails and waited for a knock on the door. The two of them were certainly taking their time. Perhaps Mr. Booth had collapsed on his way? At last, Clara crept up and looked out the kitchen window. There was Mr. Booth, seated in a garden chair; Daphne was nowhere to be seen.

Clara knew she could not sit in the kitchen forever. "Mrs. Glendoveer," she whispered, "you see what this has come to. If you can help me in any way, you must. You must!"

With that, she opened the door. Mr. Booth turned his head toward her, looking for all the world like a kindly old gentleman out to feed pigeons in a park.

"You must be Clara," he said, extending his hand. "Pardon me for not standing. I'm a bit out of breath. I've had a recent bout of bronchitis, you see."

Mr. Booth did indeed sound hoarse, but Clara kept her distance and curtseyed instead. "Good day, sir," she said.

"You have done a good deed today, my dear. I do hope that your cooperating with me does not put you in jeopardy with your mother. However, perhaps this will help." He pulled out a single bill from his waistcoat, placed it on the little table in front of him, and pushed it forward.

"Thank you. But I can't accept. Where is Daphne?"

He smiled, and his eyes crinkled at the corners. "The girl has gone to fetch me the document," he said.

"She has?"

"Yes. From that little downstairs room."

Clara could feel the blood drain from her face. "But . . . but she doesn't know where it is. I must help her."

Mr. Booth leaned back. "I'll wait."

As Clara rounded the corner, she could see that, indeed, the boiler room door hung open. Inside, Daphne stood on a stepladder with her back to Clara. She was running her hands behind the lumber supporting the wall.

"Daphne, what are you doing? Why aren't you following our plan?"

"I'm getting the document for Mr. Booth," she said.

"Stop her!" whispered Frances from above. The birds were peeping from their hiding places.

Clara put a finger to her lips and closed the door. "Daphne, look at me."

When Daphne turned, Clara could see that a spot of hair above her eyes was twisted with dirt. A streak ran down one side of her face. Her right hand and sleeve were filthy, and her boots were stuck with leaves and clots of dust.

"Daphne, you're covered with glue!" Clara said. "Get down at once!"

But Daphne seemed to look right through her. "Not until I get the papers."

"Why? Has he threatened you?"

"No," said Daphne, returning to her work. "You told me you'd hide it in the wall. Help me find it."

George peered down at both of them. "Cold eyes," he said. "Look!"

They are cold, thought Clara.

"Woodruff Booth's done it again!" said Frances. "Stupid girl. Stupid!"

Clara's sympathy for the old man evaporated. For all their planning, Clara and Daphne never considered that Mr. Booth might mesmerize them. They had been stupid, indeed. And now Clara found herself alone.

"What do I do?" she asked the birds.

"Don't look him in the eyes," Frances said.

"But about Daphne? How do I snap her out of it?"

"It doesn't matter now," Frances said. "Mr. Booth is outside. He should be inside. *That* is our problem."

Clara watched Daphne continue running her hands along the walls numbly, methodically, as she neared the corner where the envelope was hidden.

"Daphne!" Clara said. "You are searching the wrong wall. Over there."

Daphne followed Clara's pointing finger and went across the room, where she resumed her search.

"That's it," said Frances. "Keep her busy."

"I will," Clara said. "All of you keep your places. Mr. Booth will tire of waiting sooner or later."

"Arthur!" said Frances. "Go out and watch Mr. Booth. Let us know when he approaches."

The grackle fluttered up to the window and squeezed his way out. Clara kept redirecting Daphne—whose boots periodically stuck to the floor, so caked were they in glue.

Time seemed to stand still, and Clara began to doubt that Mr. Booth would ever come. At last, she saw Arthur edge through the window.

"He's coming," George said.

"Places!" said Frances.

Clara hid behind the door. She saw the knob turn hesitantly and stop, as if the old man lacked the strength to complete the task. On the third try, she heard the click of the latch. Through the crack between the hinges, she saw him with his back to the daylight and spectacles gleaming, examining the room up and down.

"Daphne?" he said.

"Yes, Mr. Booth," she said.

"Have you not found the papers?"

"No, Mr. Booth."

"Tell me, then, my girl . . . *are* there any papers?"

"Yes, Mr. Booth. Clara hid them."

Before Daphne could say more, Clara came forward, careful to avert her eyes. "I did hide them, Mr. Booth. And now I wonder if my mother has taken them back! If I cannot find them down here, we will have to search her room."

There was a slight whirring sound in the rafters—a shudder of feathers. Clara pretended not to hear, but the old man fell silent and put a cupped hand to his ear. "Are there pigeons inside?"

"No. No pigeons," said Daphne.

"Ah. Well," he said, with obvious relief. Clara imagined that he relied upon the hypnotized Daphne to tell him only the truth. He took the final step down into the room, whereupon Clara slammed the door behind him and locked it, then twirled around and seized his cane.

"Clara!" rasped Mr. Booth in a voice hot with anger.

"Quiet!" barked Frances.

That's when Mr. Booth looked up to see the birds drop down, one after another, like spiders from a web. Shrinking, he let out a dry wail.

Clara brandished his cane.

"Look away from me," she said. "Now move to the corner, sir, and be quick, or the birds will have at you!"

Chapter 28

Mr. Booth slunk to the corner, where he stood with his face to the wall.

"Set Daphne free," Clara said.

"I don't know what you mean. . . ."

George circled the old man's head twice, brushing him with his wings. "Set her free!" he repeated.

"Call off the birds!" said Mr. Booth. "I beg you. . . ."

George fluttered up to the rafters and stood watch. Cringing, Mr. Booth shaded his eyes and faced the room. "Have Daphne come here."

Clara gently led her friend to stand a safe distance from Mr. Booth. Helen and Peter perched on Clara's shoulders, ready to defend her, while Arthur and Frances paced at Daphne's feet.

"You may begin now, Mr. Booth," Clara told him.

Mr. Booth held Daphne with his gaze and hummed one low note until he had spent all his breath. And then he said these words:

"Turn aside from thy dark mirror. Daylight now awaken thee."

With a loud clap of his hands, Mr. Booth dissolved the spell, and Daphne's head snapped back in a manner that left Clara terrified.

"Daphne, it's Clara. Speak to me."

After a period of mild confusion, her friend regained her senses and looked about her in astonishment. "Where did I go?" she asked.

"Mr. Booth mesmerized you. Do *not* look him in the eyes again!"

"You evil man!" shouted Daphne. "To think I'd begun to pity you. . . ." She opened and closed her hands. "Did I fall in glue?"

"Never mind that now!" said Clara. "I need you behind me."

Daphne backed up and grabbed the umbrella. "Go on."

"Tell me, Mr. Booth," Clara said. "Where is Elliot Glendoveer? And don't dare look at me."

"I do not know," said Mr. Booth, covering his face.

"I'm going to give you one more chance to answer me, and then I will let the birds persuade you. Where is Elliot Glendoveer? Is he alive or dead?"

Mr. Booth did not say a word but drew his suit coat up around his head and cowered.

"Are you with me?" Frances asked her siblings.

Arthur let loose his eardrum-splitting laugh. "Bee-tee-TEE-TEE-EE-EE!" shrieked Peter as he dive-bombed Mr. Booth's nose.

George landed on top of his suit coat and scratched through the wool until he brought up the sky-blue satin underlining. Helen orbited his head like a meteor while Frances pecked him at the back of the knees.

"He's alive!" exclaimed Mr. Booth. "Please stop! Elliot is alive!"

"Stop!" said George, fluttering back up to his perch in the rafters. Instantly, the birds all retreated to their places.

"Where is he?" demanded Clara. "And don't try to deceive us, for we intend to hold you until he's been found."

"Answer!" Frances said.

"He is on an island. Safe. Out in the bay."

This news electrified the birds, and as they erupted in shouts of joy, Clara too felt a flood of emotion. "Where? Which one?!" she demanded.

"On Razor's Slip," he said.

"Where is that?" Daphne asked. "Do the ferries go there?"

"No, no," said Mr. Booth, still talking from under his coat. "No one does. It is the farthest southeast island and very small."

"Ask him what name Elliot goes by now," Daphne said.

A small part of Clara feared the question. Suppose this Elliot was not the man who married her mother? "You heard Daphne," Clara said.

"I believe," said Mr. Booth, "he goes by Dooley. Nevan Dooley? Yes. He was raised by one of the islanders, and this is the name they gave him."

"It *is* he!" Daphne cried.

But hearing Mr. Booth pronounce her father's name so casually stoked Clara's indignation. "How have you kept him there? Did you not know that he had a wife and child?" she asked.

"He does not remember them now," Mr. Booth said simply. "But he is well. I have arranged it so that he does not suffer."

Incensed, the birds clamored at him as Helen and Peter circled his head.

"Mesmerized him too, did you?" said Frances. "Why, I've half a mind to poke your eyes out right now!"

Mr. Booth quivered and coughed. "If you will promise the birds will keep their distance, I can explain."

"Be quick, sir," Clara said. "And know that if you make a move toward us, the birds will be back upon you."

"Yes," he said, poking his head out cautiously. Then, putting up his hands, he said, "Do not fear me."

"We do not!" said Frances.

"Of course," he said, trying to regain some of his former smoothness. "I must say that I never expected to be addressed by birds," he told Clara. "They respond as if they understand. Even the Great Glendoveer's birds could not do that outside of a rehearsed presentation."

"But these *are* George Glendoveer's birds," Clara said.

Mr. Booth's head wobbled, and he appeared unsteady on his feet. "Impossible," he breathed.

"Do not contradict her," George said.

"Yes, um, sir," said Mr. Booth, blinking. He coughed again. "What is it in the air down here? Do any of you feel a burn?"

"You shall burn, if there is any justice!" cried Frances.

"You killed Nelly," said George. "As surely as if you'd been there yourself."

Mr. Booth sputtered and pleaded to Clara and Daphne. "It was an accident! It wasn't meant to go so wrong. Why, I loved Nelly myself. I grieved over her."

"Boohoo," said Frances. "How difficult for you."

"If I could trade places with her—with any of them—I would. It was my life's greatest mistake. . . ."

Frances turned her back on him. "We don't need to hear any more, Clara; let me go get Elliot."

Clara was also growing impatient. After Mr. Booth informed them that Elliot was in a cabin on the island's north shore, Clara said, "Tell us how to wake Elliot. Is it the same incantation you used for Daphne?"

"It is always the same," said Mr. Booth.

"I would give everything," said George, "to have known those words on that terrible night. . . ."

Woodruff Booth stood for a moment. He appeared to be making some kind of difficult calculation.

"Don't even think about running," said Daphne, holding the umbrella in front of her.

"I'm not moving. Just please tell me," said Mr. Booth. "Who *are* these birds?"

"Guess," said Frances. And then, flapping up to rest on his shoulder, she spoke in his ear while he trembled: *"Victor victima fit!"*

"The conqueror becomes the conquered," he murmured. And as Frances flew to join George on the rafter, Mr. Booth counted the birds in the room. "There is one for each child," he said, shaking his head in disbelief. He turned to Clara. "Good God! How was it done?"

"Turn back around," she said. "It is you who are explaining to us. Who is the man who took the children out on the boat?"

"There is no man," he said.

At this, Arthur shrilled and launched himself at Mr. Booth. "Liar!" said Frances. "George knows! He bit him! A mean, ugly man."

"You misunderstand me!" said Mr. Booth, shielding his face. "I meant only that he is with us no longer. He is dead."

"BEE-tee-WEE!" said Peter to the rest.

"Tsip-tsip!" answered Helen.

"I agree," said George. "It is a good thing that he is dead."

Clara noticed that George did not say this with anger. He sounded sober and reflective and a little bit tired. Perhaps he'd been living with the thought of that man in his dreams for the last fifty years.

"Frances? Arthur?" said Clara. "Are you prepared to fly to Razor's Slip? Can you travel so far?"

"SQUAWWWW!" cheered Arthur as he ascended to the little open window.

"At last!" said Frances. "We're bringing our Elliot home."

The girls waved and wished them well while the remaining birds closed in on Mr. Booth, just in case.

"There they go," Clara said, looking out at the square of blue sky. She was saying a silent prayer for their safety when she felt a nudge at her elbow. Daphne's eyes were red-rimmed, as if she'd been crying.

"It's very close in here," she said with a cough. "Do you think we could take Mr. Booth to the aviary now? We've no more need of the lye."

"Lye, you say?" exclaimed Mr. Booth. "My dears! Did you mean to burn me? And here I've hardly managed to stand upright without the aid of my cane." He rubbed his back and made a pitiful face.

Although Clara saw that he was trying to engage their sympathy, she could also see he was truly weary from stand-

290

ing on his own. He certainly couldn't run far, even if he were to break away. "Very well," she said. "George, would you ride on Mr. Booth's shoulders? Helen and Peter can lead the way outside."

Helen flew down, but Peter chattered and called her back.

"What is it?" asked Clara.

"He says *not* to go," George said in a low voice.

"Bee-TEE!"

"He tells us to listen," George whispered. "Shhhh."

Daphne trained her sights on Mr. Booth while Clara surveyed the room. She heard no sound, but something about the way the light entered under the back door caught her attention. Was there a shadow on the threshold?

Clara crept nearer to the door and reached her hand toward the key still lodged in the lock when *BOOM-BOOM!* The door bulged twice in the center like a beating heart, and Clara stepped aside. With another *BOOM!* the door fell forward with a crash, dragging the frame with it. There, silhouetted against the sun, stood a man in shirt-sleeves with ropy arms.

The shock of his sudden appearance immobilized Clara. She stood there taking in everything about him: close-clipped gray hair, weathered skin, clenched fists, and a chipped front tooth showing through his snarl. And though he was old and his clothes hung on him, Clara could see by his taut neck and forearms that this man was still strong.

"Get her!" cried Mr. Booth.

Only then did Clara move, jumping back and brandishing the cane.

The man grabbed at her, seizing the cane at the end and yanking her forward.

"LET GO OF THE GIRL OR I'LL SHOOT!" boomed a deep voice.

Clara knew that this was George; but when the man loosened his grip and scanned the room for the hidden stranger, she took full advantage and ran to a corner behind some boxes.

"That's a confounded bird, Jimmy!" said Mr. Booth.

"Says who?" Jimmy growled.

"Says me! It's a cockatoo, you idiot!" Booth pointed to the ceiling. "He's up there somewhere, hiding. There are others too, so watch yourself."

Jimmy took time to scratch his head and look around. Clara climbed up on a box. Daphne was nowhere to be seen, and Clara hoped that perhaps she had found a way to run outside.

"Did you get the papers?" Jimmy asked.

Mr. Booth stamped his foot. "There are no papers! It's a trap." He shaded his eyes. "What's become of the blonde? Did she leave?"

"What blonde?" Jimmy asked. "I never saw a blonde."

Clara grabbed the envelope and waved it over her head. "I have the papers."

"Snag them, Jimmy," said Mr. Booth. "And pull out your pistol."

Jimmy put his hands on his hips and snarled. "A pistol? For a little girl?"

"Just do it!" said Booth. "If you see a bird come near me, I want you to shoot it. Shoot 'em all, as a matter of fact."

Jimmy groaned and fished a gun from the waistband of his pants. Clara's knees began to knock.

She surveyed the floor below her to her right. The rattraps she had set were massed in the shadows. She had hoped that climbing up on the box would help keep Jimmy's eyes from the floor; but now that he had his gun at the ready, she felt too exposed. Would Jimmy really shoot her?

He moved a few steps forward, holding out his free hand and wiggling his fingers. "Give it over," he said. "Don't make me come get you."

Hearing the thrum of her heartbeat in her ears, Clara shook her head. "I can't. I'm afraid of the gun."

"The sooner you give over the papers, the sooner we're gone," Jimmy said.

"Then take it and leave!" Clara said. "Please." She extended her hand and dangled the envelope. She watched Jimmy come toward her, hoping the birds might descend on him. They had been so fearless up until now. Had they been cowed by the sight of the gun?

And then she heard an echoing click—something

like a gun cocking, only louder. A rattrap going off! She watched Jimmy examine the ground, sneering, "Why, you little . . ."

Clara brought her shoulders up around her ears, sure that he would fire, when she spied the flash of a white dress. Coming at Jimmy from behind with a face full of fury was Daphne Aspinal!

Chapter 29

Daphne had leapt up from her hiding place and run at Jimmy with all her might. He toppled face-forward, setting off trap after trap, screaming. His gun went skidding toward Clara, who immediately hopped down to grab it; but there were too many set traps surrounding the weapon for her to get to it quickly.

Jimmy's face contorted as he dragged himself on his stomach toward her. His left hand still wore a rattrap clamped on the little finger.

"Stand up, you idiot!" said Mr. Booth.

"Stay down!" boomed George from the ceiling.

Jimmy twisted his neck and looked for the voice. George swooped, extended his talons, and swiped at the fallen man's head. Meanwhile, Helen and Peter buzzed Mr. Booth as he swore under his breath.

Daphne went around to Clara's other side and handed her Mr. Booth's cane.

"Disarm the traps with this," she said.

Clara tapped the cane before her but had trouble controlling her aim. Adrenaline and fear had made her clumsy. She bent low and a trap caught at the hem of her dress, but she managed to pick up the gun. The feeling of it—cold and slightly oily—repulsed her.

"Hand it to me!" said Daphne. "Quickly."

Clara saw the sense in this: Daphne could take the gun, protecting her as she backed away from Jimmy. So she turned to her friend, careful to hold the weapon with the muzzle toward the floor—but it was even heavier than she had guessed, and she shook so badly, the firearm slipped through her hands.

Clara watched the gun drop to the floor and bounce. A spark lit up the dark, and the sound of a gunshot rocked the underground room. She tried to kick the gun forward and succeeded, but a force yanked her backward.

"He's got you!" yelled Daphne.

Clara felt Jimmy's hand at her ankle and looked down. One of his fingernails was torn and bleeding, but it was the smile-shaped scar that caught her attention: a thick, jagged welt on the skin between his thumb and index finger.

George hurtled through the air, diving at Jimmy's head, but the man was willing to endure all manner of scratches rather than let Clara go. When George tried landing on the man's legs, he thrashed so violently that Clara feared for the cockatoo's life. Clara had kicked herself in the ankle so many times trying to injure Jimmy's hand that she knew she must be covered in bruises.

Finally one of her kicks struck hard, and Jimmy let loose a stream of vile curses. Clara was free of him! She ran to Daphne, who had picked up the revolver, and shouted to George. "What do we do now?"

"He's getting up, Clara," Daphne said, her small hands straining to keep the revolver upright.

"Down on the ground," said George to Jimmy, "or the girl will shoot. Tell him, Mr. Booth."

But Booth stood trembling with his coat over his head.

"I will shoot," Daphne said. "So don't make me."

"You ought to be turned over someone's knee and spanked within an inch of your life," said Jimmy, rising to his feet. "Both of you." He took two halting steps forward and gave the girls a grin. "Harder than you thought to shoot someone, eh, little one?"

Clara could see the gun quivering in Daphne's hands.

"Clara?" Daphne said.

Clara didn't know how much closer they could allow Jimmy before making a decision—but she wasn't ready yet. "One more step . . . ," she said.

"Bee-TEEEE-WEEEE!" shrieked Peter.

A glass jar streaked past Jimmy's shoulder and exploded at his feet, sending up a white cloud of powder. The man choked and wiped his hand across his mouth as another jar fell behind him.

"What the devil?" He stumbled and looked up. A third jar ricocheted off his forehead, streaking the white stuff down his nose, chin, and shirtfront.

Clara held her pinafore up to her face and pulled Daphne back.

"I'm burning," he said. "Can't breathe. . . ."

"It's lye," said Mr. Booth with a wheeze. "Don't rub it around your face. . . ."

Jimmy pointed to his mouth. "My tongue . . . Water . . ."

"There's a pitcher in the icebox," Clara said. "Cold water."

"Give me!" said Jimmy.

"I don't want to leave Daphne."

Jimmy limped out of the room as fast as he could manage, hacking, tears streaming down his face. And George flew after.

"Oh dear," Daphne said, coughing. "Do you think you ought to have let him go?"

"Definitely," Clara said. "We all have to leave before we're poisoned! Peter and Helen? Will you accompany us? Mr. Booth, you will follow me and Daphne will follow you."

"And put your hands behind your head, sir," Daphne said. "I'll be watching."

Mr. Booth did as he was told. Climbing the few steps up to the yard in this posture was difficult for him, and he nearly fell.

"Keep going," Daphne said. When they reached the aviary, Clara opened the door.

Mr. Booth stood, shaking his head. "I won't go in." But Helen and Peter circled him until he stepped into the aviary just to escape them.

Clara slammed shut the cage door and locked it tight, then gestured for Daphne to come with her to the kitchen.

"I think we should stay outside," Daphne said. "It's the kitchen. That man will have knives nearby."

The girls stood by the side of the kitchen door, which was ajar. There was no noise inside.

"I'm going to look," Clara said.

"Not without me, you aren't." Daphne crept with her up the wooden steps.

Clara peeped her head in and was thrilled at the sight. Motionless on the floor lay Jimmy while George stood guard over him from the counter.

"Come, Daphne," she said. "He can't hurt us."

Daphne peeked over Clara's shoulder. "Is he dead?"

"No! Not dead," said George. "Though he ought to be."

The girls entered the kitchen and kept their distance from the collapsed man.

Clara poked him with the toe of her boot, but Jimmy remained insensible.

"Don't get too close, Clara!" Daphne said.

"He's asleep," Clara assured her. "I put half a bottle of Dr. Pincus's Chloral Sedative in the pitcher."

"You clever girl!"

"It was Frances's idea. Wasn't it, George?"

But George remained preoccupied with the body on the floor. "It is the man. The man from the boat. Look at his hand. The marks from my teeth are there."

Clara peered again at the half-moon scar. "The kidnapper? But Mr. Booth said he was dead."

"It *is* the man," George said. "Old now, but mean as ever." He flapped his wings and flew down by the still-breathing body. "Let's find his name. Search his pockets."

Clara knelt down reluctantly while George took his place by the man's head and Daphne held the gun, just in case. Clara shuddered as she slipped her hand in the man's warm pocket and pulled out a drawstring pouch. She opened it and saw plugs of tobacco and dollar bills in a clip. She went on to his other pocket and found nothing but a box of strike matches.

"That's all there is," Clara said.

"Well, then," said Daphne, "that's too bad. But can I put down this revolver now? I hate it!"

"May as well," George said. "No need anymore."

"I'm glad we didn't shoot it," Clara said. "Here, give it to me, and we'll put it somewhere out of sight."

Pointing the barrel down, Daphne started to surrender the pistol but stopped to inspect the handle. "Look," she said. "It's engraved." After peering closely, she announced: "It says 'J. Dooley.'"

"That's . . . that's *my* name," Clara said.

George paced to and fro. "It is what I feared. The last thing I saw before I went under was this man. He floated on the box with the baby tied to his chest."

"You think this is the man who raised Elliot on the island?" Daphne asked.

"Could be," George said.

Clara didn't want to think about what her father might have endured growing up with Jimmy as his caretaker. "So we've been going about with *his* name—Mother and Father and me. It's unthinkable."

"You're still a Glendoveer," he said. "Nothing changes that, Clara. If a cockatoo can remain a Glendoveer, then so can a Dooley."

Clara beamed at him. How lovely it would have been to know George as a real, live boy.

Daphne gingerly placed the pistol in the icebox, which seemed as safe a place as any, and brought up the matter of moving Mr. Dooley from the kitchen to the aviary. Clara agreed that they should act quickly, before the sedative wore off.

"Tie a pillow round his head," George told them. "You have to drag him down the steps."

"Quite compassionate of you, George, considering," said Daphne.

But George admitted to no feelings of sympathy. He merely wanted Dooley alive should they need more information about Elliot.

After securing Jimmy Dooley's head with two goose-down pillows and twine, Clara and Daphne each took one of the man's feet and pulled him to the kitchen door. When they came to the steps, Daphne kept to the feet while Clara tried to push him from the shoulders.

"Umph!" said Clara. "Could you pull harder from your end? He doesn't budge."

"On the count of three," Daphne said, "with all your might!"

By inches, the girls got Jimmy Dooley down the stairs. With each bump, he made a snorting sound that set Clara's teeth on edge.

"Keep going," George said. "It will be easier sliding him across the grass."

When they came to the aviary, Mr. Booth was sitting on the ground.

"So you've killed him, have you?" he said. "Little savages. Makes one wonder how you were raised."

"Raised better than little Elliot Glendoveer was, I wager," George said.

Helen, Peter, and George cornered Mr. Booth as Clara and Daphne tugged Dooley into the cage. When the aviary was locked, Clara pulled up a chair to keep an eye on the two men. Daphne went to get food for their prisoners.

Clara was curious when her friend returned with half a loaf of bread under one arm and a sloshing tin bucket.

"Bread and water?" Clara asked.

"It's prison food, from what I've read," Daphne said.

"And I don't trust these two with glasses or tableware, so they'll have to make do."

After the food was inside, Daphne also pulled up a chair. Mr. Booth dunked his hands in the pail, took a few sips, and glared at the girls.

"Are you going to sit and gawk at me?" he asked. "The indignity. You realize that you cannot get away with this."

"No? How will you explain why you came here with an armed henchman to meet two little girls?"

She sounded brave, but Clara knew that Mr. Booth was right. If Elliot was not found, how could her treatment of this old man ever be justified? And Daphne—what trouble she would be in. Surely the Aspinals would never let her darken Clara's doorstep again.

But there was nothing she could do about that now. Anxiously, Clara scanned the skies for black birds, praying to soon catch a glimpse of Frances and Arthur winging their way home in triumph.

Chapter 30

The afternoon passed sluggishly. At times, Clara would try to engage Mr. Booth in order to find out more about her father, but the old man had now decided not to speak except to say that he was innocent.

From time to time, Jimmy would snore or paw the air as if in a nightmare. His injuries only worsened as he slept. His upper lip, for instance, had swollen to several times its normal size, and the tip of his nose was purple from the caustic lye. One of his eyelids grew dusky and wouldn't close properly.

Daphne and Clara would occasionally sneak each other worried looks, and once were caught by the canny Mr. Booth.

"If you let us out now," Mr. Booth said, "no one will be the wiser. I'll call a carriage and tell them my friend's had a pinch too much brandy. We'll be off, the two of us, and never speak of this sorry episode again."

The girls had no intention of letting the men go, but Mr. Booth continued to insinuate that their plans would fail.

"What time is it?" he said, checking his pocket watch. "Two o'clock? How long do you think it would take someone to row from Razor's Slip to Oddshaw Island, catch a ferry, and return to Lockhaven?"

Neither Clara nor Daphne knew the answer to this question, and Mr. Booth recognized it.

"So I'll be spending the night here?" he'd say. Or, "Do you think Jimmy might need a doctor? His breathing is dangerously shallow." Or, "If he dies, you'll be spending your next twenty birthdays in a women's prison."

This remark made Peter so mad, he chattered angrily until Booth backed down.

"When we want more out of you, we'll ask for it," George said.

Something in the harsh tone of the cockatoo's voice got through to the sleeping Jimmy Dooley. He smacked his lips and groaned, then touched his injured eye.

"Water," he said.

Mr. Booth shambled over and flicked water from the bucket onto Jimmy's face. He propped himself up on one elbow and drank greedily.

It was then that Clara thought she heard a voice in the house.

"Is that your mother, do you think?" Daphne asked.

The girls soon got their answer when they heard Ruby squeal. "What's this? Who's put chewing tobacco on my table?"

"Clara!" called Harriet, still inside the house.

Clara looked to Daphne. "Go home! Now!"

"Certainly not," Daphne told her. "I won't abandon you."

"Please," Clara said, tugging her from her chair. "Run home and don't say a word. It's important to me to know you're home safe."

Daphne stood her ground, but Clara implored her.

"Please. For *me*. If I'm in trouble now, you may be able to help me later—but only if you are free."

Daphne understood this appeal. "Then you must leave a sign when you're safe. I will be back in the morning if I don't hear from you."

"Hurry!" said Clara. She squeezed her friend's hand and let her go.

When she passed the aviary, Mr. Booth was tending to Jimmy Dooley, urging him to get up. George, Peter, and Helen stood guard at the top of the cage. The injured man groaned so loudly, Clara was sure that someone might hear him in the house. In fact, she did not know why neither her mother nor Ruby was in the backyard looking for her yet.

"Mother!" she shouted as she entered the kitchen.

"Clara!"

Harriet clutched her daughter by both arms. "What's

happening?" she asked, her face white. "Who else has been here?"

Ruby ran in from down the hall. "You found her? Ah, thank God!"

That's when Clara saw that Ruby had found Jimmy Dooley's gun. Jimmy himself was apparently awake and had found his voice, for he could now be heard pleading for help outside.

"Come," Clara said. "We must make him be quiet and then I'll explain."

Her mother and Ruby were close on Clara's heels. She could hear her mother exclaim as they spied the aviary. Jimmy Dooley was on his knees with his shirt halfway untucked, holding his head, and moistening his burned lips with his big tongue. Mr. Booth had pulled himself up and stood with his nose against the bars, shaking with rage.

"Let me out!" he cried. "Or I'll see to it that you are both hanged!"

"Who *are* these men?" asked Harriet.

"That is Mr. Woodruff Booth," Clara said, "and with him is the man who kidnapped the Glendoveer children."

Her mother appeared dazed by the announcement. "No, Clara," she said. "You didn't."

Ruby pressed forward until she stood face to face with Mr. Booth. "Is it you, sir? Are you Woodruff Booth?"

"Don't look him in the eyes, Ruby! He'll hypnotize you—"

Ruby looked up instead and saw George and his two siblings on top of the aviary's roof. "Clara, where are the other birds?"

"Enough about the birds," her mother snapped. "We're all in a world of trouble here. That man is injured."

"Your little girl burned him with lye," said Mr. Booth.

"He threatened me with a gun!" countered Clara.

"She told us that she had papers signed by Cenelia Glendoveer that could put me, an innocent friend of the family, in jail," said Mr. Booth. "She lured us here. It's extortion, I tell you!"

"Should we believe that?" Ruby asked Clara.

Clara began to explain, but Mr. Booth kept interrupting.

"Talk to me, sir," Harriet said. "I am Clara's mother."

Mr. Booth adjusted his spectacles and stood as straight as he was able. "Then you'll want to know that your *daughter* told me that you and the cook were going to sell the incriminating document to a magazine!"

"Yes, I did, Mama," Clara said. "It was for a good reason, though."

Harriet's hands crawled up to her forehead. "This is a nightmare. I can scarcely believe I'm awake."

"But he's admitted to the kidnapping, Mama!" said Clara. "And that man with him? He kept Elliot captive. He raised him on one of the Pincushion Islands and—"

"Nonsense," said Mr. Booth. "What kind of mother are you? Can you not see that the girl is ill?"

Clara's mother waved everyone quiet and paused for thought. "Ruby," she said, "I need you to go into town and get the police."

"And a doctor!" shouted Jimmy.

"No, Mama. Not yet!" Clara said.

Ruby pulled Harriet aside, and Clara stood close by. "Are you sure? Don't you think we should get more of the story from Clara?"

"There is nothing else to be done," Harriet said. "I can't release these men by myself. For safety's sake, we need the police. And then we'll sort everything out."

Clara had visions of the men being set free. They might even resort to killing Elliot just to rid themselves of any remaining evidence of the kidnapping. She broke in between the two women and implored them. "If you want to give Father a chance to return home, you have to listen to me. He's on his way! What can I say to make you believe?"

Jimmy picked that moment to howl and rock back and forth, rubbing his eye.

"You see what a position we're in, don't you, Clara?" Ruby asked.

"Yes, but you must hold off. For Mrs. Glendoveer, Ruby!"

Abruptly, before Clara could react, Harriet reached into her daughter's pinafore pocket and pulled out the aviary key. "*That*," she said, pointing to the men inside the cage, "is also kidnapping. It's a serious offense, and if we don't react quickly, it will be harder for us. Do you want Ruby and me to go to jail?"

"Don't worry. I'll go to jail!" Clara said.

Ruby pulled her into an embrace. "It doesn't work that way, girl. We will be held responsible. And then what will become of you?"

Clara's mother marched to the aviary. "Gentlemen, I'm going for the police. You will be released to them shortly."

"At last!" exclaimed Booth.

Clara did not know what else to do. She was about to throw herself at her mother's skirts when she heard a magisterial male voice ring out from the top of the aviary.

"HARRIET, DO NOT GO!"

Her shoulders dropped. She turned.

"Harriet, listen to your daughter. Wait! *Please.*"

Clara felt Ruby's grip tighten around her and watched her mother's eyes rise until she glimpsed the cockatoo, his sulfur crest spread like a fan and his wings stretched wide.

"Did the bird say that?" Harriet asked no one in particular.

"Indeed, he did," said Ruby. "Oh, my stars and garters."

Clara put out her arm, and George fluttered down to perch upon it.

Harriet glanced from Ruby to Clara. "Which one of you taught him to speak?"

"I did," Clara said. "Or maybe I should say I helped him remember."

"Damnation!" said Mr. Booth. "Are you going to listen to a cockatoo?"

"Quiet, Booth," George said sternly. "Clara," he resumed in his silky voice, "did you show your mother the gun?"

"No, George. How silly of me . . ."

"Would you get it for us, Ruby?" he asked, cocking his head.

Clara's mother looked to be at a loss for words. Ruby, however, moved with alacrity. She was back with the gun in no time.

Clara ran her finger over the handle. "It's here, Mama. See? It says 'J. Dooley.' And that man over there? He's the one who kidnapped Father."

"He raised Elliot as his own son," George said. "Changed his name to Nevan—"

Harriet put her hand over her open mouth.

"Somebody get her a chair, please," said George.

"I'll help her into the house," said Ruby.

Ruby got Harriet settled at the kitchen table, and Clara made a dash again for the door. "Peter! Helen!" she called. "Keep an eye on the men. Oh, and let us know if Frances and Arthur return."

"Leave the door open!" George reminded her.

Ruby sat in a chair beside an unblinking Harriet Dooley. "Did you say Frances and Arthur?" she asked.

"They're all here!" Clara told her. "Well, not all here now, but you know what I mean. The birds are the

Glendoveer children, Ruby. They've been with us this whole time."

Ruby's eyes shone. "So it's true," she said. She reached out her arm to George, who flew to her and bowed deeply. "You always were the prettiest of the lot," she said. "I'd never have known you were a young man."

"Don't tell Peter," Clara said. "He thinks *he's* the prettiest."

"I'm sorry!" her mother broke in. "There is no making sense of this for me. It's not in my constitution to absorb whatever is going on here."

Ruby reached over and stroked Harriet's head. "But, dear, this is good news, don't you see?"

She lifted her hands weakly and let them drop.

"Mama, we have nearly found Father. And he never meant to abandon us. Isn't that cause for joy?" Clara studied her mother's face for a gleam of happiness, but Harriet merely stared ahead. "Tell her, George," she said. "Explain it to her."

George started at the beginning—with the night of the kidnapping and his conviction that Mr. Booth had hypnotized the nanny before leaving for Berlin. He told her that he believed Elliot might well have been mesmerized too when he returned to Jimmy Dooley's for proof; and now Frances and Arthur were on their way to break the spell and bring him home, if she had the patience to wait.

Clara could see her mother leaning forward, listening closely, losing her fear. George was like that, she thought.

When he spoke, his humanity shone through, and it was easy to forget about his outward form.

"My own childhood seems so long ago. And yet, you are much older than I am. May I ask," said Harriet, "how did you do it? How did you endure those years in the cage?"

"I cannot say." George took a breath. "There were long, cold nights when I felt sick with despair. Each of us did. But when we saw that one was not eating his food, or dropping feathers, or refusing to sing, the rest of us would gather round and chase away discouragement. We always kept hoping."

"For what?" Harriet asked.

George spoke softly. "For Elliot. For release. For someone who would *believe*."

Clara saw the tears spring to her mother's eyes and felt a hand on her own. "And then there was Clara," Harriet said.

Her mother gave her such a deep, appreciative gaze that Clara blushed.

"And now we have you, Harriet," George said.

"I hope you're including me as well, George!" Ruby said. "Have you forgotten how I worked my fingers to the bone for you? Digging up night crawlers and mucking out the cage and all that."

"Our biggest thanks to you, Ruby," George said. "And you shall be rewarded if our plans come off."

Ruby folded her arms in satisfaction. "Keeping you alive and thriving is prize enough. I just wanted a little tip of the hat, is all. Now I'm going to make some proper sand-wiches for our guests out there. And, Clara, you go get some salve from the medicine cabinet for Mr. Dooley's eye. Unless, that is, someone still wants to call the police."

"No, Ruby," said Harriet. "No police. The Glendoveer children have waited, and so can I."

Chapter 31

There was no bedtime for Clara that night. Ruby provided blankets for the men in the aviary and invited Peter and Helen inside to sit with them in the kitchen.

"Your mother wasn't speaking to me this afternoon," Ruby told Clara. "Do you know why?"

"Let me guess, Mama," Clara said. "Ruby was impossible during the meeting at Mr. Merritt-Blenney's."

"She was not only impossible," her mother said, "she was also embarrassing. At one point, she fell to the floor in the most artificial swoon. You could see her peeking at us. No one was fooled for a minute!"

Clara laughed. "Ooh, that was my suggestion, I'm afraid."

"I thought you two were conspiring against me. In any case, we didn't sell the house."

Clara was glad. Anything that allowed them to hold on to the Glendoveer home and stay close to Daphne was good, in her opinion.

Ruby made endless pots of tea and brought out a big basket of mending to keep Harriet and herself busy. Clara took out her Hans Christian Andersen and read to them all until she strained her throat. Crickets sang and the late-night air so chilled the kitchen that Ruby gave the birds old tea towels to nest in. Candlelight drew long shadows across the kitchen table, and Clara could feel her chin drop to her chest.

"I'm not going to sleep," she told her mother. "I'm going to rest." And she laid her head down and dreamed.

The first moments of sleep took her to somewhere as dark and empty as an underground cave. She imagined she was waiting in an antechamber where she heard only the sound of a ticking clock. It wasn't a bad place to wait, but it was impossible to tell if she was alone or if others sat with her in the dark. She was glad, then, to feel the slightest warming and sense the rising of the sun. A subtle glow radiated at the end of the chamber until she could make out a lovely room with little beds, a small school desk, and a white armoire.

The Glendoveers' nursery! she thought.

The room grew rosy, and Clara saw a woman sitting in a rocker. A baby bundled in a blanket cooed and reached up to Mrs. Glendoveer's smiling face. To her right, on the floor, a beautiful fair-haired boy built an elaborate tower of blocks. The older sister, her brows knit in concentration, sat on the window seat reading to her two young brothers, who poked at each other and laughed at something that amused them greatly. And in the middle of the room, a girl of four sang a little song to herself while twirling and hopping over the patterned carpet.

Clara waved to them but was unable to speak. She squinted, but the light in the room expanded until she could no longer see.

"Hello? Are you still there?"

Clara heard the sound of her own voice and awoke. Her first impression was that there was a blaze in the kitchen. With a blink, Clara's vision adjusted, and she saw the source of the light: the flames on the candles were dancing! Some shot up several feet like fountains of fire.

"Extraordinary," murmured Harriet.

"Isn't it beautiful?" Ruby said. "It must be Mrs. Glendoveer, mustn't it, Clara?"

"Heavenly," Clara replied.

The birds stood shoulder to shoulder, their heads bobbing in unison with each leap of the flames. George turned to Clara.

"He is here."

The heavy rapping of the front door knocker made her jump. She saw her mother's face first twist into anguish and then expand into elation in the span of a second.

All of them ran to the foyer—except those who could fly! Clara got to the door first, flipped the bolt, and tugged open the door.

The man who stood on the threshold appeared undernourished and wore clothes that were threadbare and patched. His black hair was frosted at the temples, and his face was etched with lines that spoke of years of sorrow and loss. But when he saw Harriet and Clara, his black eyes shimmered and a smile transformed his face.

Frances flew in over his shoulder, lit at Clara's feet, and whispered teasingly: "Clara, speak up! It's your father!"

"Father," she said, hardly believing that this word was now her own.

He bent low and swept her up like a child half her age. "Clara," he said. "My baby girl." And then, extending his hand, he said, "Harriet!" And the three of them clung together as one.

Arthur flew over the threshold and led all the birds in a raucous welcome that died down when Clara's mother began to cry. She traced his face with her fingers, almost as if she expected him to disappear. "It *is* you," she said. "Nevan!" And then she amended herself. "Elliot."

The family stayed drawn close with their arms around each other for quite some time. Clara marveled at how familiar this man felt to her, though she had been only with women for all her life. Nobody wanted to interrupt the sweetness of the moment, but when Clara saw Ruby wiping her eyes on her apron, she gestured for her to come near. "Father," she said, "this is Ruby."

Elliot put Clara down and embraced the weeping woman. "I have heard all about you from Frances," he said. "She says you are a jewel and aptly named."

At this, Ruby colored so deeply that she did resemble the gem. "I've done my best by your family. We've all hoped to see you home."

"And now wouldn't you like to meet the rest of your family?" Clara asked.

"Yes, please," her father said.

George, Frances, and the others lined up on the banister from eldest to youngest. George took it upon himself to do the introductions.

"You know how brave Frances and Arthur are," he said, "but each of us down to the smallest has held you in our hearts. We never gave up on you, Elliot."

"Thank you, Brother," he said. "While I was walking from the docks, Frances flew ahead and returned to tell me that you have two men in a birdcage outside."

"Better them than us!" Frances said, which made Arthur and Peter twitter in agreement.

"We can bring them to justice now," Elliot said. "That's something I can do for you."

"Someone get his rucksack from the porch!" Frances said.

"No, I'll fetch it," Elliot said. "It's much too heavy for these ladies to carry."

Clara noted her mother's and Ruby's wry expressions and almost giggled. What on earth could there be, she wondered, that Ruby and Harriet together were *not* able to bear?

Then they all went to the kitchen, Clara holding her father's hand and her mother with her arm through his. When they entered the bright room, Elliot sniffed the air.

"Roses!" he said. "You must have a plantation of them outside."

Ruby tapped him gently. "It's your mother," she said, "telling us how happy she is."

He inhaled the scent again and declared, "Mother, I am happy too."

"She'll be even happier after we've rid this house of the rats," said Ruby. "You'll find them in a cage in the backyard."

The aviary's outline was barely visible in the dark. As the group of them approached, Clara holding a lantern high, the men inside stirred and sat up.

Mr. Booth rubbed his spectacles on his shirt and put them on while Jimmy Dooley shielded his eyes against the light.

"Who is it?" asked Booth. "I can't see a thing."

When Clara brought the lantern up to illuminate her father's face, Booth looked away and slumped.

"That's it," Elliot told him. "Better to keep your eyes to yourself."

"Nevan, boy?" Jimmy called out with a tremble in his voice.

"It's Elliot," said Clara's father, "and I am not your boy." He opened his rucksack, pulled out a gauze drawstring bag, and emptied the contents into his hand. "Harriet, I'd like to show you first."

Clara's mother plucked something golden from his palm. "Remarkable," she said. "Clara, come see!"

Shining in the lamplight was a cuff link with double Gs.

"You remembered correctly, didn't you?" Clara told him. "And they were still there!"

"I'm lucky," her father said, "that they didn't get destroyed. Dooley here has a stash of coins and jewelry that he melts down in a flowerpot furnace. He doesn't want the gold traced back to the source. I made the mistake of coming across this stash when I was a boy. I've still got the stripes on my back from that beating."

Clara glared at Jimmy Dooley. "George worried that you had been treated cruelly."

"It's the only way he knows," her father said. "The odd thing is, if he'd treated me kindly, or even with indifference, the incident with the cuff links would probably never have imprinted itself on my memory."

"I suggest we choose not to thank him for that!" said Frances.

"None of this has a thing to do with me," muttered Mr. Booth. "Call the authorities, I don't care. But you must release me now."

Jimmy's arm shot out and grabbed Mr. Booth's lapel. He pulled him so quickly that Booth tripped and teetered suspended by his jacket alone. "Now you listen here, you dog! I won't hang for you. If I go down, so do you."

"Let go," said Booth in a strangled voice.

"If I were you, Mr. Dooley, I'd get my side of the story out first," Clara said. "Before Mr. Booth throws you to the wolves."

Elliot placed his hand on Clara's head. "I'd listen to her. She's obviously a bright girl."

Jimmy unhanded Booth and let him fall to the ground. "He never treated us fair, Nevan. Never! Why, I kept his secret, and I raised up a baby too."

"Is that what you call it?" Elliot asked. "Raising me up?"

"Say what you want about me," said Jimmy Dooley, "but my wife did tend you like a mother. Lily couldn't have her own babies, you see." Jimmy studied his shoes for a bit, wiped his eye, and looked up. "Now, I don't like babies much. By God, I don't like most *people*! But we thought we could have a good life alone on Razor's Slip, with a house built for us and money from Booth. A nice setup. But after Lily died, things changed."

"Things changed for me too," Elliot said. "Being left alone with you was so frightening, I preferred it when you'd disappear and leave me for days."

Jimmy ignored him and went on. "Booth left us out

322

there, forbade me to touch the treasure, and all the while he lives like a king."

"On our stolen money?" asked Frances.

"I have my own money," said Booth. "I never touched a copper coin of the Glendoveers', and that's the truth!"

"Yes, you do have your own money—*now*," said Jimmy. "You needed the ransom money because your family cut you off. But after the bloody drownings in the bay, Glendoveer closed up shop, and the Booths swallowed their shame and brought their little black sheep back into the family."

The stark light of Clara's lamp exaggerated the crags in Booth's face and brought out what was most mean and false about him. She wondered if he was as treacherous toward his own flesh and blood as he was to the Glendoveers, or even to Jimmy Dooley.

"How could you destroy a family for gold?" Clara asked Booth. "Don't you have any family feeling?"

Booth simply scowled, but Jimmy Dooley knelt down and looked into Clara's eyes.

"He don't have feelings for anyone but himself. We Dooleys worked for the Booths three generations! Tending their grounds, fixing their carriages. When this man gave me an opportunity to earn some money, I said yes. I'll ferry your litter to Skull's Head while you wait for the ransom. So I took some treasure too while I was at it. I wanted to be sure that I got mine!"

At this, Mr. Booth lunged forward and cuffed Jimmy Dooley's ear. "Imbecile!" he hissed. "You had to steal from them, didn't you? Took your time doing it too. And then the storm kicked up! You could have moved the little brats to safety and had folding money the rest of your life! Lowlife thief and murderer, that's what you are!"

Jimmy hit the bars with his fist and began to plead. "I didn't mean to drown no children! And didn't I save you, Nevan? *Who saved your life?*"

Clara noted her father's stony expression and waited for his answer.

"Frances and Arthur Glendoveer saved my life," he said. "Not you." Then he turned and spoke tenderly to Clara.

"Little one, I would prefer that you not speak to these men anymore. You all go back to the safety of the house, and I will get the police to clean out the cage."

"It has never been more in need of a mucking out, that is certain!" said Ruby.

The police did arrive, and Clara watched the lights go on in neighbors' windows up and down the street. She wondered if Daphne had wakened too with the sound of the siren.

Elliot was forced to go with them to the jailhouse and give his testimony, and, bleary from lack of sleep, Clara lay down on the parlor sofa. Later, she heard her father and mother speaking to each other in low voices.

"Booth," said Clara's father, "has lived his whole life in terror of being linked to the crime."

"As well he should, for the devastation he's caused."

"But he claims that he never meant hurt to anyone," Elliot told her. "He felt his own family had done him an injustice, cutting him off from the Booth money just because they hated his being on the stage. Booth also believed Glendoveer was rising so quickly, he could replenish the ransom money in a season on the road. So he arranged what he termed 'a harmless kidnapping.' But the man never foresaw the deaths of the children."

Clara rose and went to the foyer, where her mother stood with her arms about her father's neck. "So it's been for nothing," her mother said. "All of it."

And Clara reflected upon that. Everything had been botched—from the original crime to the Great Glendoveer's spell to recall the children. One error after another had led to years of anguish, subterfuge, and fear.

"But we must not be bitter," Clara said. "Wouldn't that make everything worse?"

Her mother released Elliot and gathered Clara into her arms.

"No. We must not be bitter. If happiness has at last arrived on our doorstep, we must be grateful."

"Where are the birds?" Clara asked.

"In the kitchen," her mother said. "Ruby brought out the clothes-drying rack so they'd have someplace to perch."

"They don't want to go back in the aviary," Elliot said. "And I can't say that I blame them."

"I must go to them," said Clara. Being grateful was no problem for Clara, but she knew her happiness could not be complete until the birds were also set free.

Chapter 32

Clara almost hated to disturb the birds, seeing them perched on the drying rack with their eyes closed, some with their heads tucked beneath their wings. Frances and Arthur must be especially exhausted, she thought, after that long-distance flight.

Frances opened one eye, then two, and shook herself awake. Her rustling wobbled the wooden rack and woke the others, who looked around momentarily as if they had no idea where they were.

"Aww!" Frances said, lifting and dropping her wings. "Never have I been so sore in the shoulders."

"Skaaaaaawk!" agreed Arthur.

"You two are heroes!"

"My dear Clara," said Frances, "would you believe I had to rest twice on the way? If not for Arthur encouraging me with his comical loop-de-loops, I don't think I'd have made it!"

"If I had to fly on a dangerous errand, I'd proudly choose either one of you to accompany me," Clara said. "Now tell me: how did it go with Father?"

"Fortunately, the island is small. The only structure there belongs to Dooley. I was surprised—it was no lean-to, but a large cottage, well built and handsome."

"Booth had it built for him. Was Father inside?"

"He was chopping wood. Quite unfortunate, I thought at the time."

"Why's that?" asked Clara.

Frances tilted her head. "Would *you* like to be a talking bird confronting a mesmerized man wielding an ax?"

"Tsip!" cried Helen. And the rest of the birds agreed.

"Frances, tell her about the clapping," George said.

"Ah, yes!" Frances said. "I managed to light on a nearby bush and recite the incantation to Elliot, but then I could not clap to snap him awake!"

"Goodness," Clara said. "I never thought about the clapping. So, what then?"

"Arthur hunted around inside the house and found some leather bellows. They were almost too heavy for him to lift—"

"Skaaaaaaaw!" cried Arthur.

"But he managed to get them to the roof of the house. I said my spell again, and he dropped them to the ground below."

"Did it work?"

"Yes, it made a thunderous noise, though it broke the bellows," Frances said. "And then you could see a light in Elliot's eyes. He put down the ax and looked at me. Do you know that when I explained who I was and why we were there, he believed instantly. We got on from the start, didn't we, Arthur?"

"Did he remember the cuff links right away?"

"Yes. He knew just where they were buried. And there are more valuables where those came from. Elliot told us that when he returned to the island years ago, Dooley found him digging around for treasure and captured him. After that, Dooley contacted Booth, who came back to the island and mesmerized your father into a sort of willing captive. It's a wonder he didn't just shoot them both."

Ruby came in rubbing her eyes. "Good morning to you all," she said. "I've slept no more than two hours, but here is the sun again and hungry people needing to be fed."

"Morning?" said Clara. "Oh dear. I must leave a signal for Daphne that we're all well."

"Ahem!" said Frances. "Who says we are all well?"

Peter stretched out his yellow neck and chattered at Clara while Helen hopped onto the kitchen table and did a little dance of distress.

"Clara," said George, "we need to go home. You re-member, don't you?"

Clara bowed her head. "Forgive me. Of course." She looked searchingly at George.

"Do you know how it can be done?"

"Trial and error, no doubt!" he proclaimed.

"But mostly error," said Frances, "if past is precedent."

"Where *is* Elliot?" asked George.

"In the parlor with Harriet," said Ruby as she fed the stove. "They're afraid to let go of each other, it seems. It's a second courtship, I declare."

"Are you talking about us?"

Clara saw her mother in the doorway, leaning on her father's arm, and leapt up. "We're discussing you for good reason. We need Father to help free his brothers and sisters."

Elliot patted his wife's arm. "You must excuse me. I've been looking around at the house with Harriet, and I lost myself in admiration for the old place. The woodwork in the foyer and the staircase is incomparable."

"Your father can hardly wait to get his hands on the place," Harriet told Clara, "warts and all."

"So we're staying?" Clara asked.

"I like fixing things," he said. "Setting things to rights. Besides, it's our family home, and I'd like to have my time in it."

"Good," Frances said. "But first, set *us* to rights."

"I'm at your service, Brothers and Sisters. Where do we begin?"

"We can start with the clue from the mourning picture," Clara said. "I think I remember the poem by heart":

Together always to the last,
Our love shall hold each other fast.
Delivered from the frost and foam,
None shall fly till all come home.

"From the sound of that," Elliot said, "my coming back to Lockhaven should already have released everyone."

"Maybe you're meant to say the rhyme together?" Clara suggested.

"Bee-tee-WEE?!" said Peter.

"Clara," Frances said, "Peter would like to remind you that there are only two of us who speak."

"Oh yes. I keep forgetting," Clara said.

"Let's try something else," Elliot said. He spread his arms and passed his hands over the heads of the birds while reciting the rhyme. Clara held her breath and waited for a transformation. But nothing happened. So he tried next to touch the birds as he recited, but nothing changed.

Clara felt a knot of apprehension in her chest. She knew how badly the Glendoveers had longed for Elliot's help; how they had looked to it as their only hope. What if they never figured out what was required?

"All right," Clara said, "let's think hard. Is there someplace that the children considered themselves most at 'home'?"

"We did gather often in the parlor," George said.

Elliot nodded. "Let's try it."

Again, in the parlor, Clara watched as her father went

through the motions, reciting the incantation; and after each attempt, the mood of the room became more somber.

"Dear, dear, dear . . . ," George trailed off. "Not good."

Then Helen, the youngest and smallest and greenest, began to sing! She swept around the room, angling her little body so that she just missed the noses of the grown-ups as she circled.

"A brilliant idea!" Frances said. "Helen says to follow her."

The honeycreeper darted up the stairwell and down the long hall until she came to the room with the children's old furniture.

"The nursery!" said George. "We each have happy memories here."

"I have the key!" said Clara's mother. As soon as she got the door opened, she rushed to the bank of windows over the wide window seat, pulled back the dusty curtains, and opened a window to let the air in.

"What a spectacle!" said Ruby.

Coral clouds glowed in a blue sky that looked warm enough to swim in. And though dew still clung to the lawn and masses of roses below, the room took on the garden's heady fragrance as if it were two in the afternoon.

"I remember seeing the sun rise here on summer mornings," George said.

"Yes," returned Frances. "And Mother always sat there in the rocker. That's where I remember seeing you too, Elliot. We all were rocked in that chair."

Clara's father went over to the old rocker and ran his hand reverently over its dusty back. "Thank you, Frances," he said. "It does me good to know that someone remembers me as one of the Glendoveer children."

"Everyone!" cried George. "The chair."

"Yes," said Elliot. He sat in the rocker, and the birds perched around him, all bathed in the morning light. Each bird stretched out so that the family was connected, wing to wing, feather to finger. Then Elliot recited:

> *Together always to the last,*
> *Our love shall hold each other fast.*
> *Delivered from the frost and foam,*
> *None shall fly till all come home.*

And on that word *home*, Clara beheld the bodies of the birds dissolving into a dazzle of light and sparkle. She was forced to close her eyes, though she did not want to. And when she opened them, there they were: all of the Glendoveer children, outlined in a soft opalescent glow and dressed impeccably in white, down to their boots—and smiling! She had never seen such smiles.

"'Tis a miracle," said Ruby through her tears.

Clara herself could not speak. *How does one address a roomful of ghosts?* she wondered. But when little Helen stepped forward and seized Clara around the waist, she allowed her hand to rest on the girl's silky hair and found, to her astonishment, that these children felt as real as she was.

"You are so warm!" said Helen in a high, clear voice. "How good it feels to hold you."

Peter, fair and freckled, pushed his brother Arthur forward teasingly. "Go, give her a kiss," he said.

But Arthur didn't hesitate. He threw his arms around Clara too, and when he allowed her to kiss his black brows without so much as a blush, Peter had to have his kiss as well.

Handsome George stood straight, his transparent blue eyes shining. He stepped forward, took one of Clara's hands, kissed it, and bowed. "Words fail me," he said. "I am too happy."

"Me too," Clara managed to stammer. Seeing him now in all his joyful radiance was a vision that she knew she would never forget.

Now only Frances stood alone. Clara could see by her dark, intelligent gaze and sharp features that she was indeed the mynah of old. Her straight ebony hair was pulled back from her face in a white bow, and her smile was sly.

Clara and Frances advanced toward each other and clasped hands. "It's a good thing that we had you to help us, Clara Glendoveer," Frances said.

"No, I thank you, Frances. I'd never have figured out what to do if you hadn't pushed me," Clara told her. "I wouldn't have my father."

"Enjoy him, Clara!" Frances said. "Every minute you have together. Time moves by very quickly—except, perhaps, when you are spending decades in a birdcage," she added drily.

With an abrupt nod, Frances too let go of Clara and addressed her siblings.

"Now let us go to our own mother and father. I suspect they might be as impatient to see us as we are to see them. Who goes first?" she asked.

"Me!" said Arthur, raising his hand. "I'm the bravest!"

"No, you aren't," protested Peter. "I'm just as brave as you!"

"As the oldest, I should lead the way," George said.

"Don't leave before I do," said Helen.

While the children argued, Frances raised the hem of her skirt and climbed atop the window seat. With a push of her hand, the cross-paned window flew wide open, and she scanned the sky.

"Follow me!" she said.

She jumped before anyone could stop her. Ruby slumped into Elliot's arms, and Clara buried her head in her mother's shawl. And then she swore she heard a familiar voice.

"Who's next?"

Clara had to look up. There was Frances the Mynah, perched on the windowsill, canting her head jauntily, as if she was quite pleased with herself.

"Surprised?" asked Frances.

"Shocked, is more like it," Clara told her. "Oh, Frances, I thought you were all done with feathers!"

She answered with a sigh. "I know. It's a shame to put them on again, but it's only for the moment. We Glendoveers have a final flight to make." Frances, her red eyes gleaming, hopped forward to regard the others and crowed, "Come, everyone! Let's put these wings to use one last time!"

Arthur and Peter gave a whoop, mounted the window seat, jumped, and popped up again on the sill beside Frances in feathered form.

"Carry me?" asked Helen, reaching up to George.

He took her on his hip, but did not leave before shaking everyone's hand. "My brother," he told Elliot, "we shall meet again when it is your time. Until then . . ."

George took to the window seat with a bound, Helen waving at them all over his shoulder—and they were off!

Clara, Harriet, Elliot, and Ruby leaned out the casements and watched the children wheel once around the yard and launch into the sky until they became black dots, which evaporated among the clouds.

Clara turned to Ruby. "Do you think we'll ever hear from Mrs. Glendoveer again?"

"No, no," she said. "I suspect she'll be off with her children. All she ever wanted was to be reunited with her family."

"I hope that doesn't make you sad, Clara," her mother said.

"I'm not," Clara said. And she thought of Daphne, hands jammed in her pockets, declaring, "Life is for the *living*!"

"Shall we go downstairs, then, for our first family breakfast?" her father asked. "I've shifted for myself in the kitchen and would love to make you my griddle cakes."

"Lovely," said Ruby. "And Harriet and Clara and I will sit at the table and sip our tea. That's about all I'm good for this morning anyway!"

"There's never been another one like it," Clara's mother said. "Clara, you coming?"

"In a moment, Mama."

Clara walked to the window facing her friend's house and pulled the curtains open wide to let her know that, indeed, all was well at the Glendoveers'.

Acknowledgments

Thanks to Cecile Goyette, Joan Slattery, and Nancy Siscoe for their invaluable help with this book. And a special note of gratitude to Laurel Brady, to whom I owe so much.

About the Author

Kathleen O'Dell was named a *Publishers Weekly* Flying Start Author for her much-praised debut novel, *Agnes Parker . . . Girl in Progress*. She is the author of two more Agnes Parker stories and the novels *Ophie Out of Oz* and *Bad Tickets*.

The Aviary is her first historical mystery, but Kathleen took to the genre like a bird takes to the air. The past became like a second home to her while she was writing this book.

Kathleen O'Dell lives with her husband and sons in Glendale, California. You can learn more about her at kathleenodell.com.